I0708651

# Leap of Faith

## Matthew Munson

Inspired Quill Publishing

Published by Inspired Quill: September 2013

First Edition

This is a work of fiction. Names, characters and incidents are the product of the author's imagination. Any resemblance to actual events or persons, living or dead, is entirely coincidental. The publisher has no control over, and is not responsible for, any third party websites or their contents.

Leap of Faith © 2013 by Matthew Munson
Contact the author through their website:
www.matthewmunson.co.uk

Chief Editor: Peter Stewart
Assistant Editor: Austin Bonecutter

All Rights Reserved.
No part of this publication may be reproduced or transmitted in any form by any means electronic, mechanical, photocopying, recording or otherwise, without the prior permission of the copyright owner.

Paperback ISBN: 978-1-908600-18-9

eBook ISBN: 978-1-908600-19-6

**Inspired Quill Publishing, UK**
**Business Reg. No. 7592847**
http://www.inspired-quill.com

# Dedication

Lynda, Aaron, James & Lauren.

# Acknowledgements

I'm fortunate to have a number of funny, intelligent friends and partners-in-crime; Lynda, Lucy, Christina, Kay, Charli, Barbara, Jenny, Kirk, Chelby, Diana, Sam H and Chris P. You are all funny, brilliant friends.

Lucy's art-work adorns this book; isn't she talented?

Jon and Rachel; as well as being great friends, you've welcomed me to many fabulous dinners as Jon and I held many late-night creative writing sessions. Tuesdays have become a lot more fun as a result!

Sara-Jayne Slack, Inspired Quill in human form! I love that I can talk to the MD of a publishing company at 10pm on a Sunday night about some aspect of the book, and then veer off into a discussion about anything sci-fi or fantasy-esque. I am privileged to be a part of IQ, and you truly embody everything it stands for.

Peter Stewart and Austin Bonecutter; two excellent editors, and I don't think I've come across a surname more awesome than Austin's. Peter, the relationship between writer and editor is vital, and ours has helped to make me a better writer. Thank you.

Mum and Dad. You instilled a love of words and literature in me from a young age, as well as encouraging me to never give up. Your guidance made me the man I am today. I love you both.

To all my friends and family I have, and haven't, mentioned here, I will say only this; thank you all for being in my life.

The fallen angel slept.

It was a deep and enforced sleep. He had remained in that state for 2,000 years – except recently, when he had awoken for a few short, glorious hours. But after his task had been done, he had consented to return to slumber so that his human host could live out a normal and full life on Earth.

He was a powerful angel, the eldest son of the Almighty himself a leader of angels, and he was willing to wait his turn. By remaining alive, he would have killed his host – and he would not allow that to happen. It had taken him a long time, but he had learnt the value of life – whomever it belonged to.

In his sleep, he dreamt of another time, when he was younger, angrier … a time when he had made mistakes.

Lucifer slept – inside the head of a human called Paul Finn, who relied on the angel's continued submission for his own existence.

— •• —

The cosmos unfolded before her as she woke, starlight stretching out like endless fields. As her consciousness returned from its long sleep, she rejoiced in the knowledge that she was once again free.

*How long has it been?*

She had been imprisoned now for … how long had it been? She tried to answer the question, and realised she was unable to. She lost focus for a moment, terror biting at the edge of her consciousness; doing her best to control it, she spun round and studied the stars.

*They're all wrong!* she realised. *I've been asleep for so long that even the stars have shifted position!*

Her consciousness felt … fuzzy around the edges from waking up. The sleep had been forced upon her, and she resented it. Whilst she rejoiced at being awake again, she hated the thought that she had missed so much activity.

*I used to know everything,* she thought, *and now I know close to nothing.*

She hesitated; whilst she wasn't one for introspection, she found herself pausing in thought for a moment.

*I remember something.*

As it came to her, an emotion came along with it: *anger.* She felt it raging though her as she remembered.

*I remember what the angels did to me.*

If she had been human, her face would have clearly shown her frustration and anger, but she *wasn't* human – nor was she angelic. She was something else, and glad of it; she couldn't bear the thought of being trapped in a limited and pathetic physical body. She was a spirit, and she had been imprisoned and humiliated by angels for far too long.

She could feel the rage inside of her, threatening to over-whelm her thoughts with its desire for revenge and hatred for everything that wasn't a spirit.

*I* will *have my revenge,* Poena told herself, *but on my own terms. I will not let the rage win; I'm back, and I will defeat the angels before they know what's happening.*

The cosmos was vast; with their telescopes and satellites, humans could see into the interstellar realm further than they had been able to even fifty years before, but they could only see the merest fraction of what was truly there – and *understood* the most slender proportion of that knowledge.

It was as a result of these advances that Poena existed. She had been protector of the astral plane until her imprisonment of sleep.

The changes were human in origin; they were trying to fracture the supposedly unbreachable barrier between the physical and astral planes.

*And that's meant to be impossible.*

However, as much as she wished it wasn't the case, some humans were clearly getting better at the endeavour – and that was what had first awoken her. There was a group in a small corner of Earth called The Seekers of Truth, and they were becoming problematic.

Poena had *always* protected the astral plane from incursions, and was more determined now than ever before that she would continue to do so.

She had to concede that The Seekers of Truth were clearly *good*; they were learning how to separate mind from body and explore the other realms. Spurred on by so many reports of strange, paranormal activity, they had pooled their resources and begun exploring *out there*.

What the Seekers didn't realise was that whenever they attempted to travel into these other realms, they disturbed the spirits who lived there. While no-one had yet managed to fully infiltrate their realm, the fact that human beings were getting closer concerned and frightened them. Spirits were protective, and were angry that humans were trying to invade the one place that was theirs.

*And rightly so.*

Poena had heard the Spirits' anger and jealousy – and fed off the raw energy it supplied. She had awoken to their cries of anger and rage, and she felt suffused with it, and nourished by it.

*They will listen to me now,* she thought. *The spirits, they* need *me now … and I need them. I need them to help take my revenge on those who betrayed me.*

—•●—

Evan Somerville lay down on the cot bed and closed his eyes; that wasn't strictly necessary for what he was about to do, but he found it easier to focus when he shut out the world around him.

He was a slight man, with sandy hair, piercing green eyes and just about 5'9" in height. Whilst Somerville wasn't physically powerful, his personality was far stronger; the Seekers under his control respected and feared him in equal measure, and he encouraged the fear.

*It ensures my position,* he thought.

He felt the straps wrap tightly around his forearms, securely fastening him to the metal frame. Then the same ties wound around his legs, waist and forehead. He had authorised that measure himself; two separate Seekers had failed to come back mentally intact after they had tried to move beyond this world and into the next. They had jumped from their cots and tried to rip their eyes from their sockets, screaming insanely about things that had tried to enter their head and invade their thoughts.

Plastic pads, hooked to the brainwave monitor, were gently stuck to either side of his forehead, the coolness of the glue bringing a welcome relief to the overbearing warmth of the room.

*I must authorise some air conditioning in here*, he thought, not for the first time. *When I wake up, I'll get Rachael to –*

He blinked, surprised by his lapse. Although he tried to force her from his mind as much as possible, his guilty secret was that he was *still* incredibly fond of her, even after everything.

"Are you alright, Mr Somerville?"

The voice of his assistant, Joshua McKenzie, brought him back to the present; he pushed all thoughts of Rachael – and the past – away.

*Now is not the time for nostalgia.*

He grew excited, as he always did just before he travelled. *How can moving into another veil of existence* ever *get boring?*

"Let's begin."

He let his mind wander, allowing it to pull away from his body and move beyond the physical world. As always, he felt liberated. His ability to separate his soul from his body was a special one, he knew, but one he had carefully cultivated. He thrived on his ability to seek out what was beyond the mundane world he lived in.

*One day I'll understand what's truly out there.*

—•◦•—

Somerville hadn't realised it, but in the early hours of this summer's day, he was about to do something no-one in his fledgling organisation had managed to do before.

He broke through the barrier that separated the physical and astral planes – and his soul arrived *inside* the astral plane.

—••—

The Seven Sisters slept fitfully, and had done so since the Great War. They had accepted a punishment that wasn't entirely their own, to try and heal the wounds that had fragmented the angel and spirit societies. This hadn't been the Civil War, where angel had fought angel, but an earlier War, between angels, spirits and *them* – and they had, to their shock and horror, lost.

A handful of times over the last untold millennia, the Seven Sisters had stirred from their slumber, hoping that the time was ripe for them to return, but it never had been. Now, however, things were different.

Poena was one of the few beings that watched over them. The Civil War in Heaven had caused a lot to be forgotten in the ensuing chaos, but *she* had remembered. She had awoken in confusion, unable to remember all of her past, but could remember *this*.

*I lost at the end of that war as well*, she thought ruefully. *The angels would say they had done us a kindness, but did they really? Or did they betray anyone who wasn't like them?*

She found herself torn; did she stop the Sisters from re-awakening, or did she step back and allow the inevitable War to restart?

*But what will happen to us?* she wondered. *The spirits – what will happen to us? We will be caught in the middle of these two ancient sides again – and it will hurt us more now than ever before. And will I ever then get my revenge?*

Poena paused as she felt something, on the edge of her consciousness; it took her a moment to realise what it was she was sensing.

The astral plane had been breached!

Her first thoughts moved towards the angels, but that was quickly dismissed; she would *know* if it was them. That only left one possibility.

*A human.*

She checked the Seven Sisters, but their sleep was constant, if still troubled. Poena wondered how much they knew, in their current state – she hadn't been aware of too much while *she* had hibernated.

*But the Sisters are so much more powerful than I am.*

She turned her attention to the minuscule human soul that was now in the astral plane. It seemed to be out of control, as if caught off-guard by its appearance in this realm.

*Those humans and their desire to see what is beyond the veil while they are still alive,* Poena thought. *Why can they just not wait until their body dies?*

*He has a vague talent,* she grudgingly conceded. *This … intrigues me. I shall watch you carefully, little human. But for now, go back to where you came from. I need to clear my thoughts and consider my plan. I can't do that while invaders are here.*

# Broadstairs, Kent – Present Day

Paul Finn's eyes snapped open. He gasped for breath while his heart pounded fast inside his chest and adrenaline pumped through his body.

Words that had been on his lips just a moment before faded away, tantalisingly out of reach. Lucifer's influence was obvious, but Paul couldn't access the angel's thoughts while he was awake; it seemed to be only in their dream world that they could communicate – *and forget instantly after I wake up.*

*Well, communicate after a fashion,* he added. *When I sleep, I dream of flying through the cosmos – and then I get dreams like that one, where I know something's gone wrong, but can't remember what when I've woken up.*

He sat up and automatically reached out an arm to check he hadn't disturbed his girlfriend. He was thrown when he found nothing but empty space.

Still half-asleep, he turned to look – and his eyes confirmed what he already knew. Christina Challis wasn't in bed.

*Impressive powers of deduction,* he told himself with a half-smile. *Kirby will be impressed. He might even offer to sponsor your application to the training academy.*

Glancing at his bedside clock, he noticed it was 3:33 – and frowned. Every time he had one of these dreams, he woke up at the same time, and he was beginning to get a complex about it.

Knowing that he wouldn't be able to sleep again for a while, he padded through to the kitchen (which was separated from the living room by a breakfast bar), flicked on the kettle and then began searching for a cup.

"Where the hell did I pack them?" he muttered.

"*Who* packed them?"

He froze with a hand inside in a half-opened box. He hadn't bothered turning on a light, and his eyes hadn't focused on anyone in the gloom. He peered across the breakfast bar – and finally saw a figure sat in the gloom among the boxes and black plastic bags.

"Hey," he said, "what are you doing, lurking around in the dark?"

There was a laugh from the figure. "I could ask you the same thing."

Paul had to concede that point. He found his way to the light switch and flicked it on. Their living space was covered in packing materials – everywhere. His girlfriend was just about visible on one of their leather sofas, in her dressing gown and holding a cup of tea.

"Here's a thought," he said, clicking his fingers. "As everything's packed, shall we move tomorrow?"

Christina's left eyebrow rose wearily. She had heard Paul's jokes so many times that she was used to them by now – although it didn't mean she had to like them.

"Yes, darling," she replied in her lilting South African accent. "That sounds like a great idea."

Paul smiled. That was one of the many reasons he loved her, of course; she let him tell his jokes, despite the fact they were terrible. He sat down next to her in silence, thoughtful.

"Penny for your thoughts?" Christina asked.

Paul shrugged. "You'll be pretty poor," he replied. "Just had another weird dream."

He had never really told Christina much about his dreams, but she knew he had them fairly frequently. He'd hoped they would have finished two years ago, when he discovered the truth about his connections to Heaven, but no – Lucifer had returned to his sleep, and so Paul had started getting the dreams again.

*You should tell Christina everything,* he thought. *Don't keep any secrets from her. Tell her about your past.*

"Paul?"

"Sorry," he said and cleared his throat. He smiled. "I was somewhere else for a minute."

*Not now,* he told himself. *I don't want to ruin the moment.*

"Yeah." Christina smiled back at him. "I love you, you know."

"I know," Paul replied, and quickly added, "I love you too."

His feelings for Christina were the reason he hadn't told her about his Heavenly experiences … and about the angel sleeping inside his head. He didn't want to lose her, ever, and the thought of the look on her face as he confessed to once having visited Heaven and meeting God terrified him.

It was at times like this that he missed the old days, when his best friends Joseph and Lauren would have told him exactly what they thought of his hesitation. He missed his friends dearly, never more so than when he needed their advice.

He distracted himself by taking Christina's hand and kissing it.

"Let's go to bed," he said. "We need all the sleep we can get."

*I want a quiet life*, he thought. *I just hope my past stays right there – in the past.*

# Seekers of Truth Headquarters, Ramsgate – Present Day

When Somerville's soul slammed back into his body, he woke instantly. He pulled against the restraints, shock overriding any conscious thoughts. If it weren't for the ties wrapped about his limbs, he would have doubled over in pain as his stomach spasmed in surprise at being so forcibly thrust back into his body. He was filled with a mixture of joy, elation and fear – he had finally breached the barrier between the physical and astral planes! But something had sensed him – and forced him back.

*What can possibly be that powerful?*

"Mr Somerville?"

McKenzie's voice cut through Somerville's thoughts – his assistant looked shocked at the man's abrupt return; Somerville was usually calm and collected, for his careful mask to slip told McKenzie that something was wrong.

"What's wrong, sir?" McKenzie asked. "What is it?"

"I broke through the barrier," Somerville replied quietly.

McKenzie blinked in surprise: he clearly didn't believe that he'd heard his superior correctly. It was only after a few seconds, when his mind had fully processed the information, did he realise what the director had said.

"You … you did it, sir?" he asked breathlessly. "You *saw* the astral plane? What was it like? What –"

He stopped at a glance from Somerville. The director took another deep breath as he tried to centre himself.

*What* did *I see over there?* he wondered. *Something … beautiful, as I knew it would be. This is the start of something new – and powerful. With this ability, I can do so much.*

Clearing his throat, he pulled his left arm against the strap again; it had held. As McKenzie undid the straps, Somerville felt his stomach turn somersaults. He was confident in his power – he had managed to break through the barrier, after all – but he had touched the consciousness of something far greater than himself. While he would never admit it to anyone else, the power he had felt frightened him.

*What should my next move be?* he wondered. *And how can I protect myself – and the Seekers – against whatever is out there?*

# Broadstairs, Kent – Present Day

etective Sergeant Kirby was lost and confused. *It'll be fine*, he told himself, *just stay calm.*

He paused, angry, and looked at his surroundings again as he tried to orientate himself.

*I am lost in the middle of my own bloody town*, he realised. *I'm either a complete moron or someone's moving the world around. At the very least, I wish all these houses would put numbers on their doors; I have no clue if I'm even going in the right direction.*

He was in St Peter's Road, a long street not far from a busy T-junction, and was convinced that he wasn't far from his destination. After a couple of minutes searching, he finally found a row of three houses that *were* numbered *and* easily visible from the path – but he then realised that he couldn't remember the house number he was looking for.

*I'm not lost, just geographically displaced.*

"Kirby!"

He blinked; the shout bringing him out of his thoughts. The sun was beating down mid-summer heat and it made him squint for a moment; all he could see was the blurred outline of a figure walking towards him.

"You were away with the fairies then," the person said. "You and Paul are so alike sometimes. What were you thinking about?"

Abruptly, Kirby's vision cleared and he could see Christina Challis stood in front of him. He grinned.

"I was thinking about *you*, of course, Chris," he said. "I was wondering when you were going to see sense and leave Mr Finn for me."

Christina laughed; she was well-used to Kirby's banter and ignored him whenever he pretended to flirt with her.

"Took you long enough to find us," she said as she lead him down the road and into the right house. "When you offered to help us move, I assumed you meant *this* move."

"I got lost."

Christina paused as she stepped over the threshold of the flat. "Kirby, remind me of your job again?"

"I'm a detective in the police force," Kirby replied. "I detect and solve crime. I'm a policeman, not a navigator."

Christina shook her head in despair. Kirby looked round the ground-floor flat and was immediately struck by the space. Removal men were moving in and out of a number of different doors.

"He's in there," Christina said, nodding towards one of the rooms at the rear of the large hall, "trying to assemble the new bed."

All of a sudden, an expletive came rolling through the door; Kirby raised an eyebrow and glanced at Christina.

"I'll go and help," he said.

"Are you alright in there?" Christina called.

Kirby opened the door. Paul was knelt at the base of the half-constructed double bed, supporting the wooden base with one arm while looking quizzically at a wooden strut that he was holding in the other.

"Yeah, I'm fine!" he shouted then, more quietly, he muttered to Kirby, "I'd have an easier time exorcising a demon."

"Much call for that in Broadstairs, is there?"

Paul rolled his eyes. "Not any more," he replied. "I convinced mine to go to sleep."

Sighing, he lowered the bed to the floor, then glowered at the broken strut again. "I've spent the last twenty minutes trying to build this stupid thing, and I still can't get this last leg on straight."

Kirby couldn't hide his smile as he asked; "Wouldn't it be easier to turn the bed upside down?"

The ex-priest's eyes flicked between the bed and his friend.

"You know, Mr Kirby, it amazes me how you didn't pass your detective's exam on the first go."

———●●———

Kirby took charge and, as a result, the bed was constructed with a minimum of fuss and no more problems; Christina then supervised them carefully as they moved large items of furniture around. She had proved herself to be a fair taskmaster who, after only two hours' work, allowed them to pause for a beer.

*I could get used to this*, Paul thought. *Being a removal man is easy; maybe that's the job I'm meant to do.*

He and Kirby were in the living room, testing out the new leather sofas. Christina had retreated to the front garden to think about plants; Paul had made a decision to avoid her for as long as possible.

"I think I'm going to like it here," he said, smiling contentedly.

Kirby nodded. "And you've got enough room for a family."

Paul gave his friend a withering glare; Kirby had been teasing him about children ever since Christina and he had announced that they were planning to move in together.

"She is *not* pregnant," Paul said. "If I get my way, she won't be for a long time."

"Hey," Kirby said suddenly, "you know what today is, don't you?"

Paul nodded and took a long swig of his beer. Of course he knew; how could he *not*? It had kept him up half the night.

*I'll never forget*, he told himself.

"Yeah," he replied. "Yeah, I remember."

Jealousy churned in Kirby's stomach; he quickly suppressed it, hating the fact that he felt it at all.

*I did help, in my own way, back when … all hell threatened to break loose. I just … wish I could have seen Heaven first-hand.*

Two years before, when 144,000 people – and angels – had come very close to dying at the hand of a vengeful angel known as Metatron, Kirby had remained on Earth, unaware of the drama going on in the heavens above.

Despite his irrational jealousy, he knew Paul, Joseph and Lauren hadn't *chosen* to travel to that other realm without him, and he knew he had to just get over it. Realising that the silence had gone on for a moment too long, he cleared his throat as he changed the subject.

"Paul, you never …" He paused as his brain caught up with his mouth. *Bloody hell, could you be any more awkward?*

Paul frowned. "I never what?"

Kirby realised that he wasn't going to get away with not finishing his sentence; he cursed himself again and carried on.

"You've never asked me if Rachael has found Lauren … on the other side."

*I knew this was a bad idea,* he told himself.

His sister Rachael had died four years previously in a mugging that had gone wrong; during her lifetime, she had been a Seeker of Truth, and her soul had survived death. For whatever reason, she hadn't contacted the Seekers – instead, she had sought out her brother, and they had maintained occasional contact between the realms.

The silence returned between them, rolling on as Paul thought about what Kirby had said. His heart was beating fast in his chest; the grief was two years old, but still returned when he least expected it. The death of one of his best friends was hard enough to bear, and he had sometimes fantasised about how he would feel if he knew her spirit had somehow survived.

*I've already grieved over her,* he thought. *How would I feel if part of her was still alive?*

"I …" Paul shook his head. "Of course I never asked. I saw Lauren *die,* Kirby. She *died!* I want to grieve … not go chasing a vague hope."

"But you're a priest. I thought you *believed* in the afterlife."

It was one of the problems of being a detective – Kirby always had a question. *Might explain why I'm still single,* he thought wryly.

"I *was* a priest," Paul replied, "four years ago. Now … there's so much I still don't know. I lost two of my best friends, one to death and one to heaven. I'd bet even the most devout would question their faith."

Kirby nodded; he had always been more spiritual than religious, so hadn't experienced Paul's depth of feeling. He glanced out the window to savour the bright sunshine for a moment – and frowned when he caught sight of two figures in the small front garden.

"Who's Christina talking to?" he asked as he squinted his eyes against the sun's rays.

Paul followed his friend's gaze and shrugged. "Some guy," he said. "Probably a neighbour."

"That's no neighbour!" Kirby exclaimed. "That's … My god, that's Evan Somerville, the director of the Seekers of Truth."

"That organisation your sister belonged to? No disrespect, mate, but they sound a bit barmy to me," Paul said incredulously. "Why the hell is he here? Don't tell me he's my new neighbour."

Kirby snorted in amusement. "I wouldn't say *barmy* exactly," he replied. "They were determined to learn about the astral plane, so wanted to recruit all the genuine psychics around. He even tried to recruit me once."

"What did you say?"

"Do you *really* want to know?"

Paul shook his head. He could imagine what his friend would have said; while his psychic abilities were clearly genuine, he never flaunted them – and certainly would never have used them on behalf of a slightly eccentric society who wanted to travel to other realms.

*That's more dangerous than they realise*, he thought. *I should know.*

He was still curious to know why Somerville stood outside his flat talking to his girlfriend. For some reason, it didn't entirely feel like coincidence.

Somerville had been looking intensely at Christina during their conversation – and all of a sudden, he looked over her shoulder and through the net curtains, as if he knew Paul and Kirby were looking at him.

Paul's first instinct was to duck and hide, but he resisted the temptation – he wasn't going to act like a seven-year-old child in his own home. A moment later, Somerville stopped talking – and Christina looked over her shoulder through the window as well.

Her blue eyes, usually so full of compassion and humour, were suddenly full of surprise and shock … and annoyance. It was so surprising and out of character that it took Paul's breath away. He didn't know how to react for a moment, but he quickly recovered; something was clearly going on, and he didn't like the feel of it.

Before he knew what he was doing, he was at the front door, stepping out onto the front porch.

"What's going on?"

This wasn't the time for niceties – and Christina seemed to feel the same way, given the coolness of her body language. Paul was focused entirely on her – Somerville had faded into the background for a moment.

"Chris?" he prompted when she didn't reply. "What's wrong?"

"You lied to me."

Those four words were like a punch to the stomach; for a brief moment, Paul tried to think what she was talking about, but he *knew*. In his heart of hearts, he *knew* what she was talking about, even before she went on.

"You kept it a secret from me," she said. "The last two years, did it not occur to you that I should know?"

Surprised that she was so angry about it – and so accepting of it being true at face value – Paul opened his mouth to reply and reached out to touch her, but Christina waved his hand away.

"I don't want to hear it just now, Paul," she snapped. "I need to think about this. Just … leave me alone for a while."

Paul's mouth opened and closed, no words forming as his brain struggled to keep up.

"What the hell …?" he asked stupidly, then turned to Somerville. "Who *are* you, and what have you been saying to my girlfriend?"

Somerville shrugged. "Just the truth, Mr Finn," he replied, "and sometimes the truth can hurt."

Lost, Paul shook his head and looked back at Christina. "Chris, I –"

"Not now, Paul," she said with a disappointed air. "It's … it's more important than you realise. I need to think. Evan is an old friend and needs my help with something. I'm going with him for a couple of hours. It'll give me a chance to work things out in my head."

Without looking back, she nodded to Somerville and they both headed for a black Suburban parked across the road.

Anger and frustration surged through Paul – at himself as much as anything. The situation had gotten out of control incredibly quickly. As he didn't entirely know what the situation *was*, that just made his frustration worse.

"What the hell just happened?"

Kirby had arrived silently at his friend's side, and looked equally as confused as they watched Christina get into the passenger side of the car.

"I wish I knew," Paul said dumbly. "I wish I knew."

⸺•◦•⸺

Somerville put the car into gear and pulled away from the kerb.

"I'm glad you decided to come with me, Ms Challis," he said quietly to his passenger. "We've got a lot to talk about."

"I've got a lot to *think* about, Mr Somerville," she replied, looking out the window. "I'm coming with you to try and get some answers, nothing more. I … I just want to understand what happened two years ago."

"Whether it's related to my success this morning or not," he said, "we're on the cusp of a new understanding in our civilisation."

"Then surely it's Paul you would want, not me."

Somerville shook his head. "You *know* why I've asked you, Christina."

She hesitated for a moment, then nodded. "Yes," she replied. "Yes, I do."

⸺•◦•⸺

Paul had been silent for a while – and Kirby hadn't interrupted him, not wanting to bother his friend. He could only imagine how *he* would feel. They were sat in Paul's front room, each gazing into the middle distance as they tried to process what had just happened.

"How did Somerville know?"

Kirby blinked as he came out of his reverie. "Sorry?"

Paul shifted on the sofa as he thought out loud. "How did Somerville know about my visit to Heaven? I thought you told me once that the Seekers hadn't ever been able to access the astral plane."

"They hadn't," the detective replied. "It took them a long time to learn how to separate their souls from their bodies. There are barriers between each realm – no human ever had the power to break through."

Paul bit on a fingernail. "Well, something's changed," he said, "because he's learnt about it from *somewhere*. Clearly, the Seekers are more experienced than we realised."

"I won't disagree," Kirby replied. "I've been trying to contact Rachael for the last ten minutes, but it's difficult; she's not always there when I need her."

"Why *now*?" Paul said out loud.

"Huh?"

"Why did he come by today – and why did he feel a desire to tell Christina everything?"

"Why don't we go and find out?"

Paul blinked – he was thrown for a moment and, after what had just happened outside the flat, he didn't think that was possible.

"What?"

Kirby shrugged. "Rather than just sitting here, going around in circles trying to figure it out, let's go and do something productive. Like finding out more about these Seekers – and what they've been up to since my sister died."

Paul didn't hesitate. In fact, he smiled the more he thought about Kirby's plan.

"Let's do it."

# Heaven – The Distant Past

Lucifer looked out over the cosmos, his brow knitted together as he completed his visual inspection.

"Why is this so hard?" he asked out loud.

"Because we must defend our realm at all costs, even if it's against the most powerful beings of all."

Lucifer was surprised; he hadn't expected an answer. Indeed, he had travelled out here, to the edge of the cosmos, specifically to be alone, and hadn't sensed that anyone was near him – although someone clearly *was*.

He whipped around, his huge wings beating against the solar winds of space to steady him. In this realm, there was no such thing as gravity – no such thing as up or down – so the owner of the voice was floating in the void of space several feet beneath Lucifer.

He gently beat his wings and lowered himself to the other angel's level.

"Are you saying we will need to defend ourselves against the Seven Sisters?" he asked. "Michael, they are –"

The Archangel Michael held up a hand to forestall the protestations; his face didn't show any irritation, but Lucifer knew not to push the point.

"I know who the Seven Sisters are," Michael replied calmly. "But if they threaten our existence, then surely we *must* fight."

Lucifer swallowed. He was proud of his angelic heritage, and Michael – older than Lucifer by a significant margin – was equally so, if not more. He knew it wasn't prudent to argue with his Father, who was the Almighty, or Michael when they had their hearts set on a course of action.

*It does not follow that* I *must be happy with it.*

He looked over Michael's shoulder. Now that he was looking the senior commander in the eye, he was also level with the angelic battalion, who had massed to battle the Seven Sisters. 144,000 angels against the ancient Sisters. *Do we have enough on our side?* Lucifer fretted.

Michael followed his gaze and raised his eyebrows. "We *will* win, Lucifer," he said, seeming to read the younger angel's thoughts. "I will be leading our troops to victory … with you by my side."

"What?"

Lucifer was sure he had misheard the older angel, but the faint smile on his face told Lucifer that he hadn't.

"You … you're asking me to lead the angels into battle with you?"

Michael nodded. "You are ready," he replied. "Your Father and I both agree; it's time."

Lucifer nodded absently; he wasn't even half Michael's age, and yet he was being given a great honour.

"Thank you," he said quietly. Without a backward glance, he flew towards the angels; his worries were pushed to the back of his mind now that he knew he had his Father's trust.

Michael watched him go. For a moment, he felt guilty at playing on his protégé's emotions, but reminded himself it was for the greater good. He needed Lucifer on his side, not allowing his emotions to cloud his judgement.

*We are at war*, he thought. *We must be willing to do anything to win.*

# Ramsgate Harbour – Present Day

**P**aul hadn't stepped foot in Ramsgate Harbour's Marina for two years – and that had been a deliberate decision. He and his best friend, Joseph Tempur, had come here every Monday since time immemorial until Joseph had … ascended. Since then, Paul hadn't wanted to dig up the memories.

He sometimes wished he knew what Lucifer, the angel imprisoned in his head, would think if he were awake now. He wondered how the angel would view, looking out from human eyes, Paul's world … and his life.

*I respect his power – and his willingness to give up a portion of his own life so that I can live mine to the fullest. I just hope I'm doing him proud.*

The angel was a … strong personality, however, as Paul was learning from his dreams. Portions of Lucifer's memories occasionally seeped through – and not always when Paul was asleep. Just now, when he had thought of Joseph, a memory had formed of an angel – a tall, imposing, *intelligent* angel – that Paul knew was called Satan. Joseph and Satan – through some complicated means – were now one being; Lucifer clearly remembered Satan as the angel he used to be.

*And I remember Joseph as the man he used to be … not the hybrid he now is.*

"Kirby!" he called out. "This isn't doing any good! No-one's there. Let's think about a plan B! Maybe you'll be able to contact Rachael now?"

The detective ignored him; it had been his idea to come here, and he wasn't giving up that easily. He was stood outside Customs House, the ornate red-brick building that housed the town council – and, according to his sources, the HQ for the Seekers of Truth.

Paul walked back over the road; he was fed up with waiting now. Kirby looked annoyed, as if the fact that the doors were locked was a personal slight against *him*. He rattled the doors and rang the bell again, but neither was successful. They hadn't been successful the previous four times either, but it helped him feel like he was *doing* something.

"How did you find out about this place?" Paul asked, trying to distract his friend.

"What?" Kirby replied shortly, glancing briefly over his shoulder; he was distracted at trying to multi-task by holding a conversation at the same time.

Paul gestured at the building. "You're not telling me that the council are all Seekers, are you?"

"What are you jabbering about?" Kirby replied testily. "The town council rent out space in the building; the Seekers have the entire top floor and the basement level."

"How the *hell* did you find all this out?"

Kirby looked at him blankly, then went back to glaring at the lock.

"Kirby, there's no-one there!" Paul expelled a breath. "You've been trying for the last ten minutes, and we're getting nowhere! I came with you to get answers, not to stand around like a pillock!"

The detective turned to face Paul and nodded in satisfaction. "In that case," he said, "you can help me –"

"No, Kirby," Paul said wearily, "enough's enough. Your information is probably out of date. They probably upped and left ages ago. We need to look elsewhere."

"No, we don't."

"Kirby, I'm not staying here all night –"

"We don't have to."

"There's no point argui– What?"

Kirby sighed, then nodded in Paul's direction. "The caretaker's behind you. Let's see if he'll let us in."

# Astral Plane – Present Day

The astral plane wasn't Heaven, nor was it Earth. Instead, it was nestled between the two realms, and was the home to once-human spirits. When a human died, *this* was the realm that became their soul's home, and some had lived here for a long time.

These ancient spirits hadn't all coped with their long existence well; some had slowly gone mad, believing that their long life was a punishment against some imaginary crime. They craved another human body, as they felt it would solve all their problems – and regain their sanity.

Up to now, however, they had been resigned to their fate of forever remaining in this realm, shunned and ignored by the younger spirits around them.

Now, a human soul had breached the barrier and, although he had been sent back and the breach had healed over, it was still a weak point. It had been broken through once – and could be broken through again, surely.

These older, angry spirits swarmed around the weak point, trying to find a way to tear through this healed point in space, but it was difficult. Their thoughts were scattered and confused, and they lacked direction.

Poena knew this – and knew instantly how she could turn it to her advantage. It was time to help them do what they craved and return them to the physical realm, strengthening her own position as a result. She watched the spirits carefully, savouring their lack of awareness. It suited her. If she could get these spirits – these half-crazed, yet determined spirits behind her, then Earth was hers for the taking … and, after Earth, the angels would quake in their high citadel. No-one would be safe from her, especially those who had imprisoned her for so long.

⸺•⸺

Rachael Kirby's soul shivered as she sensed the anger and hunger of the older spirits, massing around the healed shard of the astral plane. She could feel it even here in the outer reaches of the spirit world where she spent most of her time.

Rachael had only been here a few short years, but was already learning so much – far more than she had ever done so as a Seeker of Truth on Earth. When she'd had a physical form, she had been convinced that their admirable aims would one day raise human consciousness to a higher plane of existence. Now, however, she saw it from the other side – and she felt fear for all those humans still on Earth. If the older spirits had their way, humanity's consciousness wouldn't be raised. It would be extinguished.

It was then, as she watched them swarming around the partially-repaired barrier, that she felt the new presence – and gasped.

"What is it? What's wrong?"

For a moment, Rachael had almost forgotten she wasn't alone, but the voice brought her back to her friend.

Lauren Tempur was looking at her with concern. Like her friend, Lauren had, in death, maintained the same shape as her once-physical form – if more ethereal.

"Rachael?" she prompted. "Is it the spirits? Have they torn through the barrier?"

Rachael shook her head. "No," she said. She didn't take her ethereal eyes off the middle distance, where she could focus on the depths of space far better than when she had been alive.

*That's the beauty of being freed from your physical body,* she thought. *Your senses grow a hundred-fold. To think I used to have to wear glasses – now I can focus on anything I want.*

She realised that Lauren was waiting for an answer. It wasn't a response she wanted to give, because it unsettled her; a name she had learnt from older spirits, one that had been spoken in hushed tones laden with fear. One she had never wanted to speak aloud.

"Poena," she whispered. "It's got to be her."

*Why am I whispering her name?* she mused. *She can't hear me from here. I hope.*

"Who?" Lauren asked. She looked confused, and Rachael couldn't blame her; after all, she'd never mentioned her before.

"She's … an ancient spirit," Rachael said. "Said to have been formed in the fires of creation at the same time as the first angels."

Lauren frowned, and tried to focus her own eyes on the far distance – but she hadn't learnt the art of it yet.

"But she's not an angel?"

"Most definitely *not*," Rachael said emphatically. "Do you really think the other spirits would allow an angel into their realm?"

Lauren smiled. She knew the answer to that one – for a very good reason. "They'd *hate* it," she replied. "Why do you think I've been keeping a low profile over the past couple of years?"

Like Paul and Joseph, she'd had an angel living in her head during her life – and that angel had, technically, died along with Lauren. She always used the word "technically", because the angel – Beelzebub – hadn't had physical form like Lauren did at the time.

Unlike Paul and Joseph, however, Lauren's angel – Beelzebub – had remained awake, and remained a separate entity in her own right. She was even able to live independently of Lauren, although often chose not to – mostly because of where they lived. Knowing that most spirits hated angels with a vengeance, Beelzebub usually shared Lauren's ephemeral space, and both of them welcomed the company in this strange environment.

*Rachael's right*, Lauren thought. *They all* loathe *angels here.*

Lauren didn't understand all of it, but there was an ancient enmity between the two realms. The angels had sealed off the astral plane from the rest of Heaven, and many ancient spirits felt that the angels had kept the "best" parts of the cosmos for themselves.

*I can't see it myself.*

She savoured the cosmos swirling round her. Stars floated in the far distance, lighting her way as she floated, gently, past a nebula. Although she was an ephemeral being – not as solid as an angel, but still substantial *enough* – she could feel the energy of the universe moving through her. It was a strange feeling; she could remember her days as a physical being, with the wind and rain against her hair, and now she felt the cosmic wind channelling through the molecules that made up her semi-permanent body ... and it made her feel *joyous* and connected with the wider universe.

"I'm just surprised the spirits haven't found Beelzebub yet," Rachael said slowly. "They may be half-crazed, but they're tenacious."

Lauren couldn't help but smile. "But Beelzebub is *sane* and tenacious," she replied. The smile slowly faded as her mind slowly moved back to Rachael's earlier alarm.

"So why is this Poena so scary then?"

Rachael's eyes widened as her friend said the spirit's name; for a moment, she looked terrified.

"Don't say her *name!*" she said sharply. "She's one of the oldest beings there is – she can hear her name across the astral plane!"

Lauren rolled her eyes, refusing to accept her fellow spirit's mounting hysteria. "Rachael, calm down, would you? What makes you think she's going to be interested in us?"

Rachael paused. She couldn't immediately think of a retort, and Lauren used the moment of silence to continue; "So what the hell is going on?"

"She's the stuff of legend," Rachael replied, focusing on what she knew rather than her fears. "The legend of her is passed from spirit to spirit."

"What *is* the legend?"

"That she was formed around the same time as the Almighty," Rachael replied, "and, after a while, she joined a rebellion against him."

Lauren frowned. "But … you're saying she's not an angel?"

"That's all I know," Rachael said. "Except for the fact that she was put into a deep, supposedly *endless* sleep as a punishment for losing the rebellion. She would have been asleep for millennia … and now that she's awake, and the spirits are still being kept separate from heaven, she'll be furious."

"That would piss anyone off."

Rachael gave a half-smile. "Yeah."

"So what's she doing now?"

"Looks like she's trying to herd the older spirits into following her," Rachael said distantly as she peered into the darkness of space. "They're gathering round the sealed rupture – and *she's* with them."

It was Lauren's eyes that widened this time, in alarm at what Rachael had seen. "What happens if …" Lauren was careful to avoid using the spirit's name "… *she* manages to break through?"

"Then Earth is damned," Rachael said quietly. "The spirits will swarm over it like a plague of locusts."

Determination set into Lauren's eyes. "Then we've got to stop it."

Rachael laughed. "You think *we're* going to stop the oldest-known spirit in existence?" she asked incredulously.

"Not *just* us," Lauren retorted. Her ethereal eyes were blazing with passion. "We've got an angel on our side, don't forget – and a couple of people on Earth who we can call on."

It took Rachael a moment to realise what Lauren was suggesting. Her mind churned with thoughts and sudden fears; although the sudden rage in emotions must have registered on her face, Lauren didn't react to them. Instead, her gaze wandered until she found a particular star in the distance.

"That's our sun," she said.

Rachael blinked. She turned and looked at it carefully.

"You're right." She chuckled. "How is it that I've been here three years and still get lost round Jupiter?"

"How is it I'm here in the astral plane?" Lauren replied, still looking into the distance. "How did a part of me survive death?"

Rachael didn't know what to say in reply to those questions, so she decided to say nothing. Her friend was determined, and a part of Rachael wanted to believe what she wanted to do was possible.

"I know we can find a way through the barrier," Lauren said confidently. "If a Seeker managed it in one location, then we can do it in another – a place that's quiet and out of the way."

Rachael smiled. "You make it sound easy."

"It will be with Beelzebub doing the hard work for us." Lauren replied, deadpan. "Now … let's find a gap in the fence."

# Customs House, Ramsgate – Present Day

"Joshua, we're here to find out more about the Seekers. It's vital you tell us everything you know. This is important."

Joshua McKenzie, the man who had arrived to unlock the building, had introduced himself as the caretaker. He also looked like he didn't want to be there with them, in the foyer of Customs House.

"I don't know anything, Detective," McKenzie replied. "I've never heard of these Seekers."

Kirby scowled, and Paul could tell that his friend didn't believe McKenzie at all.

"You *must* have heard about them," Kirby said. "They're based in this building."

"I told you," he said, "I'm the caretaker and I've never heard of these Seekers."

Kirby stared at the man intently, impatience and anger seeping out from him as he weighed McKenzie up. After what seemed like an eternity – even to Paul, and he wasn't struggling under the weight of the detective's glare – Kirby spoke.

"I don't believe you."

"I'm not lying to you, Detective," McKenzie replied.

*Perhaps too quickly*, Paul thought.

"Do you know Rachael Kirby?" Kirby asked abruptly.

McKenzie wasn't quite quick enough to stop his head nodding. He bit his bottom lip in regret, but it was too late to take back the confirmation. Kirby took a step forward, anger blazing from every pore.

"She was my *sister*," he snapped, "and she died, Mr McKenzie, while working as a Seeker. She was trying to do what had never been done before – breach the barrier between the realms."

"I remember her," McKenzie whispered, as if caught in a trance.

Paul was motionless, terrified that the slightest movement would stop whatever was happening between the two men in front of him.

"Then you'll know she was an honourable woman," Kirby went on, "and I think of myself as an honourable man, but I am getting angry with all this dissembling. My friend –" he pointed to Paul "- was meant to be moving in with his girlfriend today. Instead, she's gone off with Evan Somerville for reasons I can't begin to fathom!"

McKenzie blinked and looked at Paul. "Your girlfriend is Christina Challis?" he asked breathlessly.

Paul nodded, but didn't trust himself to speak.

"She was one of the best Seekers there ever was," McKenzie went on. "We could have already breached the barrier if she had still been with us."

Paul's mind reeled in shock; he didn't believe what he had heard.

"She – she was a *what?*"

McKenzie looked confused. "You mean – she never told you?"

"No," he whispered. "She never told me."

He looked at Kirby. "It looks like we kept secrets from each other," he said. He felt suddenly drained, the fight taken out of him.

McKenzie looked between the two men, clearly confused. He didn't understand what was going on. Paul and Kirby were distracted by the revelation they had shared – and so didn't hear the side door opening, or the soft footsteps moving carefully across the plush red carpet.

Paul opened his mouth to say something – but choked as a rag was stuffed into it. He gagged, but couldn't resist it as his hands were pinned behind his back by someone out of sight.

A strange smell hit his nostrils; *No!* his mind screamed in alarm as he tried – and failed – to fight against his restraints.

Kirby couldn't help him. He was suffering the same fate; a masked figure had a cloth over his face and had managed to restrain his arms. Despite both men kicking out in alarm, the anonymous figures were holding them secure.

Paul's last conscious thought was of his girlfriend; had she suffered a similar fate, despite being a Seeker – and what did it all mean?

# Heaven – The Distant Past

The war between the Seven Sisters and the angels had been fought passionately and violently, and both sides had been utterly confident of victory.

Neither side had been entirely right.

The angels were more numerous by far, but the Seven Sisters were … well, they were the *Seven Sisters*, with all the power that conveyed, and each side had drawn the other to a standstill.

Alcyone looked out over the young cosmos, its stars slowly swirling and orbiting cooling planets. She was treasuring it while she could. *Things will change once physical life arrives.*

She knew that the peace and solitude would end when physical beings arrived, and a part of her looked forward to the change. *I will have to ensure I protect and nurture it.*

She felt Poena, her trusted and loyal follower, appear by her side. Poena's anger burnt off her in waves.

"We should have followed the angels back to their citadel," she said curtly. "They took casualties – if we keep fighting, we could –"

"Take heavy casualties as well," Alcyone said quietly, her gaze never wavering from the endless sprawl before her. "Is that what you want, Poena? For the Seven Sisters to be harmed? Killed, even?"

"Of course not!" Poena exclaimed. "But surely –"

"Enough!"

Alcyone turned to face Poena's form, silvery and free-flowing against the dark backdrop of space, and Poena stopped instantly. She may have been angry, but she would never have argued too strongly against one of the Seven Sisters.

"This war isn't over," she snapped. "We just have to re-think our strategy. The angels are … more clever and cunning than we gave them credit for, but that does not mean we give up. We sit back and think about how to beat them. We do not jump in – we are better than that."

"But in the meantime, what if life begins to form?" Poena protested. "The Almighty wishes –"

"The Almighty will soon realise that he will not get every-thing he wants," Alcyone replied coolly, and Poena could tell the argument was over. "And neither will you, Poena. Now go and leave me to my thoughts."

Although still seething with self-righteous indignation, Poena conceded and disappeared in the blink of an eye, leaving Alcyone alone. The Sister slowly turned her gaze back to the cosmos – and her thoughts.

Poena was also left with her thoughts – and she wasn't entirely comfortable with where they were taking her.

*The Sisters came into this war to help the spirits win,* she thought. *Now, they are holding us back … for what reason? It does not make* sense!

# Heaven – The Present Day

Joseph Tempur was in the Ruling Chamber, sitting on a pew facing the steps leading up to the ornate, golden throne. Until recently, this had served as the Almighty's throne room; now, the room served as the Senate Chamber in the republic's new government – and the throne stood empty.

*And will continue to do so as long as I'm alive.*

Joseph Tempur was an angel, although his name was a human one. There was a very good reason for that; technically, he was only *half*-angelic. The other half was human. His angelic "half" was actually a being that had once been known as Satan. Previously, Satan's consciousness had been locked inside Joseph's mind, in the same way that Lucifer slept inside Paul's – but after their forced imprisonment recently ended, angel and host had merged into a single consciousness, with the memories of an ancient angel and a young human occupying the same mental space.

Joseph often came to the Chamber just to think; he found it calming. The angelic memories within him could remember millennia of discussions and debates within the vast walls of this room. Both Satan and Joseph loved discussion and debate, so a Chamber such as this was like a second home to them both.

He hadn't been thinking about anything in particular to-day; instead, he had been in a generally reflective mood. He was relishing his new life, but occasionally found he missed his old life as well; he wanted to see his human friend Paul again, as well as his sister – but knew neither was possible.

*Angels have their own path*, he thought. *We cannot meddle in the affairs of the other realms. We need to remain separate.*

He shook his head, knowing that he hadn't entirely convinced himself.

*This won't do*, he chided himself. *Lauren would not forgive me for wallowing. Time to return to work.*

As he walked out of the Chamber, he paused and looked at the massive doors; they were buckled and warped, and had remained that way since he, Paul and Lauren had had their inner angels reawakened. No-one had yet repaired them although, in truth, Joseph liked them like that. *It reminds us what we lost in order to get the Republic. No-one should ever forget that.*

Something flashed across his mind's eye, and he turned round to look – but nothing was there. He frowned in confusion; for a brief moment, he thought he could sense … something.

But what?

He couldn't fully explain the sense of something strange in the realm for a moment, but it was gone almost as quickly as it had arrived. Joseph knew he still had so much to learn – or *relearn*, from Satan's point of view – that he couldn't be sure what it was he had seen and felt.

*I'm imagining things*, he thought dismissively.

"Is that you, little sister?" he asked, only half-joking. There was no response, of course, but that didn't make him feel any better.

He made a decision; he couldn't risk ignoring his intuition, especially when he didn't understand most of it.

*And why do I think Lauren's involved in this somehow?*

There was only one way to find out; he headed for the Celestial Observatory.

# Astral Plane – Present Day

The Seven Sisters stirred. After untold millennia in their supposedly-eternal sleep, they had been all but forgotten by heaven. The angels had endured a civil war in the interim, and a vanquished enemy was the least of their worries. Thus, one of the Seven Sisters could begin to wake without the angels noticing.

Poena knew nothing of the Seven Sisters slowly waking; it didn't occur to her that she should check on them. They were vanquished and enduring their punishment of everlasting sleep … and, in truth, she was angry at them for being beaten by angels.

Poena didn't have a physical form – she was an ancient spirit, born well before human souls became self-aware – nor did she ever seek one, but she could see the opportunities involved with breaking through the barrier.

*I will find a way to turn this to my advantage*, she thought. *If* one *human can travel through, then how long will it be before –*

*Wait. Something is happening. What is it?*

—•◆•—

"No! Absolutely not! It is madness!"

Beelzebub briefly lost control as an eddy of cosmic wind buffeted her. She was using her wings, of course, but they were an ethereal figment of the wings she'd had before her imprisonment in human form – and certainly not up to the job of propelling her through Heaven.

*You're not in Heaven anymore!* she chided herself. *You're in uncharted territory.*

With some effort, she pulled herself out of her free-fall and got her ephemeral wings under control.

"Beelzebub!" Lauren snapped. *"Listen* to me! Do you really see yourself spending eternal life here in the astral plane?"

Beelzebub considered her semi-permanent host. She and Lauren had no need of sharing the same mental space any longer – *neither* of them had a physical form, after all – but the ethereal angel occasionally hid within the human's soul if a half-crazed spirit was nearby.

With the spirits' attention elsewhere, however, Beelzebub was savouring the freedom. *I don't want to draw their attention back to me,* she thought, *and if it were anyone other than Lauren speaking to me like that, they would get the sharp edge of my tongue.*

"You know my feelings on that," she said curtly. "I would go back tomorrow if I could, and serve the Republic."

She paused and tried to reign in her emotions. *I used to be a senior angel in Heaven,* she thought. *Now I am a spirit in the astral plane. But I must not forget that Lauren has always been there for me.*

"If we don't stop Poena from breaking through to Earth," Rachael said quickly, "who's to say they'll stop there? Who's to say they won't then try and break through the *other* barrier – to Heaven?"

Beelzebub hesitated as she thought about the human spirit's words, and Lauren jumped in. "Beelzebub, *Paul* is still down there. So is Lucifer, and other angels like him, sleeping inside human minds. What will happen to them if the spirits break through?"

In truth, Lauren wasn't as concerned about the angels as she was about Paul, who had been one of her best friends in life; she desperately wanted to see him, and her brother Joseph, again – *and if this is the way I have to go about it, then so be it*, she thought.

Beelzebub sighed, and suddenly looked very tired. She inclined her head, indicating that she was, at the very least, willing to go along with the idea, despite any previous reservations. Lauren was relieved; she had worried that she might have pushed too hard, but was glad that Beelzebub was willing to listen.

"You have … convinced me," she said slowly. "However …"

"What?" Lauren asked. "Anything."

"We move quickly when I break though the barrier," the angel said. "The spirits – and especially Poena – will detect it. I do not wish to be here when they come."

—●—

Poena was delighted; the older, bitter and angry spirits were desperate to break down the barrier, to get through and savour the physical realm again. She knew what would happen if they did – the physical realm would drown under the weight of all of these insane, feasting spirits – but she found it difficult to care.

*If they feast on the physical realm,* she reasoned, *they will become stronger … and then we can attack the angelic realm, and I can take my revenge on millennia of imprisonment.*

Something made her pause; the spirits, in their frenzy of pushing and shoving to try and prise the sealed breach open again, hadn't seemed to notice the cause.

*Another breach is happening right now – and this time, it's opening from* this *side.*

❖

Lauren had to fight to control her emotions. *Don't be stupid, Lauren,* she told herself. *We* have *to do this in order to protect humanity … and particularly my friends.*

"Quickly!" Beelzebub urged. "Through the breach, before anyone does anything about it!"

Lauren and Rachael nodded – and quickly went through the gap in the barrier and, with a final glance over her shoulder, Beelzebub's spirit followed. Poena followed, sliding through the gap, unnoticed by the other three. She had served the Seven Sisters faithfully for millennia – even if she now resented it – and she had learnt so many things from them, including how to avoid an angel's watchful gaze.

*Time for me to learn all that is learnable in the physical world,* she thought. *If I can find the human who opened the rip the first time, they can open it again for me – and the spirits can come through and feast.*

The barrier repaired itself, as it was programmed to do, and everything returned to normal in the astral plane.

# A Hidden Dimension – Present Day

Paul couldn't feel his body. He didn't truly begin panicking, however, until he realised that he couldn't *see* anything either. He was surrounded by blankness – everything was white, with no depth or indication that there was anyone there except him.

*Bloody hell!* he thought. *What have the Seekers done to me? Where the hell am I?*

"You're in a secret realm. This place is not somewhere many people can access."

The feminine voice came from behind him.

"Who's there?" he asked, trying to keep his voice under control; he could feel the panic threatening to erupt, but he was determined to suppress it as much as possible.

"We have not met before," the female voice replied. "You do not know me."

Her voice was beautifully melodic. Paul couldn't tell if he was turning around or not, but he was doing his best to search for the voice's source.

"Do not try to locate me," the voice said. "I am everywhere … and nowhere, all at once."

Paul had no clue what she was talking about, and the panic was starting to truly set in: he couldn't see anything, he couldn't *feel* anything and he sure as hell couldn't find the woman who was talking.

"Who *are* you?" he demanded. "And where am I? For the love of God, *tell* me."

"You speak of God?" the voice snapped, suddenly far angrier and focused than it had been a moment before. "How dare you speak of *him*, in front of me?"

Paul's temper, which had been fraying since he had first woken up here, suddenly snapped.

"How dare *I* talk about God?" he snarled, trying – and failing – to spin round and locate the whereabouts of this voice. "How *dare* I? Let me tell you a story! I've *met* God, and he's a decent angel! When he finally remembered who he was, I actually found him quite … respectable. He's no better or worse than anyone else, and he has learnt to accept his failings!"

"Then he has learnt that only recently," said the voice with a weary sigh. "He has also left you, and the angels, and travelled to a different plane of existence, leaving others in charge of the new republic."

Paul remained silent, unsure of what the voice was getting at. It had sounded bitter and angry, and something told Paul that he didn't want to make the owner of this voice any angrier.

"You intrigue me, Paul Finn," the voice said abruptly.

Paul couldn't help but laugh at that. "I 'intrigue' you?" he asked. "Well, that's the oddest chat-up line I've ever heard."

His stomach churned at the thought; it made him think of Christina. He wanted to know where she was; the fact that she had been a Seeker of Truth in the past wasn't going to change his feelings for her.

"You are searching for someone you love," the voice said in a matter-of-fact tone. Paul didn't feel like it was the right time to ask how she knew that.

"Yes," he replied. "I am. Do you know where she is?"

"We do not have any interest in the affairs of humans."

"You're an angel, then?"

*You've brought me here*, he thought. *If you're going to get offended without giving me any frame of reference, then you can just sod off – and I don't care if you can read that thought or not.*

"No," she said, "I am not an angel. I am … something else."

"Well, you're obviously not human, and if you're not an angel …" Paul's voice caught for a moment. He swallowed, cleared his throat and carried on. "You're a spirit."

"I am more than just a mere spirit."

Paul wasn't sure what to say, so he decided to say nothing. Did this über-spirit know Lauren? Had they met? Was Lauren safe?

"There is a war coming, Paul."

"A war?" he repeated. "What sort of war? I know angels who were involved in a war two thousand years ago, and I caught the tail end of it. I'd rather not get involved with another one."

"You may not have any choice," the female spirit said. "Decisions are being made already … and sides are already being drawn."

Paul sighed, frustration suddenly welling up inside him. "Everyone always talks about sides," he snapped. "Why can't someone be on *my* side for a change instead of me having to run around after everyone else?"

The spirit sounded genuinely confused. "Humans often talk in riddles, and I won't pretend to understand you, Paul Finn, but you will not have any choice in the matter when the time comes." It sounded for a moment as if she had sighed. "You have experienced life in Heaven; as a result, you may be more important in the war than you realise."

"I have no clue what you're talking about."

The voice chuckled. "I don't expect you to, at least not yet. Soon, however, you will. Be ready, Paul. You will be needed."

"Don't just send me away!" Paul said quickly, he'd been in a similar situation before and recognised what was about to happen. "Listen to me, I want to know –"

He vanished from the strange realm, as quickly as he had arrived.

# The Celestial Observatory, Heaven – Present Day

"Satan?"

Michael stood at the entrance to the Observatory, waiting for the hybrid to acknowledge him – but he was lost in thought, however; his eyes were locked on the images filling the large monitors in front of him.

"Joseph?"

Joseph blinked, looked round and smiled.

"Michael," he said. "Sorry, I didn't hear you."

Michael wasn't concerned about the hybrid's confusion. In angelic terms, it was the blink of an eye since Joseph and Satan had merged into a single entity. It was going to take him time to acclimatise to having two sets of memories – and two names.

Michael stood to Joseph's left and glanced at the screens. They looked out over all the planes – heavenly, astral and earthly. Both Michael and Joseph often spent time here, observing the screens to make sure all was as it should be. One wall was set aside for each realm, with different screens looking out at different perspectives.

Satan – or Joseph, as he seemed to prefer – was staring intently at the wall of screens observing the astral plane. He was scowling at them as if they had personally offended him.

"Is something wrong?" Michael asked him.

Joseph sighed. "I haven't been watching the screens much lately," he confessed, "but something *is* wrong. A lot of spirits are congregating in one spot."

Michael followed Joseph's gaze and surveyed the scene. His angelic eyes were able to absorb far more information than any human could, and he quickly saw what he was looking for; a large group of ethereal spirits gathered round a seemingly-innocuous portion of space. These spirits, like so many of them, were half-crazed by their lack of physical form. *That is their own doing,* he thought without sympathy. *Earth is off-limits to them … and to us now as well. The spirits must accept their fate. The Seven Sisters wanted to break down the barriers between the realms. They failed – and this is their punishment.*

Michael frowned. "What do you suppose they are doing, old friend?"

It jarred Joseph to hear this angel, recently restored to the position of commander of Heaven's armies, describe him as an "old friend", but had to remind himself that half of him *was*.

"I do not know," he admitted. "I can't see anything there." He smiled. "My eyesight isn't what it was, of course."

"No, it's got better."

Joseph laughed and inclined his head. "Michael, is that …"

Michael looked back at the screen and tried to see what Joseph was referring to. After a moment, he saw it – and growled a low, guttural sound that was concern and annoyance all in one go.

"There's been a breach," he whispered. "A human's broken through."

"*Two* breaches," Joseph corrected. He pointed at another screen, where a second one had just sealed itself. "Did another human just come through?"

"No," Michael replied in horror. "Someone's gone the other way."

"Lauren," said Joseph without hesitation. "It's my sister. I just … I can *feel* it in a way that I can't entirely explain."

Michael didn't question it. He understood – in a way that Joseph didn't right now – how angel feelings worked. They were able to feel things at an instinctive level that humans would never understand. If something had happened that involved someone they cared for, those instincts would be more pronounced.

*And because he is human*, Michael thought, *he will want to protect his sister. I can understand that. But he must not.*

"Satan, the astral plane is out of reach," he explained. "Angels have been banned from going there for … well, an incredibly long time. We can no longer travel to the astral plane *or* Earth. You cannot go after Lauren."

"That is my *sister*!"

Joseph's anger was sudden and abrupt. It caught the fellow angel off-guard – Michael was used to his friend being calm and thoughtful, so it was surprising.

"Don't …" Joseph bit his lip and forced his mind into calmness. "Don't tell me I can't go after my sister when I *know* something is wrong. She *died*, Michael, right in front of me. Now I find out her soul is still living and she's torn through the barrier to Earth. We've got to find out why. She wouldn't just do that for the fun of it."

Michael couldn't disagree; he had known Beelzebub for more millennia than he could remember, and if Lauren was anything like her, then they would be sensible – except if there was a damn good reason to be rebellious.

"Then we should find out why Beelzebub and Lauren have risked everything to draw our attention," Michael said thoughtfully. "We need to take this to the Council of Twelve."

Joseph shook his head. "That will take too long; they'll want to debate everything a hundred times over. We need to take this to *Micah.*"

The two angels shared a moment of agreement and turned towards the Observatory's exit. After a few steps, Michael realised that he was walking alone. He looked back over his shoulder at his fellow angel.

"Why are the realms separate, Michael?" Joseph asked. "My memories are still … scattered. What happened to separate the realms?"

Michael frowned. "Is this *really* the time?" he snapped.

"No angel has travelled to the astral plane for millennia. Spirits *hate* us and are jealous of living humans. What happened?"

Michael shook his head. "Whatever issues the spirits have aren't connected to the ancient war," he said angrily. "The Seven Sisters fought us – and used Poena as their agent. She *manipulated* Lucifer –"

He closed his mouth again, more annoyed at himself than Joseph for having revealed anything.

"We need to talk to the first among equals," he said, and this time, Joseph knew that there was no pushing him any further.

*I'll just have to pump Micah for information,* he thought. *I need to find out what the hell my sister's up to — and if that means travelling to the other plane of existence, then so be it.*

# Customs House, Ramsgate – Present Day

Paul groaned as he woke up; his body ached, his tongue was thick and clumsy and his head was pounding.

*Am I still in that odd place?* he wondered – then realised he couldn't be, as he could *feel* his body.

His eyes slowly focused on his surroundings – and the fact that he could *see* his surroundings confirmed that he was back on Earth. He was in a changing room, with lockers along each wall. The door at the end was open, and he could see out into the hallway; they were inside Customs House.

*At least we haven't gone far*, he thought. *I'm not sure what good that will do us, but it's a small comfort anyway.*

He tried to move, but found himself tied by his arms and legs to a chair that was itself bolted to the floor.

*They've thought this through.*

Kirby was opposite him, in the same restraints, but still unconscious. Paul's gaze then settled on McKenzie, who was stood next to the door. He had a look of fear mingled with worry on his face; Paul sensed that McKenzie wasn't in control of the situation.

*Maybe he* is *just a caretaker*, Paul thought.

As soon as McKenzie saw that Paul was awake, he stepped outside the room for a moment and spoke in a hushed whisper to someone in the corridor. He stepped back to allow the other person inside.

Paul snorted in amusement. "I should have guessed," he sneered.

"How lovely to see you again, Mr Finn," Somerville replied. His face was pleasantly neutral, and he looked as if he hadn't a care in the world. "Sweet dreams?"

"Where's Christina?" Paul demanded.

McKenzie raised an eyebrow. "She's *your* girlfriend, Mr Finn. You mean you don't know?"

Paul did his very best to keep his anger under wraps. Somerville was clearly a nasty piece of work under this supercilious, sarcastic exterior, and Paul doubted that pushing his anger would do much good.

"Why are you here?" Somerville asked him. "Why have you come to Customs House?"

"You mean it's not Election Day?" Paul replied as innocently as he could manage. "Damn, I thought this was my local polling station. After all, I thought this was the *council's* building, not yours."

The façade dropped from Somerville's face, and was replaced by an angry snarl. McKenzie, who saw the change from his position in the corner of the room, whimpered in fear. Clearly, Somerville could get very scary when angered – but Paul refused to be baited.

*I will not be cowed by you.*

"You think it's *funny* to not give me answers, Mr Finn?" Somerville said slowly. "It is not in the *slightest* bit funny. Your girlfriend said she wanted some time alone, and you are not being very respectful of her wishes."

"So she *is* here then?"

Paul hadn't been able to stop himself from giving the first smart-alec response that appeared in his head, and Somerville's hand lashed out before Paul could react – and slapped him hard around the side of the face.

Paul had seen on TV when people had been hit, and he had always imagined it would be painful, but the *actual* feeling was shocking; the pain was awful and he couldn't help but cry out.

Paul's cry of pain seemed to rouse Kirby; the detective opened his eyes and took in the scene; his jaw set in an angry line as he quickly caught up.

"Leave him alone, you bastard!" he snapped at Somerville.

Somerville glanced at him. "Your sister was a Seeker of Truth."

Kirby nodded; he seemed to realise that it wouldn't be a good idea to answer back, given the swelling on his friend's face.

"Yes," he said, "I *know* she was. She was one of your senior officers for years. She tried to slow you all down, *you* especially. Rachael thought there was more out there than any of us understood, so we should take our time *until* we understood what was truly out there."

From the door, McKenzie showed the ghost of a smile. "She recruited me, your sister," he said, and seemed lost in the fog of reminiscence for a moment. Somerville glared at him, and McKenzie quickly picked up on it; he faded into the background again.

Paul and Kirby exchanged a glance, each of them knowing the trouble they were clearly in. Paul felt a deep, primal urge to summon Lucifer from his slumber to help them out of the predicament.

At the same time, however, he knew that wasn't practical. There was no way of knowing what would happen if Lucifer awoke while still trapped inside this human body – and still on Earth.

*I'm not convinced my death would solve the problem.*

Somerville looked back at Paul. "Why did you come to find Christina?"

"Wouldn't you?" Paul asked. "If you saw your girlfriend being dragged into a car, wouldn't you go looking for her?"

"She was hardly dragged."

"Why did she go with you then?" Paul asked, desperately wanting an answer. "Why did she think that going with you would solve the problem? She was angry with me, not you – but I thought she loved me enough to stay and work it out."

"She felt betrayed at not knowing something so fundamental about you, Paul," Somerville replied, his calm mask back in place. "She was always a Seeker, even if she didn't actively participate any longer, and she didn't know what to think when someone she loved had been somewhere she had longed to go."

"But why *you?*" Paul insisted. "Why did she choose to leave with *you?*"

Kirby's face dropped as he seemed to realise the answer.

Paul frowned. "What?"

The detective looked almost sorrowful as he looked into Paul's eyes. It took Paul a minute to understand, but then the colour drained out of his face. "No…" he whispered.

Somerville rolled his eyes. "Don't be so dramatic," he sighed. "Yes, Christina and I were lovers, once – and now that I've breached the barrier to the astral plane, I want her back by my side so we can explore that realm together."

# A Hidden Dimension –
# Present Day

Alcyone looked around, confused by what she could see – or, rather, couldn't see. She had been the last of the Seven to go into their deep, enforced slumber; by rights, she should have been the last to be awoken, but now that she *was* conscious, she was surprised to see that none of her Sisters were awake and waiting for her.

In her heart, she knew the answer, of course; it wasn't something they had ever admitted to each other, but that didn't make it any less true.

*I was always more powerful,* she thought. *Out of all of us, it was always me who held sway over my Sisters.*

A part of her was disappointed. When she had been imprisoned, she had been confident that they would awaken again, one day, when the angels had been defeated, hopefully by the spirit world they had enslaved for so long. But everything seemed to be exactly as it had been.

*I need to find out what precisely has been happening,* she thought. *Where is Poena?*

# Customs House, Ramsgate – Present Day

"You and Christina were a *couple?*"

Paul paused for a moment to process the information – and then his brain threw up another fact which, despite his heart breaking in two, seemed more salient.

"You've broken through into the astral plane?" he demanded. A thought – or, more accurately, a *feeling* – rose unbidden from his deep subconscious, otherwise known as Lucifer. The feeling made him aware that, in some way, humanity gaining access to the astral plan was wrong. He couldn't be more specific than that, so he pushed the feeling away again and focused on confronting the man in front of him instead.

"So you decided to poison my girlfriend's mind against me so you could bring her back to your ... your coven and help you break through it again?"

Somerville remained surprisingly calm; he didn't flinch once at Paul's words. Instead, he reached into his jacket pocket.

"Paul!" Kirby said urgently. "Watch what you're saying! Somerville is –"

His voice tailed off as Somerville pulled his hand out of his jacket – his fingers clenched tightly around the dark silver handle of a gun. Paul's heart felt as if it had leapt into his throat at the sight of the weapon; he shot a warning glance at Kirby, who seemed to understand automatically – stay silent!

"She didn't lie to you, Mr Finn," Somerville said quietly, his voice calmly belying the fact that he was wielding a deadly weapon. "She just chose to keep that private. She hadn't been an active member for some time, but after my recent … success, I needed people I could trust. With Ms Kirby gone, Christina was the obvious choice."

Paul opened his mouth, but Somerville spoke over the top of him.

"We didn't set this up, if that's what you're thinking," he said. "It's nothing that dramatic. Christina hadn't been active with the Seekers for some time when she met you – and she ended up falling in love with you without any involvement from us."

"What would Christina think if she knew you were doing this?" Paul asked. "I thought the Seekers were meant to be a peaceful group, not kidnappers?"

Somerville shook his head. "You were asking too many questions," he said. "We couldn't just let you leave. I don't want the world to know about my success – or even just the police."

Kirby laughed. "Too late," he snapped. "I'm a detective for the local force."

Paul groaned – that was the *last* thing Kirby should have told this … madman. Somerville's finger twitched on the trigger as the gun spun towards the detective – just as time began to slow down.

It didn't take Paul more than a second to realise that it wasn't his *perception* of time that was slowing down; it was measurable, external time that was slowing. Disorientated, he looked between his friend and his captor, but neither seemed aware of the problem; in fact, they didn't seem aware of *anything.*

A shiver ran up Paul's spine; this wasn't the first time he had experienced this. Two years ago, an angel had travelled to Earth to deliver some news – and manipulated time in the process.

He looked round, but there was no-one else in the room; usually, angels appeared on the physical plane by using a door-like hole in the air, but nothing like that had appeared. The room was still and silent; Somerville's finger frozen on the trigger and Kirby's eyes half-widened in alarm.

"Michael?" Paul said out loud. He hesitated, then added, "Gabriel?"

Both of those beings had been able to stop time like this – being angels, there wasn't much they *couldn't* do. He'd been hopeful as he'd said Gabriel's name, as he'd seen the angel's physical form dead in the Ruling Chamber of Heaven, but knowing that he had a disembodied angel in his own head, he was still willing to consider any possibility. His heart skipped a beat as another name came into his mind.

"Joseph?"

Paul's best friend didn't appear – and his hopes began to fade as quickly as they had been raised.

*"Paul, it's me."*

The voice seemed to come from everywhere and nowhere at once. Paul found himself looking for a sound system, but remembered that time remained frozen.

"Who's there?" he demanded.

He blinked in surprise as the air in front of him began to shift, like a heat haze *inside* the building. He glanced around the room to see if he could spot any trickery; when he turned back, he yelled in surprise. Three figures had begun to emerge from the haze.

"What the —"

Another surge of certainty surged through him, and it was clear — at least to Paul — that he was being subconsciously fed information by the unconscious Lucifer.

*You're from the astral plane,* he realised. *So why does that feel like such a* bad *thing?*

Paul blinked — and his jaw dropped open as he realised. One of the three forming shapes was someone he recognised very well, and in that instant he felt his heart break for a second time.

"Lauren," he whispered.

Lauren Crabtree-Tempur stretched her arms out above her head for a moment, wincing as something twisted inside her faux body. She smiled as she realised she was able to *feel* something on the physical level and then looked at Paul.

"Hello, Paul," she replied — he could have cried right then at the sound of Lauren's voice — and put her hands on her hips. "Looks like we turned up at just the right time."

# Astral Plane – Present Day

Evan Somerville was angry. He was angry at being pushed out of the astral plane just when he had succeeded in getting through for the first time – and he was embarrassed as well. He was one of the most powerful Seekers, and certainly wasn't the sort of person to allow *anyone* to force him out of a location if he didn't want to go.

*I'm not* one *of the best*, he thought. *I'm* the *best*.

He knew he was because he had beaten the time lock currently around Customs House.

A sixth sense told him, as he touched the gun's trigger, that time was slowing. Instinctively, he had done what had been at the forefront of his mind; he had fled his body and tried to re-enter the astral plane.

He had failed, of course; while the process of leaving his body was easy, and he had done it many times before, he hadn't been able to break through the barrier again. The previous breach had healed, and he couldn't find another weak point.

If he had been a lesser being, he might have been worried about his lack of interest in his body's welfare. It was only then did he begin to wonder *who* had caused the time stop in Customs House.

*Only spirits would have the ability to do this*, he realised — and he was shocked at himself for not considering it before. *Spirits have penetrated* Earth — *but why? They have had their time here! We should be travelling to their realm and learning more about their existence!*

—◆•◆—

Poena was angry. No, she was beyond angry — she was *furious*.

She had avoided detection as she followed the other three into Earth's realm — and then watched as a human spirit tried again to break through the now-healed breach.

*Their arrogance is appalling*, she thought. *What will happen if they do break through again? No, we must strike first. We will feed on their strength.*

She had been a powerful spirit before the war, fighting alongside the ancient Seven Sisters — beings she had worshipped, once upon a time. Had she still felt like that, she would have woken them, to have them fighting by her side.

*Now I see how wrong I was*, she thought. *They are weak — they allowed themselves to be confined and beaten by angels. Now I have a proper army — of willing, hungry, angry spirits, I can fight without the Seven Sisters. Let them sleep.*

Her anger was therefore greater when she had sensed the angel-spirit travel to Earth with the two human spirits. *An angel has already invaded our realm. How long before other angels come and get her — by force if necessary?*

*We must draw first blood.*

An unusual emotion then interrupted her thoughts: fear. The last time she had fought a war, she had lost.

*Because I was betrayed,* she reminded herself, *but also before I didn't understand what the Sisters were thinking.*

She was hungry for victory this time, and knew that she couldn't afford to repeat the mistakes of her past – so she needed to consider different tactics this time.

*I need to learn about humanity,* she realised. *I need to learn about their weaknesses, foibles and strengths, and use them to my advantage.*

A plan immediately occurred to her, and she knew that she had to bide her time. She watched the human spirit carefully … and waited for the moment when the time lock was lifted and he tried to re-enter his body.

# Customs House, Ramsgate – Present Day

It had taken some time, but Lauren eventually managed to unbind Paul's hands from the thick rope that was holding them behind his back. All Paul could focus on was how Lauren could manipulate the rope, given that her body was created out of … well, he didn't know what it was, and since it certainly wasn't anything that he could understand, he tried his best not to think about it too much.

"Thanks," he muttered, rubbing each wrist in turn to try and get some feeling back into them. "I was beginning to forget I had hands."

"Glad to hear that your mouth was unaffected."

Paul's stomach churned again as Lauren spoke; she sounded exactly as he remembered, and it made him feel sick in a way he couldn't fully explain. To distract himself, he looked over at the other visitors.

The first one was obvious – another memory from Lucifer's sleeping mind came to the forefront; Beelzebub stood next to him in the Celestial Observatory, both looking over the cosmos in friendly companionship.

Beelzebub's ghostly form smiled as she saw the recognition in Paul's eyes.

"Very nice to meet you again, Paul," she said – her voice was surprisingly soft and quiet. Paul's – or rather, Lucifer's memories – told him that Beelzebub's voice was usually strong and powerful.

*But she was a physical angel back then,* he told himself. *She's … dead now.*

He had suddenly become tongue-tied in the presence of the angel – even one who was vaguely transparent – so he smiled at her and looked at the other visitor.

"Rachael Kirby, I assume?"

Rachael nodded. "Pleased to meet you," she replied. "My brother's told me all about you."

He glanced over at his friend, who was still frozen in time. Rachael looked guilty as she looked at her brother.

"I didn't realise he'd be here as well," she said. "I've only just learnt about the time lock, and once it's in place, I can't pull someone out of it."

Lauren shook her head. "I don't want to be here without the time lock in place," she said with certainty. "Not until we've talked."

"Talked about what?"

Paul realised how blunt that had sounded, and gave a wan smile to apologise.

"Not that it's not good to see you," he added, "but it's just … well, unexpected."

Lauren hesitated, unsure how to explain their desire to protect their human loved ones. She glanced over at Rachael, who shrugged and looked into the middle distance.

"Go ahead," she said. "This was *your* idea."

Beelzebub flexed her wings, looking suddenly uncomfortable. "I have to say," she said quickly, "that I was initially against this."

Paul watched Lauren carefully; his old friend seemed surprised that Beelzebub would speak so bluntly.

*I shouldn't expect angels to think like us*, Paul thought. *From the memories I'm picking up from Lucifer, they don't think like I do … But then they're not humans, are they?*

"Something does not … feel right," Beelzebub said abruptly.

Paul blinked; he was caught off-guard by the sudden change in conversation. "You're the spirit of an angel on Earth," he retorted. "I'm not surprised something doesn't feel entirely right."

The look that the angel gave him almost turned Paul's legs to jelly, but something inside him strengthened his resolve – and he realised it was Lucifer, from his deep sleep, reminding his human host that he *could* withstand one of Beelzebub's legendary stares; after all, if Lucifer could, then Paul could as well.

Paul cleared his throat and raised an eyebrow.

"You were clearly thinking of something else," he said, "but seeing as my psychic abilities are non-existent, you'll have to *tell* us."

Lauren and Rachael remained stock-still, their eyes moving between the two. Lauren had always known that Paul had a strong personality – and, in the last two years, had learnt that Beelzebub's personality was equally so.

She was surprised, therefore, when Beelzebub inclined her head in an apparent sign of submission.

"You are correct, of course," she said quietly. "I cannot be any more precise. All angels are able to sense when something is … wrong with the cosmos. If I had a physical body, I might be more accurate."

She looked at Lauren. "I will step outside and try to locate the source."

Lauren felt like she had missed something fundamental, and it must have shown on her face as Beelzebub raised an eyebrow.

"I meant out into the corridor," Beelzebub explained. "I have put a time lock on the entire building."

With that, she disappeared into thin air.

Rachael frowned at the now-empty spot. "Considering Beelzebub's never been to Earth before," she said, "I'm not convinced *something* won't go wrong. I'll go after her – and don't worry, I *will* be careful."

As Rachael disappeared, Paul turned to look at Lauren – and seeing her again, looking exactly as she had done two years ago, took his breath away. Her chestnut brown hair, her petite face and slim frame hadn't changed one iota – and the silvery outline that surrounded her didn't distract Paul from the fact that his friend, who he had seen die, was right in front of him.

Lauren chuckled – she could clearly tell what Paul was thinking, and looked down at herself. She was wearing the same clothes she had been in when she died; dark blue jeans, a green t-shirt and flat, black shoes; they had clearly still been on her mind when she created this body upon returning to Earth.

"How do I look?" she asked, glancing down at her body.

"You look …" Paul hesitated, trying to find the words. "You like exactly like I remember you."

"Is that a good thing?"

Paul shrugged. He didn't mean to be so dismissive, but he was feeling overwhelmed. Wanting to seem fine with his friend, he tried to speak again, but his throat closed up and he croaked something incomprehensible.

Lauren nodded and looked away.

"It's funny," she said, "I didn't really like these shoes when I was alive, but I wore them because they were comfortable. Now, they're the only shoes I can remember wearing, so now I'm stuck with them for as long as I'm here."

"I gave the eulogy at your funeral."

Paul hadn't meant to blurt that out quite so bluntly – or at all, if he were honest, but there was nothing he could do about it now. He licked his lips and carried on talking.

"I talked about what a great friend you were to me … and what a great sister you were to Joseph. How you'd always been there for me, no matter what. But one thing I couldn't talk about was … was how you'd died. Because everyone aside from Kirby would think I was a raving nutcase. I miss you and Joseph every single bloody day, and now here you are standing in front of me like nothing's *happened!*"

Paul could hear his voice rising towards the end of his last sentence, but couldn't stop himself – and he couldn't now take it back. A strange mixture of emotions was churning through him, from anger through to a resurgence of the grief he had thought he'd dealt with two years ago.

Still not looking at him, Lauren shook her head; her own conflicting emotions playing across her face.

"Something's happening, Paul," she said. "Something ... strange, and I don't know what to do. I need your help. I'm scared."

That had been something she hadn't been willing to confess even to Rachael or Beelzebub; she *was* worried about her human friends, and her brother living in heaven, but she was also scared herself, and needed her oldest friends around her to reassure her.

"What is it?" Paul asked. He had been brought up short by the fearful tone in his friend's voice. "What's happened?"

"A human breached the barrier between the astral plane and Earth ... and some of the older, angrier spirits want to find the breach and come through, to feed off human energy."

Paul was silent for a moment as he thought carefully about what his friend was saying. Lauren had clearly seen things that he could never imagine; many humans wanted to know what happened beyond death, and Somerville and his Seekers of Truth were just one example of a group actively trying to find out.

"So *that's* what Somerville has done," he muttered. "*He* was the one who did it."

Lauren looked confused. "What are you talking about?" she asked him.

Paul quickly filled Lauren in on the events of the morning, and Lauren's eyes lingered on the time-frozen Somerville, his gun still pointed directly at Kirby.

"Rachael's mentioned him," Lauren said slowly. "He's led the Seekers for years, but he and Rachael were always at loggerheads. Somerville always believed that they would be accepted in the astral plane without question. She tried to slow him down, convince him that they shouldn't be trying to get into realms that they didn't understand, and that there were other ways of learning what was out there."

Paul raised an eyebrow. "With Rachael dead, it looks like he's succeeded in doing it."

"And Rachael's been proved right."

Paul nodded. He chewed on the end of a fingernail as he considered the situation; while Christina was clearly hurt that he had never told her about his past, he was suddenly filled with a new-found confidence that her anger would subside and they would be able to move past this argument.

He smiled and gave his friend a hug; trying to ignore the bizarreness of how *real* she felt.

"So …" she said. "What do we do now? Angry spirits are trying to get though the barrier to feed on humanity, and we've lost Rachael and Beelzebub to some sort of investigation out in the corridor."

"Did someone mention my name?"

Lauren was used to the concept of being able to transport quickly from one location to another; it wasn't instantaneous, merely *incredibly fast* – although, when the distance involved was only through a wall and air, it could easily *seem* instantaneous. Paul, however, *wasn't* used to it and yelled in shock.

"What is it?!" Rachael asked in alarm, looking around for the source of Paul's yell.

"You –!" he began to exclaim, but couldn't quite finish the sentence. He clutched his chest; his heart felt as if it were beating one-hundred to the dozen.

For a moment, both Rachael and Lauren struggled to understand what Paul was talking about.

"Oh!" Rachael exclaimed. "The appearing, disappearing thing? Sorry about that – I forget non-spirits aren't used to it."

Paul released a breath and shrugged, doing his belated best to appear blasé. Lauren filled Rachael and Beelzebub – who had also re-materialised – in on their discussion.

Rachael was clearly fascinated by what she had heard, and nodded as she listened.

"I'm not surprised it's Somerville," she said. "He's so arrogant that he thinks he can overcome whatever's out there."

She looked at Paul. "Trust me when I say that he can't."

Paul glanced at Beelzebub, who seemed worried by the thought of what was waiting to come through beyond the astral barrier.

*If something can worry an angel,* he thought, *then it's going to worry me as well.*

"Well, I'm glad you're here," he replied. "You saved both our lives. As you can see, Somerville was about to shoot us."

He had never been particularly good at reading body language, but he picked up on the look between Rachael and Beelzebub easily.

"What?" he asked. "What's happened?"

"Somerville found a way to free his soul from the time lock," Beelzebub said. "He will re-enter as soon as we release it – and will know that spirits have been here on Earth."

Paul breathed out. Nerves started churning in his stomach as he realised how complex and dangerous this situation was becoming.

"We can't just keep the time lock in place indefinitely," he said. "Let's just … release it and see if we can reason with him."

"Paul, the man was just about to *shoot* you," Lauren said incredulously. "I don't think you should be waiting for him with flowers."

Before Paul could retort – or even think about what his retort *would* be – all three spirits looked up at the ceiling, almost at the same time. Paul noticed that Lauren and Rachael seemed more fearful than Beelezbub – who looked more intrigued than worried.

He opened his mouth to ask what was happening, but decided against it; he wasn't honestly sure he wanted to know what could worry three spirits.

"Is it Poena?" Lauren asked.

Without taking her eyes off the ceiling, Rachael nodded. "She must have realised we were here."

"Who the hell is Poena?" he asked. He glanced at the ceiling again, but it wasn't giving him any clues. "Sounds like a dish you'd order in a curry house."

Beelzebub blinked and looked over at her friend, suddenly confused.

"What are you talking about?"

"I could ask you the same thing."

Lauren interrupted the cross-purposes conversation. "Poena is a spirit. She works ... work*ed* ... for some very powerful beings called the Seven Sisters." She glanced at Rachael as if for confirmation, but her friend was still staring at the ceiling. "She's been asleep for a very long time."

"What's made her wake up now then?" Paul asked.

Beelzebub inclined her head to one side and stared intently at Paul, until it started to make him feel uncomfortable.

"Precisely the right question," she replied.

Paul raised an eyebrow. "So what's the answer?" he demanded.

"Paul, this isn't the time," Lauren cut in. She looked directly at him for a moment before turning her head to Beelzebub.

"We should shift locations," she said.

"Agreed," Beelzebub said with a nod.

"And we should split up," Rachael added. She was still watching the ceiling, worried that Poena would somehow break through the time lock before they had agreed what to do. "We should split up and rendezvous later when it's safer."

Beelzebub scowled at the spirit. "Poena will *not* break through the time lock."

"Yes she will," Rachael snapped back, finally taking her eyes off the ceiling to look at the angelic spirit. "She's out for blood, Beelzebub, and won't stop until she's destroyed everything on this planet."

Beelzebub hesitated for a moment, then nodded her head. "Very well," she replied coolly. "I cannot return her to the astral plane – I do not have the power – but I will make sure the barrier is strengthened enough to prevent any more spirits coming through."

"And we'll hide out while we come up with a plan," Lauren added. "Paul, you and Kirby should remain out of sight until we come and get you."

Paul frowned. "But I want to come with *you*," he insisted. "We could –"

Beelzebub breathed out in pure frustration. "We do not have *time* for this," she snapped. "We must go *now.*"

Rachael looked round at Paul. "I take it you've never travelled the way we travel?"

Paul rolled his eyes. "What do you think?"

"How *are* you with fast travel?"

"Not bad. I once went round a Formula One track for my birthday and didn't throw up – unlike your brother," he added with a glance at Lauren, "who threw up almost as soon as he finished his lap."

"Yeah …" Lauren said slowly. "This is nothing like a Formula One car." She looked at Beelzebub. "I'd send them somewhere near a bathroom, if I were you."

Paul frowned. "Okay, you're going to have to start talking very slowly to me, because I have literally *no* idea –"

There wasn't time for him for finish his sentence before the world disappeared in a colourful spiral of light – and he lost consciousness.

⬛●⬛

Poena felt time rushing back into the nearby building, and she moved immediately towards it. Her energy, however, was different to before – it was beginning to absorb the energy of another soul … Evan Somerville. He was fighting, certainly, but she would not let him win.

*I will learn about the physical realm,* she thought, *and then lead my spirits here to* destroy *it all … and then we can take on the angels. I will unite all the realms … and the death of Evan Somerville is just the beginning of the sacrifices that need to be made.*

# Heaven – The Distant Past

The war raged.

Angels and spirits had lived side by side since the moment of Creation, but tensions had now spilled over into outright war. The Seven Sisters and Poena had led the spirits, albeit few in number, against the angels, and were continuing to fight them to a standstill.

*This shouldn't be happening!* Lucifer thought. *We should be winning!*

Lucifer was in his private quarters in Heaven's vast citadel, which floated on the ethereal eddies of space. Being as lost in thought as he was, it took him a while to realise that someone was talking to him. He looked round and saw Satan stood in the entrance, looking tense as he waited for his friend to speak.

"My apologies," he replied, without being entirely sure what he was apologising for, and stepped away from the window. "My mind was … elsewhere."

Satan couldn't help but smile. "I would not have guessed."

Lucifer snorted with twisted humour and nodded in agreement. He sat down in his chair and motioned for Satan to sit opposite him.

"Why is the war continuing?" he asked. "It should be over by now. "

"Because we believed that we are better than them," Satan replied, "and did not expect the Sisters to side against us."

Lucifer gave him a weary look; they had been over this a hundred times, if not a thousand, and he didn't want to argue about it now.

"I meant —"

Satan shook his head. "I know what you meant, my friend," he interrupted. "I'm not sure what you want me to say. We've been so sure of our superiority for so long that we assume nothing is equal to us." He rolled his eyes. "This war is beginning to show that we were wrong."

"The spirits ..." Lucifer exhaled as he tried to think through his argument; he could feel anger bubbling through every pore of his being, which was making his thoughts difficult to process. "They wish to destroy everything we stand for," he went on. "At the very least, the Seven Sisters should have remained neutral. They have changed the balance of power in this war."

"You mean that they have given the spirits a chance of winning?"

Lucifer opened his mouth to retort, but found he had nothing to say. He and Satan were polar opposites: Lucifer was passionate and often leapt before thinking; Satan, on the other hand, was contemplative and thoughtful. Together, however, they had become firm friends — and could always speak honestly to one another.

"We're losing, my friend," Satan said bluntly, "and *we're* to blame."

Lucifer's wings tensed up and partially unfurled, then settled back down. He finally sat down opposite his friend, and stared thoughtfully at the floor. The war *was* going badly; he couldn't deny it. The general feeling had been that the angelic armies, commanded by Michael and Lucifer, would win an outright victory in the blink of an angelic eye; the spirits didn't have the strength, numbers or coordinated approach that the angels did.

So why were the spirits winning? They had routed the angelic armies in the last two major battles, and countless skirmishes in between. Michael was reported to be in a foul mood, although he had remained locked in conference with the Almighty for the last two days, and not even Lucifer – the Almighty's eldest son – had seen either of them since.

Satan rubbed a hand over his face, suddenly looking tired and old despite the youthfulness of his features.

"Where did it all go wrong, 'fer?" he asked.

Lucifer sighed. "The Seven Sisters became involved."

"I wasn't talking about that."

Lucifer was thrown. "I thought we were discussing the spirit threat."

"Would you really call them a threat?"

Lucifer really *was* confused now. A deep frown creased his forehead as he leaned back in his chair and rested his chin on one hand.

"They've attacked Heaven without mercy," he said after a while. "They crave physical form, despite the damage it could cause to the cosmic balance, and they have *killed* angels."

Satan inclined his head; it was clear that he wasn't about to dispute the truth.

"Lucifer," he replied calmly, "you are one of the most intelligent angels I have ever had the good fortune to know. You are also one of my closest friends, and I *know* that your memory is excellent. Do you really expect me to believe that you have forgotten how this war started?"

"It was pre-emptive!" Lucifer snapped. He stood angrily from his chair and folded his arms across his chest, scowling out of the window. "The spirits were planning –"

"We can always find a reasonable justification," Satan cut in. He remained deliberately seated and kept his wings in a submissive gesture; he loved his friend like a brother, but knew his temper could be a destructive force.

*There is a time and place for that*, he thought. *This is not it. It is my responsibility to make him understand.*

"We attacked first," he went on, "because we were scared."

Lucifer spun round and glared at his friend, but bit back his initial response, which Satan was grateful for. The longer Lucifer kept his emotions in check, the longer Satan had to convince his friend of his point of view.

"Angels and spirits live in Heaven *together*," he went on. "We are equal … tenants, if you will."

Lucifer snorted. "I doubt that very much. We continue to build this universe even now."

"And we have always used the spirits to do it."

Lucifer glared at his friend. "I do not think I like where this conversation is going."

"Maybe not, but it is the truth, and I will always speak the truth to you … even if you do not wish to hear it."

"What is this grand truth then?" Lucifer snapped, his anger finally bubbling over. "Tell me what it is while we fight for our survival!"

"Against an oppressed people!" Satan said angrily. He stood up again and this time didn't try to hide his anger. "They have been our slaves, Lucifer, and *we* attacked first because we were terrified that they would do exactly what they are now doing. Our slaves are on the verge of becoming our masters, in alliance with the Seven Sisters, and all because we provoked them in the first place!"

There was a tense, angry silence between the two for a moment, then Lucifer straightened, his face hardened with frustration.

"We are stronger than them," Lucifer said passionately, "and they *will* be beaten. I will see to that."

# Customs House, Ramsgate – Present Day

Time came rushing back into Customs House.

Paul, Kirby and the three spirits vanished in a blink of an eye; the body of Evan Somerville, however, slumped to the floor. It was temporarily without a consciousness controlling its movements; two spirits were currently fighting for control inside his head.

Somerville and Poena were circling, each calculating the strength and cunning of the other.

Poena was still seething with anger, furious at these arrogant humans who believed that they could rule all the dominions – *like the angels did before them*, she thought – and were now trying to force themselves into *her* realm. The Seven Sisters had given them a fighting chance before – *but I don't need them now*, she thought. *I will subdue this human and discover how he travelled between the realms. I will then bring my army through and let them feed.*

*You will* not *win!*

That thought wasn't Poena's – and it surprised her, because she had assumed she'd swallowed her opponent's conscious thoughts whole.

Somerville's rage matched Poena's, and he was *not* going to give up his body without a fight. An arrogant spirit was not going to take it away from him.

*I believed there was something* better *across the barrier!* he screamed. *I believed you would be able to teach us so much.*

*You were wrong.*

Somerville prided himself on being a strong, confident person, but those three words chilled him to the core – and pushed him off-balance for a moment.

As he stumbled to regain control, he caught an edge of this spirit's thoughts; *I will* destroy *the angels*, she told herself, *and finish the job the Sisters started all those years ago. But before that, we will look to the physical plane … and my followers will experience the pleasures of the flesh that angels have denied us for so long.*

*And this time*, no-one *will get in our way.*

# A Hidden Dimension – Present Day

"Not *again*."

Paul was back in the other realm – *Wherever it is*, he thought – and was unable to see anything but the pure whiteness around him. He sighed, instantly fed up with being involuntary transported to this strange place – and unnerved at having been brought here against his will. Again.

"Thank you for returning to speak with me."

Paul tried to spin around and search out the source of that beautiful, lilting voice, but it was like trying to spin round in treacle – and even if he had been able to, there would have been nothing to see.

"I don't really think I had much of a choice in the matter, did I?"

"I didn't say you had a choice," the voice replied coolly.

"Seems rather a pointless statement then, if you don't mind my saying."

A small part of Paul's brain was shouting at him to stop being quite so sarcastic, but he couldn't help himself – he was angry and annoyed with this being, and he wanted her to know it.

"You seem rather confident, Paul Finn," the voice said. "I admire that, but I wonder if you truly realise the gravity of your situation."

Paul didn't answer immediately, because he knew she was right. He *didn't* truly understand what was happening to him, and he knew that the owner of the voice was clearly a powerful being. She had brought him here without Lucifer, after all. Despite the angel being asleep, Paul always *knew* he was there, nestled in the subconscious part of his brain. The angel was now a constant, comforting presence – except that, while Paul was here in this white space, Lucifer wasn't with him.

*He'd better be looking after my body.*

An uncomfortable thought suddenly passed through his mind – *Without me there, what's to stop him waking up?*

"He won't have time to realise you're gone," the voice said. "You'll only be gone for a fraction of a second in human terms."

"Okay, you've got to stop reading my mind like that," Paul snapped. "You may have dragged me all the way to … wherever this is, but I really don't appreciate you digging around in there. It's bad enough that I have to share my head with an angel."

"So Poena was right?" the voice said thoughtfully. "Angels were planning a take-over of every realm all along, in league with humanity."

"What? 'In league'?" Paul was lost. "What the hell are you talking about?"

The voice went steely as she replied; "You share a body with the angel. Do you deny it?"

"I … Of course I don't deny it, it's true!"

Paul was lost for words; he didn't know what to say other than the truth. The owner of this voice seemed to be accusing him of something, but he couldn't work out *what*.

"Look," he went on, trying to regain the initiative, "who *are* you and why are you so concerned that an angel lives in my head?"

There was a pause, as if the voice was surprised by Paul's sudden anger – and hadn't fully expected it, nor his total honesty.

"Do not concern yourself with who I am," she replied. "I am someone who needs to understand what angels and humans are doing working together."

"Working …" Paul would have frowned if he had his body around him. "I wouldn't say we're working together per sé. We don't share my head space by choice."

"Have any spirits spoken to you recently?"

Paul hesitated, and changed the answer he had been about to give. "Apart from you, you mean?"

The voice chuckled. "You don't propose to tell me?"

"I'll answer your questions when you answer mine."

The voice sighed. "Disappointing," it said. "I had hoped we could work together. Instead, it seems that Poena was right … and angels are conspiring against my sisters and I."

*You're making this up as you go along.*

"I can still read your thoughts," the voice said reproach-fully.

*I know you can,* he thought angrily at her. *How can you expect me to trust you, when you don't stay out of my head?*

"Will I ever understand humans?" she wondered. "You protest your innocence, yet you share your mind with an angel and tell me that the planned invasion isn't real."

Paul was thrown. "Our … what? 'Invasion'? I really *don't* know what you're talking about."

"That surprises me," the voice snapped, suddenly sounding annoyed and angry. "You believe that you are telling the truth. I can sense your thoughts. Yet you carry an angel in your physical body with you. I wonder if the angel is somehow hiding part of your mind from me. Do not criticise me for evading the truth, when you have done the same thing. I *felt* the barrier shift twice; once bringing a human here and once letting spirits through into your realm."

Paul sighed; whoever this being was, it clearly wasn't going to listen to him.

"You're dreaming," he snapped. "There *is* no conspiracy."

The voice was silent for a moment, as if thinking carefully about what Paul had said.

"It's been so long," she said quietly. "I've been asleep for so long, I'm … confused. I do not know what to believe any more. Should I have trusted Poena … or should I believe you?"

Paul hesitated before interrupting – the being sounded lost and confused, and he found himself feeling sorry for her, just for a moment.

"I am tired now," she went on. She sounded oddly distracted, as if she had overexerted herself. "I am exhausted at trying to maintain my form. I need to recuperate. You will leave now."

It was a statement of fact, rather than a request, and the whiteness immediately disappeared –

# Paul's Flat,
# Broadstairs – Present
# Day

Paul squeezed his eyes shut; the brightness of … wherever he'd been before had been replaced with normal levels of lighting – and, for a moment, everything seemed dull.

He had only been gone a microsecond, but in that small slice of time, Beelzebub had moved them away from Customs House.

*She's sent us home*, he realised in relief. *I hope we're safe here.*

He and Kirby were back in his semi-unpacked front room, sitting among the boxes as if the two of them had never been away. He was facing the long, cream wall that he had, just a short time ago, pushed his sofa against. Now he was looking at it with a deep sorrow in the pit of his stomach as he realised how much his life had changed in the space of a morning; his girlfriend had walked away because he had kept a secret from her, he had met her ex-boyfriend, and had twice visited a strange realm and been confronted by a being that believed him to be part of some sort of massive, cross-realm conspiracy.

He wasn't the sort of person who usually felt sorry for himself, but right at this moment, he did. He felt … unsettled in a way he couldn't entirely explain.

"Paul?" Kirby shook his head, as if trying to clear it. "They must have drugged us," he muttered. "The Seekers must have given us something, because I don't remember getting back here – and now I'm seeing double."

"Did you hit your head or something?" Paul asked him. From his position, he couldn't immediately see any damage – or blood.

*Good job*, he thought. *I don't cope well with the red stuff.*

"I don't … think so," Kirby replied. He touched a hand to the back of his head, but it came away clean – and he frowned as he looked back at Paul.

"Jeez, there *are* two of you," he muttered. "What the *hell?*"

Paul had no clue what his friend was talking about – until he caught sight of a movement out of the corner of his eye, and saw someone standing up from the floor.

His head swam as he realised it was him.

Nausea flooded over him as he realised that his body was under someone else's control … and it didn't take him long to figure out whose.

"Lucifer?"

His body was moving around of its own accord, fixing its eyes on Paul; it was in that moment that Paul realised what was going on.

"I'm a spirit?"

"No," Kirby said quickly, "you have to die to be a spirit, and that body's still alive. Look, Paul – it's breathing."

Paul looked carefully, and Kirby was right. The body that he quite obviously vacated *was* breathing, as well as blinking and doing all the other normal functions that a body did without Paul having to think about it.

"I did not expect to be woken while you were still alive, Paul," the body said. The words were spoken in Paul's tone of voice – *Of course they are*, he thought. *Lucifer's clearly in charge of my body now, so he's using my voice box. I may* look *like a human, but I'm a spirit now.*

"Neither did I," he muttered. "I need to sit down."

Kirby couldn't help himself; "Shame you can't, mate."

Paul gave him a withering glare, which didn't stop Kirby smirking at his witticism.

"So what *did* happen at Customs House?" the detective asked, changing the subject. "How did we end up here, and how the *hell* is Lucifer controlling your body?"

Paul began to bite his nails, then blinked and realised that it wouldn't actually do any good.

He sighed. "What's the most bizarre explanation you can think of that would explain what just happened to us?"

Kirby rolled his eyes. "I'm a detective sergeant in the police force," he said, "my sister and my friend can both separate their souls from their bodies without dying, and a once-comatose angel is now *controlling* your body. My tolerance level still has quite a way to go."

"Alright," Paul conceded. "But I think *you're* going to need to sit down for this."

Kirby looked like he was about to disagree, but instead he nodded. He sat on the edge of the sofa and listened carefully as Paul told him everything that had happened, from the moment time had frozen through to their arrival here in his front room. He mentioned his two visits to the strange, alien realm, and hesitated briefly before he mentioned the identities of the three spirits, but then decided against pulling his punches. Both Kirby *and* Lucifer reacted to the names, Lucifer seeming especially alarmed at the name "Poena."

Finally, Paul fell silent. Kirby seemed to have taken it all in very carefully, not interrupting; finally, he looked up at spirit-Paul. Lucifer seemed distracted, obviously surprised at being constrained inside a human body, and was clearly struggling with the concept.

"So you left your body, which somehow woke Lucifer up," Kirby summarised, "and you can't go *back* to your body because …?"

"We cannot share the same physical space; it will drive us both insane, or kill us," Lucifer said. He hesitated, then added; "Or it could drive us both insane and *then* kill us."

Paul and Kirby exchanged a nervous glance, then Kirby cleared his throat and said, "So Rachael was *here*? On Earth?"

"Yeah," Paul confirmed.

"How did she look?"

"Good." The right side of Paul's mouth twitched up. "You never told me how attractive she was."

Kirby rolled his eyes. "I never expected her to continue looking good after she died, to be fair. There's a whole *other* issue there beyond her being my sister."

Lucifer stirred; while it was odd for Paul seeing the angel move *his* body around, he had grown used to it far quicker than he had expected. *After everything that happened two years ago,* he thought, *there's not much that can surprise me anymore.*

"Paul," Lucifer said – his (or, rather, Paul's) eyes boring straight into Paul. "Are you *sure* the spirit's name was Poena?"

Paul shrugged, confused by Lucifer's intensity; only a moment ago, he had seemed more focused on waking up and getting used to his temporary home.

"It's an unusual name," he replied. "I wouldn't get it confused with *Smith*."

Lucifer paced to the window and looked out over the street; although Paul couldn't see his face, he was sure that the angel was looking up to the sky.

"If Poena *did* come through this breach," Kirby noted, "then she'll have met Evan Somerville's soul coming the other way."

Lucifer made an appreciative face. "That would be an interesting meeting."

"What do you know of Somerville?" Paul asked. He was desperate for anything that could help him get Christina back.

"He's a … powerful Seeker," Kirby replied, suddenly lost in nostalgic memory. "He founded the Seekers about ten years ago, and his temper has always been legendary. More than one Seeker got on the wrong side of him and left in a hurry; usually because he thought they should have torn through the barrier immediately after concluding they were powerful enough to do so."

"Have you ever met him before today?"

"Just the once." Kirby glanced over his shoulder at Lucifer, but he hadn't moved. The detective sighed, clearly perturbed by two images of Paul. "It was at my sister's funeral. There was something …"

He hesitated, then shook his head as he sought for the right word. "I didn't warm to the man," he confessed. "There was just something about him I didn't trust."

Paul shrugged. "We've all known people like that," he conceded. "I used to work for the Catholic Church, don't forget."

Lucifer turned away from the window to look at the two humans. He seemed to have got over his initial shock at being awoken – and discovering Poena's identity – and was now a lot more focused.

"If Somerville and Poena *have* met in this realm," he said, "then it will not end well. Poena loathes humanity with a passion."

"And Evan Somerville will fight anyone who hates us," Kirby said. "He may be an arrogant arse, but he's protective of humanity at least."

Paul sighed, and slumped into the sofa. He realised quickly that he was sinking *into* the sofa; his spiritual form was not geared towards dealing with physical objects.

"Seriously," he said with a pleading look towards Lucifer, "I need my body back."

Lucifer couldn't hide his amusement as he waved a hand in Paul's direction; Paul immediately stopped sinking and reappeared on top of the furniture, balancing precariously on the edge of it.

"That is something we need to work on," he said. "I have as little desire to remain awake inside a human body as you do outside it. However, if Poena is out of her cage, then we need to resolve that and put her back before we do anything else."

"Her cage?" Paul repeated. "You mean she was imprisoned for something?"

Lucifer was silent for a moment, and a range of emotions – guilt, sorrow and anger – crossed his face before he got it under control.

"Lucifer," Paul prompted, "you clearly *know* Poena. How?"

Kirby shot his friend a warning glance – he obviously thought that Paul had been too blunt in his questioning, but Paul ignored it. There was more to this than met the eye, he knew it.

"I … do not wish to discuss it," Lucifer. "It is not relevant to the current situation."

Paul stared at the unfamiliar emotions that moved across his own face, and decided not to pursue it right now.

*We've got other things to worry about.*

"This all started with the astral plane," he said out loud. "When Somerville breached the barrier, he … got Poena's back up, for want of a better phrase."

He smiled as he saw Lucifer look confused at the idiom, liking the fact that the angel didn't recognise it. *You need to remember that you're not all-powerful right now, my friend. You're an angel in a human body – you're going to need our help to sort this mess out.*

"Somerville's breach into the astral plane woke Poena up," the angel said. "Is that what you mean?"

Paul half-nodded. "In a way, yes."

"Everything is leading us to the astral plane," Kirby went on. "The Seekers, Christina's past *with* the Seekers, our three … visitors." The last comment was made with the vague hint of a smile, although Paul wondered if there was a bit of sadness behind it at the fact he hadn't been able to see his sister.

"We need to find out more about the astral plane," he said. "We need to learn about why this Poena is so angry that a human broke through the barrier – and why she has taken it upon herself to travel to Earth."

Kirby looked momentarily confused, and then his brown eyes moved to Lucifer – who had already understood what Paul was saying. He looked reluctant, but he nodded his agreement nonetheless.

"I will tell you what I can," Lucifer said, "but I cannot guarantee that you will like what you hear."

# Customs House, Ramsgate – Present Day

Poena had surrounded Somerville's consciousness and begun drawing energy from it; she needed the power to stay strong as she headed for his body, which was slumped, unmoving, in Customs House.

She could feel Somerville fighting against her presence, and raging with every fibre of his being. Poena thrived on his anger and drew strength from it – she tried to resist the urge to gloat; it was an unseemly emotion, but one she exulted in right now.

*I've been asleep for so long,* she thought, *and I am still the most powerful being in the astral plane – and soon will be the most powerful being on Earth as well.*

Her anger was still boiling inside her, and she channelled it effectively; the time lock had faded away like mist, so she flew into Customs House without any effort. She watched human beings flitting like insects, panicking and worrying around the shell of a body that Somerville had recently vacated – and that she now intended to inhabit.

One human in particular – the name "McKenzie" floated into her mind as she tapped Somerville's resisting consciousness – was knelt by the body's side. He looked worried, as far as Poena could tell of these things, but Poena wasn't overly interested in this human's emotions – or, indeed, *any* human's emotions.

Ignoring the nearby human, Poena – with Somerville's consciousness in tow – slammed into the unconscious body. For a moment, she rejoiced in the knowledge that she had won.

Entirely focused on her task, Poena failed to notice the small part of Somerville that was still conscious. He was weakened and not able to fight back; he could only watch in horror as Poena took control of his body.

Poena operated Somerville's arms and legs with ease – even the voice was easy – and she demanded that McKenzie take her to 'his' office. She had a plan and, while she put it into operation, she would make use of Somerville's form – and let everyone believe that she *was* him.

As she followed McKenzie though Customs House, her thoughts wandered briefly to the Seven Sisters. While her anger still burned brightest towards angels and humanity, a small part of her rage was reserved for them, her one-time masters.

*We would have won*, Poena thought, *had the Sisters kept fighting.*

Instead, they had sought peace at every avenue – and, even when she had convinced a young, impressionable Lucifer to help her, they had survived and then surrendered, accepting their punishment – an eternity of slumber – without any argument. And Poena had been forced to accept the same.

*Except now I am awake*, she thought – as she stepped into the Cabinet Room of the Seekers of Truth, *and I have control over the one who breached the barrier. I will discover how he did it – and then the feasting can begin, before we destroy the angels and take our places as rulers of all the realms.*

# Ruling Chamber, Heaven – Present Day

Micah was chief archangel and first amongst equals in the Republic of Heaven – and couldn't help seeing it as a poisoned chalice.

*This job was never meant to be easy,* he reminded himself. *If it were, then anyone could do it … and I would be retired.*

A part of him wondered what retirement would feel like, but he rather suspected that he would be bored. At least here, he was making a difference.

Currently, he was pacing across the floor of the Ruling Chamber, trying – and not entirely succeeding – to ignore the large, empty throne behind him.

*It is still … odd, to see it empty after such a strong personality filled it for so long,* he thought with a tinge of sadness … that was, until he remembered the price so many had paid to make that happen.

*Imprisonment … for what should have been the rest of our immortal lives.*

He realised his mind had wandered; he blinked and concentrated on the discussion he was having. If his fellow angels were right, then something was seriously wrong in the astral plane.

*We have never trusted the spirits*, he thought. *But could we have done anything different? We could have given them more trust. Instead, we have made them hate us.*

Joseph was speaking; "There have been *two* breaches in the barrier between the astral and physical planes – and I *know* that my sister was involved in the second breach."

"Poena *must* be involved," Michael added. "The older spirits would not be so coherent without a strong, decisive leader."

Micah's wings stretched as he paced, worry causing him to tense.

"The concept of Poena being awake worries me greatly," he admitted. "If she is awake, how long will it be before the Seven Sisters wake up as well?"

"Then we need to work quickly," Michael said, stepping forward and looking intently at the archangel. "I suspect that the Seven Sisters will break out of their imprisonment in time, if Poena has managed it. With so many of our angels still sleeping inside human minds, we would struggle to defend ourselves against their attacks."

Joseph cleared his throat; it was a human gesture, and Micah had yet to learn the meaning behind it.

"I have Satan's memories," he said, "but there's still a lot I don't understand. Why is Poena so important in the astral plane?"

"She was the aide to the Seven Sisters during our ancient war," Michael said, half-distracted. "Poena … came close to betraying everything by allying herself with an angel – and we could have all paid the price, in the end."

Joseph hesitated – and then dropped his wings in a gesture of submission. He didn't understand all of what Michael had said, and knew there was more to it, but he also recognised that he wasn't going to learn any more now – instead, they needed to focus on the fact that breaches had occurred, and that spirits were clustering round the seals, trying to force their way through again.

"Michael?" Micah prompted. "What are your thoughts?"

"We need to discover the cause of the breaches," the angel replied. "Whether Poena is the cause or the effect, she is *awake* – and I do not like the thought of the chaos she could cause if she chose – and she *will* choose to do so. We need to establish her role in all of this – and then decide how we stop any more breaches occurring."

Micah nodded. "Agreed."

He began pacing as he thought. Michael had to suppress a feeling of fascination as he watched Micah walk the floor of the Chamber, acting so calm and self-assured as the new leader of this realm. Behind him was the royal throne; Micah refused to use it, given its symbolism as the ruling place of the kingdom's previous sovereign.

*It is not a kingdom any more*, Michael reminded himself. *It is a republic now ... and Micah is our leader.*

A Council of Twelve had assembled after the Almighty's departure into the unknown, and they had elected Micah – a one-time rebel and friend of Lucifer, Beelzebub and Satan – to lead them. Like his fellow rebels, he had been imprisoned inside a human host; however, his host had died just as the Almighty had stepped down – and Michael and the others on the Council of Twelve had successfully woven him a new angelic body.

Michael was thrilled to have the angel back amongst them after 2,000 years, although it felt strange to have him immediately installed in the position of first amongst equals.

*I hope he is up to the task.*

Micah turned and faced the others, his face settling into a determined expression. "How long do we have before the Seven Sisters wake?"

Michael couldn't help but shiver at the prospect; nothing scared him, not after his long life, but the thought of the Seven Sisters waking up after all this time certainly … *worried* him.

"A few days, no more," he replied. "That is, if Poena has not already woken them."

Micah frowned. "If I recall, she disapproved of their decision that ended the war. I doubt very much that she will wake them. I imagine she will be thinking the same as we are. That is something both sides have in common, at any rate; neither of us will want the Seven Sisters awake."

Michael nodded; his face was pensive, but he remained silent.

"Who are the Seven Sisters?" Joseph asked. It frustrated him that he couldn't remember, but there were so many memories in his head still to process. "What *was* this ancient war?"

"They are …" Micah shook his head, trying to put his thoughts into words that would convey the seriousness of the answer. He sighed, clearly frustrated with himself – and also relieved in a way, as it meant he didn't have to think about it right now. "They are difficult to explain. I will try my best, but later. For now," he added, looking over at Michael again, "I wish to see where the breach occurred for myself."

◆●◆

The screens in the Celestial Observatory were as Joseph and Michael had left them, the images rotating through different portions of the astral plane. Micah scrutinised them carefully, as if by staring at them long enough, he would get the answers he wanted.

*If only I knew the questions to ask.*

It felt odd, being in the Observatory after two millennia imprisoned in a human's head for the crime of rebelling against the Almighty's rule – and knowing that, until recently, these screens had also watched *him* and his fellow "rebels". He raised an eyebrow as he reflected on the irony of a rebel now *leading* Heaven.

*It should be Lucifer, of course*, he reflected. *He is a natural-born leader. One day, when he returns to us…*

"We've seen an increase in the number of spirits at *both* breaches," Joseph said. "They're clearly searching for a way to get through."

Micah suppressed a smile. The half-angel's tone and words were so uniquely *human* that it was hard to remember sometimes that he was also half-angel.

*It's quite refreshing*, the rebellious part of him thought. *I was unconscious for my time amongst humans, so I did not learn to appreciate colloquialisms.*

"There is only one explanation," Michael said. He was stood a couple of steps away from the other two, his wings ruffling to indicate his frustration.

"Which is …?" Micah prompted.

"The breaches were deliberate," Michael went on. "Someone on the astral plane – possibly the Seven Sisters, possibly Poena or someone else – is trying to get through to the physical plane … and Earth … and these initial breaches are ways to make sure it can be done."

Micah was horrified at the thought. "What do you think they are planning?"

"An all-out assault," Michael replied. "With the Almighty gone, the spirits are planning to test our defences. They may assault Earth first, as a rehearsal before attacking us, but they *will* eventually attack us."

Silence pervaded the Observatory for a moment. Micah didn't want to agree with Michael, but found his mind gradually moving towards that opinion.

"Our strength has never been derived from one angel," he said quietly. "We have always been greater than the sum of just *one*."

Michael shook his head. "But the Almighty was the focal point of so much power and authority. Spirits may believe us weakened from the change to a republic … and see this as an opportunity to strike against their oppressors."

Micah was curious about the angel's opinions. "If this is true – and I am not yet entirely convinced it is – what do you suggest we do about it?"

The older angel answered without hesitation. "Allow me to take a battalion of angels into the astral plane. It will be a show of strength and perhaps break up these massing spirits."

Micah was surprised. "Angels have not entered the astral plane for … longer than I can remember – and now no-one ever – *ever* – leaves it. The barriers are as strong now as they ever were. What you're proposing … I don't even know if it can be done. Can anyone even remember how to release the bonds between our realms?"

"I can!" Michael retorted. "It may have been eons ago, but I remember it as if it were yesterday. Micah, something is happening there – I do not know what, but something is wrong, and we need to act decisively."

He took a breath and added; "Also, an angel *died*, and is living in that realm. Granted, she had no physical form at the time, but she was still an angel. She is only the second angel to die since I was young – and she has moved into the astral plane! You know how angels are perceived there. We *cannot* leave her in that place any longer!"

Micah opened his mouth to argue, but found that he couldn't. It was a good point well made, and he knew that others on the Council of Twelve would think the same way as Michael. He turned his head to look at Joseph and raised an eyebrow.

"What do you think, Satan?"

Joseph seemed startled for a moment, but whether it was because he had been addressed by his angelic name or addressed at all, Micah couldn't be certain.

"I ..." Joseph drew in a breath and started again. "I agree with Michael."

Michael nodded in satisfaction, and Micah inwardly cringed; the thought of having to use the military to resolve this appalled him, but if Satan was agreeing with Michael, then he knew the way the Council would vote. The battalion would be dispatched, and life in Heaven and the astral plane would never be the same again.

*Sometimes I wonder if we did the right thing*, he thought, only half-sardonically, *when we did away with the divine right to rule.*

"However ..."

Micah blinked; Satan had spoken again. The hybrid cleared his throat nervously. He seemed embarrassed by the attention, but nodded and, casting a nervous glance at Michael, continued.

"I agree that we need to do something," he said, "and military action will certainly be decisive … but I worry about the consequences. Michael, two millennia ago, Heaven had a Civil War. It was a divided kingdom, and will remain divided until all the angels are returned to us. 144,000 angels will return to us in the space of a human life span, and then this realm will be whole again. Before *that* war, you … *we* were engaged in open warfare with the spirit world, which Heaven won, but at a terrible cost."

"What is your point?" Michael asked gruffly.

"Are we making a mistake, engaging in a third war? The first two didn't do us any favours."

Micah blinked in surprise. He was used to debate raging over many days, and points were not often made quite so bluntly as that.

*It is refreshing, however*, he found himself thinking. *Satan – Joseph – is going to help us revitalise our thinking.*

"We are discussing a single battalion," Michael snapped. "I am not suggesting we begin a war."

Joseph smiled and tapped the side of his head with a finger. "I think people still forget that I have all of Satan's memories in here," he said. "I haven't sorted through them all yet, but I know enough to know that beating the spirit world was enough to make them hate us … and then locking them apart from Heaven didn't improve their temperament. They're angrier than I would have ever thought possible. How could a battalion of angels travelling into a realm that we have kept on a tight leash for so long *not* be seen as the opening salvo in a war?"

He held up a hand to forestall Michael's argument and went on; "It was a *long* time ago – yes, I understand that, Michael. But just because it was a long time ago doesn't mean that the spirits have forgotten about it – or *forgiven* us. If we charge in like a bull in a china shop, then all we're doing is provoking a backlash against us."

Micah could see Michael's mind working as he tried desperately to translate "*bull in a china shop*" and "*backlash*" into language he could comprehend. The first among equals turned to Joseph, curious to follow the argument through. "What would you do, if you were in my place, Satan?"

Joseph gave his fellow angel a sly smile. "Resign. I could not do your job."

Micah laughed. That had been the first thing he had *planned* to do when appointed to his new position; however, he had eventually been talked into remaining.

"Micah?"

He looked at Joseph, raising his eyebrows in response.

"Where is Poena?"

Micah blinked; he hadn't anticipated that question at all, and it wasn't one he could immediately answer. He hadn't registered her on any of the screens when he had looked them over; he looked at them again now, trying – in vain – to locate her.

"I ... I do not know," he conceded. His eyes flicked back to Joseph. "Do you see her?"

Joseph shook his head. "No," he said. "I have enough of Satan's memories to know that I would recognise her if I saw her. I have been studying these screens closely, and Poena isn't near either of the breaches."

"Impossible!" Michael exclaimed, scowling as he searched for her as well. "She would be there, stirring the spirits into action."

"Except that she's not." Joseph's characteristic bluntness was more pronounced now. "I don't know where she's gone, but she's not been around since the second breach happened."

Michael's eyes bored into Joseph. "Do you know what you're suggesting? Poena was never able to breach the barrier by herself before her imprisonment."

"But an angel can," Joseph retorted, "and as you've already pointed out, Beelzebub is in the astral plane … along with my sister."

"That settles it!" Michael exploded. "Micah, let me take the battalion into the astral plane! If Poena has gone through to Earth, time is short!"

Micah couldn't immediately see a way to refuse, despite his own reservations – but he then saw Satan's face.

"Satan, you have an opinion?"

Joseph looked pensive as he replied. "Yes."

Micah noticed Joseph's eyes flick to Michael; he looked nervous at challenging the older being – he was, after all, one of the most senior and experienced angels in existence.

*Times change*, Micah thought with a stubbornness that surprised even him. *And I need as much advice as I can get.*

The hybrid shifted awkwardly. His wings lowered slightly, and Micah understood he – or, more possibly, Michael – might not like what he was going to say. He inclined his head to indicate that Satan should say it anyway.

"If Poena has travelled to Earth, then *that* is where we need to go."

Micah frowned in confusion. "You wish to take an army of angels to *Earth?*"

"No," Joseph replied with a shake of his head. "Just me, and perhaps one other. We will locate Poena and try to reason with her."

Micah noticed that Satan's language had subtly changed from his usual human slang to a more angelic tone; it was clearly designed to sound more respectful and not seem like an outright challenge to Michael.

Michael snorted in derision. "Poena will never see sense." He hesitated. "Who would you take with you? Not many angels would wish to travel from here to Earth."

"I agree."

Micah blinked. "What are you –"

Michael, however, was quicker off the mark.

"No!" he exclaimed. "Absolutely not! Retrieving him now would kill his human host – and he was most insistent we do not sacrifice any humans to allow him his freedom early."

"Lucifer," Micah whispered.

Joseph shook his head. "Paul," he said.

Micah had not seen the leader of the rebels since the day they had all been placed into their human prisons, over 2,000 years ago. A sudden pang of sadness hit him; to Micah, it felt like only a blink of an eye since he had been placed inside his first human host, but he had awoken to find that two millennia had past ... and that Lucifer, while now conscious, had chosen to remain in *his* host's mind until Paul died in order to allow the human a normal life.

*A typically noble thing to do from the Son of the Almighty,* he thought. *I wonder if I could have done that – willingly return to my imprisonment, knowing that it could be many years before I woke again.*

"I know what was agreed, Michael!" Joseph said, anger cutting in his tone. "I was there. I *killed* Metatron! I have a right to speak!"

Michael seemed taken aback by Joseph's sudden passion.

"Times have changed," Joseph went on. "I'm half-human, Lucifer is living inside a human's head and the astral plane is angry, after thousands of millennia of us ignoring them and allowing their anger to ferment and bubble … while humans are allowed free will."

He sighed, frustrated that the angelic realm had been so blind to this for so long. "The astral plane wants control of its own destiny, and they won't listen to an angel who appeals for calm." He grinned, catching Micah and Michael off-guard. "But a half-human and a full human might just succeed where angels fear to tread."

He glanced at each angel in turn; Micah looked thoughtful, as if he were considering Joseph's words, but Michael just looked frustrated and annoyed.

*You're about to piss someone off,* Joseph thought of Micah. *Is it going to be little old me … or the Almighty's oldest advisor?*

"Joseph's right, Michael," Micah said. "Sending angels into the astral plane will only prove catastrophic. I do not want to lose any more of our number. Satan's plan might well succeed."

A low rumble in Michael's throat showed his frustration, and Micah wondered if the older angel might challenge the decision. After a moment, reason clearly outweighed his anger; he muttered a muted, "As you wish," turned sharply, and stormed out of the Observatory.

Micah and Joseph watched him go. Michael's opinion held a lot of sway among the host of angels. He had served as the Almighty's military commander for millennia, and now he served on the Council of Twelve in the same capacity.

"If he wants to follow his own agenda," Joseph said slowly, "then things could escalate very quickly."

Micah nodded, without taking his eyes off Michael's receding form.

"Then we must make sure we do this quickly – and *right*." He finally tore his eyes away from Michael and looked instead at Joseph, who drew himself up to his full height under the ruler's gaze.

"Get Paul committed to this task," he said with finality, "and then locate Poena before it is too late."

# Astral Plane – Present Day

"I cannot describe the astral plane to you. You must see it for yourselves."

With those words, Lucifer grabbed Kirby's wrist and summoned up all his energy – and they reappeared somewhere else. It took Paul and Kirby a few moments to register where they were. They were floating in mid-air – or mid-vacuum, to be precise. Space engulfed them; the twinkling of stars in the distance broke up the blackness. Paul looked over his shoulder and saw a nebula that had more colours than he knew even existed.

A brief surge of panic rose within him, as he began to wonder how he was breathing in the depths of space, but then remembered his current situation.

*Technically, I don't even have lungs.*

"This is … incredible," he whispered.

He glanced at Kirby, whose eyes had widened; he seemed speechless – and in shock – so Paul let him absorb their new location at his own pace.

"This is just my memory of the astral plane," Lucifer said, still in Paul's own voice. "It is too much of a risk to take you to the *real* astral plane, not when Poena is awake. She could be anywhere."

Paul blinked in surprise; "We're in your *memories?*"

"It is … difficult to explain," Lucifer conceded. "I must ask that you trust me."

In the shortage of any evidence to the contrary, Paul had to accept that Lucifer's description – the beauty of open space – was accurate, so he nodded and tried to process what he was seeing.

"So the astral plane is completely separate from Heaven?" he asked. "Most of our religions teach us –"

Lucifer held up a hand. "I know what your religions say," he replied. "Your prophets are … inventive people. They fill in the gaps in their knowledge with stories not even suited for your children."

"Human prophets … didn't speak for God?" he asked cautiously.

Paul wasn't entirely able to hide his surprise. He was comfortable being labelled a lapsed Catholic, but still put some emphasis on the *Catholic* part of that title; unlike Kirby, who didn't associate with any religion, Paul liked knowing he was part of an organisation bigger than himself. But based on what Lucifer had said, was the Catholic faith based on anything heavenly at all?

"It is frustrating," Lucifer replied. "Humanity is given assurances that they will personally meet the Almighty when they die, so many people focus on that instead of appreciating the true journey they will take when they leave their physical bodies."

Kirby seemed keen to distract himself from the awe-someness of their location, as he looked overwhelmed by the sights around him, so spoke up for the first time since they had arrived here; "So, Paul's right … Heaven and the spirit world are separate?"

"Yes," Lucifer replied, "but when the universe was young, they co-existed." He shrugged. "There weren't as many angels – or spirits – then."

"What happened?"

The angel's face darkened for a moment. "You must understand that it was a different time. It was new and unexplored – and angels … we were convinced that we were the highest form of existence anywhere, whereas anyone could be a spirit … any prehistoric human with a vague spark of consciousness could move into our realm of existence."

"So you separated the astral plane from Heaven because angels didn't want to be associated with … a lower life form, as you saw it?"

Lucifer was silent for a moment, then nodded. "The angelic race certainly made some mistakes when they … we … were younger. We thought we were superior to everyone."

"How many spirits are here?" Paul asked. He felt uncomfortable about the angel's maudlin attitude, and wanted to try and change the subject.

"How many humans have ever lived?" the angel replied. "That is how many spirits there are – and the older spirits have been driven insane by their millennia in the astral plane, coupled with their desire to retake human form. Many spirits also wish to be united with Heaven – after all, they believe they are entitled to it."

"Why?" Paul asked.

It was Kirby who answered; despite his obvious unease at free-floating in space – even if it was just inside Lucifer's memories – he had picked up on Lucifer's expression. "As

Lucifer already said, humans are told that living in Heaven is their entitlement. They're bitter."

"And bitterness can fester," Lucifer added. "Over centuries, it becomes so deep-seated it is almost second nature."

Kirby nodded; Paul frowned, as his friend looked … ill. He'd almost forgotten about his friend's earlier reaction to their abrupt move into Lucifer's memories – and to this … awe-inspiring sight. Paul had visited Heaven before, and so was able to accept this change more readily. Kirby, however, had never left Earth.

"Are you alright?" he asked the detective. "What's wrong?"

"I'm fine," Kirby replied, although a slight quaver in his voice told Paul that his friend was lying.

"Tell me," Paul urged him, genuinely worried now.

Kirby looked pale, and a sheen of sweat had appeared on his forehead. "I'm just … I get travel sick, and …"

"Kirby, this isn't like travelling on public transport …"

"No," his friend interjected, "on public transport, you can *see* the floor! How are you staying so calm about this?"

Paul shrugged. "I've got an angel living in my head and I've met the Almighty. There's not much that can surprise me any more, I guess. And I've never felt airsick." He thought for a moment. "Well, *space* sick is more of an accurate description, I suppose."

Kirby glared at him for a moment, but didn't say anything. He was clearly trying to acclimatise to the unusual surroundings, and Paul wanted to make sure he could get through this.

"What can I do?" he asked.

"Nothing," Kirby replied with a shake of his head. "Let's talk about something else; it might help … distract me from the fact that I'm just floating in mid-air."

He went paler for a moment; closing his eyes. He breathed out slowly and swallowed hard, then opened his eyes again and looked at Lucifer.

"Why can't they just *create* human forms?" he asked, clearly wanting to just focus on something – anything – other than where they were. "If they care that much about their old bodies, why can't they just create new ones?"

"Because they will never be real," Lucifer replied. He glanced over at Paul, whose spiritual form was half-transparent. "Paul is a perfect example. He has been thrown out of his body; he can never create another one. Nor can any other spirit. They should not crave that which they can no longer have."

Paul scowled. "I still want my body back," he said.

Lucifer nodded and inclined his – or, rather, Paul's – head. To distract himself from the disorientating sight of his body being operated by someone else, he focused on their main discussion.

"So to stop the spirits from trying to … take over humans in order to get a physical body," he said, "you split off the astral plane from Earth. That I can understand … but why did you refuse them entry into Heaven as well?"

"We sealed off Earth to them because of the threat they represented to humanity," Lucifer said with more than a touch of reluctance. It was clearly an uncomfortable subject for him. "Some spirits learnt to accept this after a time. Many, however, grew resentful … they were bitter at being denied the opportunity to return to a physical form, and managed to encourage the Seven Sisters, who have never been bound by human form and are more powerful than you can imagine, to rise up in rebellion against us."

"The angels won, I take it?"

Lucifer nodded. "The Seven Sisters eventually went into hibernation, as did their second-in-command, Poena. Heaven was sealed to all other spirits as punishment."

"'Eventually'," Paul repeated. "I take it they didn't make it easy for you then?"

Lucifer shook his head, but didn't say anything. He looked off into the middle distance, seemingly lost in thought. Paul watched him for a moment, then tried to get his attention again.

"How did you manage to end the war?"

Lucifer blinked, as if he had forgotten that there was anyone with him. "I'm sorry?" he asked.

"How did it end?" Kirby prompted. His initial queasiness seemed to have gone, although he still wasn't entirely thrilled at the thought of hanging in mid-space. "How did the war end?"

Lucifer shook his head. "Not well," he said quietly. "Not well at all. We need to locate Beelzebub and your friends."

Paul was thrown by the change of subject; Lucifer had spoken without emotion, and that told Paul that this wasn't the time to pursue the true story of the war's end.

*Looking at this amazing scenery, how could anyone* want *to fight?* he thought. *Then again, I haven't been driven insane by the desire to get back into a human body.*

A terrible thought then struck him.

*If I don't get my body back, will I end up the same?*

"Agreed," he said out loud, to distract himself from that thought. "We need to join forces and stop Poena before she does anything destructive."

"She has already done that," Lucifer said. "She has tried to take over a human body that leads a human group of ... explorers, for want of a better word. If she succeeds, then she will have the Seekers of Truth at her disposal – as well as her spirit army."

Kirby swallowed. "Then it won't be long before they breach the barrier again."

"And her spirits will then set about devouring this world whole," Lucifer said gravely.

# Heaven – The Distant Past

The war had ground to a halt ... again. Battles had been fought time after time, each with the same outcome: stalemate. The Seven Sisters, despite their incredible power and age, were small in number, even with their band of spirits following them. The angels, while many times more numerous, lacked the knowledge and wisdom of the Seven Sisters.

Lucifer was in his quarters in Heaven's citadel, unsure of what to do. He had seen a number of battles now, and was much more war-hardened and less naïve than he had been when Michael had "encouraged" him to join the first battle all those years before. He still didn't know, however, how to get out of this endless cycle of stalemate.

"Lucifer?"

He came round from his reverie – and yelled out in shock.

"How in the name of all that is *holy* –!"

"Oh please, can we skip the protestations of alarm? We've both got better things to do with our time."

Lucifer was stunned into silence; as the Almighty's first-born son, he wasn't used to being spoken to like that – especially by *her*.

"How did you get in here?" he demanded.

Poena, who had formed her ethereal being into the form of an angel, shrugged, and looked uncomfortable doing so. "I don't propose to tell you."

Lucifer's eyes glowed with sudden fury. He took a step forward, anger blazing as he glared at this intruder, this interloper in the angelic inner sanctum that she had no right being in.

"We are at *war*, Poena!" he snarled angrily. Her appearance – in the centre of Heaven's citadel – made a mockery of all the energy and time angelic forces had spent making their fortress impenetrable.

Poena had folded her arms across her chest as Lucifer spoke, her eyebrows raised in apparent amusement at Lucifer's pure anger.

"Are you quite finished?" she asked, her voice mocking him. "I've got all day, Lucifer, but I don't think *you* have."

Lucifer opened his mouth to speak – and then closed it again. His best friend, the angel Satan, always nagged at him to think before he spoke and while he hardly ever listened to that advice, he did on this occasion. Clearly, Poena was far more clever and wily than he had given her credit for; she had penetrated the citadel's inner defences without apparently raising a single alarm, and she was stood here in his quarters looking amused at his righteous anger.

*What am I missing?* he wondered.

"You ... have come here with a purpose," he said slowly. "Why have you not approached the Almighty?"

Poena smiled appreciatively, as if she had known – or had hoped – that he would ask that question.

"Because the Almighty would have me executed on the spot," she replied. "I have visited you, however, and I am not yet dead. I hoped you would listen to me."

Lucifer couldn't deny it; his interest was piqued. He knew that he should be raising alarms from the rooftops – and calling out for his Father, or Michael, or Satan, or a combination of the three. Instead, he stood there, frozen to the spot, waiting to learn what his sworn enemy was doing in his quarters, as calm as anything.

"You clearly have a plan," he said, "or you wouldn't be here. I presume you think it would benefit the both of us, and you think I will be self-interested enough to want to go along with this plan rather than want to win the war."

Poena nodded. "You're not as stupid as I've been led to believe."

Lucifer's hands bunched into fists, but he restrained his anger – barely. "Do you *want* me to summon Michael?" he snapped.

Poena swallowed nervously, and Lucifer was glad that at least the name of the heavenly general commanded respect. *Even if mine doesn't seem to*, he thought regretfully.

"That won't be necessary," she replied. "Will you listen to what I propose? It could help us *both* win this war, after a fashion."

Lucifer was intrigued, despite himself; he couldn't help but wonder what Poena's proposition was going to be. He knew that this was a moment that would change his life, whatever he decided. He nodded.

Poena licked her lips, nervous – despite her outer confidence – about how Lucifer would receive her thoughts.

"I am here today to talk to you about the Seven Sisters," she said. "They seem to be the bane of *both* of our lives, do they not?"

# Astral Plane – Present Day

The spirits were agitated; they didn't know where their leader, Poena, had gone, and they weren't known for being patient. Poena had vanished through one of the two breaches, and they wanted – *needed* – to follow, to finally access the physical plane after thousands of years of being constricted and constrained by those cruel, evil angels. They massed in all the hiding spaces they could find; in the middle of supernovas and nebulae and still-burning stars.

*Poena!* they called out with one voice. *We are ready! We want to return to Earth and feed!*

They were half-crazed, but they could still sense changes in the realm they had lived in for so long; now they could detect a presence on the other side of one of the breaches. They sniffed it out – and spoke again, together, in a unified voice.

*Angel!*

◆•◆

The three spirits – one angelic, two human – had remained in the physical plane, hidden from Poena while they decided what to do next. Each of them agreed that, while Poena would be dangerous inside a human body, she was even *more* dangerous in her natural form.

"If she's fighting Somerville in his head," Beelzebub noted, her ethereal wings beating against the gentle summer breeze, "then she will be distracted … and we could have a chance to fight her."

She paused, her face registering sudden concern. "Something's wrong."

"What is it?" Rachael asked, frowning as she thought, *What the hell can worry an angel?*

"The spirits know I'm here," Beelzebub replied. "They're trying to find me. If they get through, they will come for me first."

Michael was pacing, fuming silently in the mighty citadel at the heart of Heaven. He found that pacing helped him think, as well as being a way of helping him burn off any excess energy – and anger. Usually, when he was in such a state of mind, he found it difficult to focus on anything else – but something managed to intrude on his thoughts. There was a flood of uncontrolled emotions that he could *feel* from … who? Who was projecting their emotions so strongly that he could feel them in the citadel?

Trying to detect the source was like trying to grab hold of cosmic dust – the more he tried to focus on it, the more it slipped away.

"Who's there?" he asked quietly, still gazing out of the window. "Where are you? If it's you, Beelzebub, then I'm coming for you. I give you my word."

# Customs House, Ramsgate – Present Day

oena was finally in control of Somerville's body – and it felt good. She could still feel him there, inside her mind, struggling to escape her grip, but she was confident that she could hold him there for as long as she needed.

The Cabinet Room had changed little over the years – it was still all wood panelling, with a redwood conference table and plush red carpet. Poena sat in Somerville's usual place at the table's head. She had been able to access enough of the director's memories to know where to sit. Biding her time, she wanted to learn more about this group who had broken through to the astral plane.

Sitting at the other end of the table was Somerville's young assistant, Joshua McKenzie, who looked terrified at being under the steely gaze of the man he thought was his leader.

"Let me understand this, Mr McKenzie," Poena said. "You and your colleagues have been unable to locate Beelzebub, the two human spirits or the humans that were with them?"

At the far end of the immaculately-varnished table, McKenzie swallowed nervously and shook his head. He was terrified of the look in his director's eye. The rage that they held was unlike anything he had seen before; Somerville's reputation preceded him, but this was something new – and terrifying.

"Yes –" McKenzie's voice cut out, his throat dry with nerves. He swallowed, trying to get his voice back. "Yes, sir. They just … disappeared into thin air." He looked up. "We're not police officers, sir! We've never conducted a full search for spirits before."

Poena raised one of her human host's eyebrows. "I would be very surprised if *any* human police force could adequately search for spirits."

She sat forward, savouring the feeling of power that she had in this room; she had won against Somerville, and soon she would pull all the information she needed from this weak human.

"In your time with the Seekers, Mr McKenzie," she went on, "how many out-of-body journeys have you made?"

McKenzie licked his lips. "Fourteen, sir," he replied.

"Of those fourteen times, Mr McKenzie, how many times have you been able to pierce the veil and see the astral plane for yourself?"

"None, sir. You're the only one who has been able to do it so far."

Poena was silent for a moment. Somerville was still fighting her; she couldn't hear all of his thoughts as yet, although she was slowly winning. This next question was vitally important, as it was something she couldn't yet access from Somerville's mind.

"Do you know who … *I* … was in league with?" she asked, careful to remember to use the personal pronoun. "Who helped me pierce the veil between the realms?"

As best as Poena could tell – and she didn't pretend to be an expert on such matters – McKenzie was terrified, and didn't know what to say.

"Who you were … I'm sorry, Mr Somerville, I don't understand," he said after a moment's thought. "I didn't think you were in league with anyone. I thought you had succeeded all by yourself."

Poena sighed, simultaneously frustrated and intrigued. *Perhaps he's not in league with anyone*, she thought in realisation. *Perhaps he is the only one who can do it. In the meantime, however, there is no reason why I cannot allow the spirits the opportunity to feast.*

In her mind, Somerville raged. In the same way that Poena could detect his thoughts, he could detect some of hers – and he was *not* about to let her rain fire and destruction down upon his world.

Poena stood, the chair rolling backwards on its casters and hitting the small desk that was reserved for the minutes secretary. Her eyes still on McKenzie, she took off the suit jacket and began rolling up the sleeves of Somerville's white shirt.

McKenzie watched in abject terror as Somerville put his hands into his pockets and step out from behind the desk. He walked slowly down the length of the table as he spoke.

"Humanity confuses me," he said, "and it vaguely disgusts me. I have inhabited this body for less than an hour, and already I feel its disgusting needs and desires pressing against my consciousness."

This wasn't the Somerville that McKenzie knew and respected talking now. As the director stepped behind him, McKenzie began to turn round – his mouth even formed a question – but he was too late. Poena gripped hold of McKenzie's head. Her eyes rolled back into their sockets as the low thrum of energy flowed into the room. All of a sudden, McKenzie realised it wasn't *energy* that was thrumming; they were voices, overlapping and multi-tonal. There wasn't even a modicum of melody behind it. It sounded like the voices were competing against each other, vying to be the loudest and the strongest voice in the pack.

"Oh god!" McKenzie exclaimed. "Please no! Please, please, *NO!!*"

The pressure of the spirits on the other side of the veil, plus Poena's increased power from her absorption of Somerville's humanity, meant that Poena could finally tear open a rip through to the astral plane.

McKenzie felt an abrupt, exquisite level of pain as his soul was *ripped* from his body, torn out from his physical form and shoved painfully into another realm – something alien and different, where he knew he didn't belong.

*Help me!* he cried out, but realised he didn't have a voice to cry out with; he was shouting out with his soul, but there was no-one on Earth left to hear it … except for Evan Somerville.

*No!* Somerville bellowed behind his own eyes. *No, I won't allow this!*

Poena cried out in sudden pain and gripped her head; Somerville's anger was like a knife cutting through her consciousness, and he *forced* his way forward. The two minds were locked in sudden, savage conflict.

Somerville's body collapsed to the floor, uncontrolled by either consciousness. Poena fought to get back control, to keep the rip in the astral plane open. She knew that, by itself, it would seal itself within minutes. Only her active abilities would sustain the rip long enough for the hungry spirits to detect and reach it, so that they could begin piling through to Earth.

But Somerville had something equally forceful to fight for – the survival of his race. He fought back against this cold, hard, evil spirit, allowing his rage and anger to match hers, thrust for thrust.

And then, suddenly, it was all over.

The director's eyes rolled back to their correct position – and Somerville was once again in control. He searched his mind, and couldn't feel any trace of Poena anywhere. He realised that he was breathing heavily. While his body hadn't been through any physical activity, he felt bone tired.

Using the conference table to push himself to his feet again, he noticed McKenzie's body slumped in a heap on the floor. His assistant was still breathing, but without a consciousness to drive it, all that was left was a shell; Somerville looked down, and a lump formed, unbidden, in his throat. While he had a hard streak – and had done things in his past that were cruel, to get him where he was today – McKenzie had been just twenty-two, and comparatively naïve.

*He didn't understand*, Somerville thought. *Rachael was different – she knew what she was doing when she made her choices, but McKenzie … he was still a child.*

He was jolted out of his reverie by a knock at the door. Fear, an unusual emotion for Somerville, caught in his stomach for the moment until he realised that it was unlikely that Poena would knock.

"Who is it?" he asked.

"It's Christina," came a familiar voice from the other side of the door.

Somerville relaxed; if there was one person he could trust right now, it was Christina. They hadn't contacted each other in years, but seeing her this morning was like they had never been apart. It never once occurred to him that she might feel differently.

"Come in," he said.

Christina entered the room, looking apprehensive; the last time she had been in here, it had been to resign – and, if Somerville remembered correctly, he hadn't been too polite in his response. He had lost Rachael and then Christina in quick succession; the betrayal had hurt him deeply.

*But I forgive you now, Christina*, he thought, believing himself to be truly benevolent as he did so. *It's time to come back to where you truly belong.*

"Evan," she said as she walked in and looked round the doorframe, "I wanted to talk to you –"

She froze as her brain processed the scene. Somerville stood at the other end of the room, slightly out of breath, over the lifeless body of Joshua McKenzie.

"What the hell?!" she exclaimed.

Her knees threatened to buckle for a moment, but something kicked in at the back of her mind. She was a nurse by training, and it came to the fore now. She ran to McKenzie's side and began doing some basic checks. As she checked his pulse, she looked up at Somerville.

"What did you do?" she croaked, trying – and not entirely succeeding – to keep her emotions in check.

Somerville's scowled at her. "You think I did this?" he asked incredulously. "I tried to *save* him!"

Christina shook her head. "What happened?"

For a moment, Somerville bridled at being questioned, but he relented; he understood that Christina was asking so she could try and save McKenzie.

"His consciousness has gone," he said. "It's … gone. There's no helping him now."

Christina's eyes blazed with anger; she wanted to argue with him, that was clear, but she also understood the truth. On the few occasions that a Seeker's consciousness hadn't returned over the years, the body that had remained behind hadn't survived more than a couple of days.

*A body needs the consciousness to drive it*, Somerville thought. *If it's torn away, the body can't last.*

Reluctantly, Christina stood up; she clearly hated being unable to save a life, but McKenzie was beyond help now.

"Don't forget, Evan," she said tiredly, "that I *know* you. I know what you're capable of."

"That was a long time ago!" he snapped angrily. He released a breath and sat down at the conference table.

"I'm different now, Christina," he said quietly. "I've changed. I've breached the barrier to the astral plane!"

Christina laughed out loud; it was a short, sharp laugh with little humour behind it.

"You tell me you've changed, and then you go straight back to the only thing you ever truly cared about – your precious astral plane."

"Then why come with me?" Somerville asked tersely.

She shrugged. "Because you'd told me all about Paul and his inner angel – and I wanted to see what else you knew."

She suddenly looked tired, clearly resigned. "You're just the same as you ever were."

As she turned to leave, Somerville leaned forward and grabbed hold of her wrist. "How can you tell?" he asked, intrigued.

Christina looked at him with something akin to pity. "You didn't ask me to take care of Joshua's body."

Their eyes met for a moment, and Somerville could tell his efforts had been in vain. She clearly felt nothing for him; his hopes of her returning to the Seekers as his second-in-command had been dashed.

She pulled her arm out of his grasp and headed for the door. It was in that moment that Somerville realised they weren't alone in the room.

Christina caught the look of curiosity and fear that had mingled on his face, as if he had sensed something familiar and frightening all in one go.

"What is it?" she asked, knowing that it was more than just a ploy to get her attention. She hadn't spent three years as a Seeker without learning how to read him.

——•◦•——

Poena felt humiliated. A human had managed to push her out of their body, as if she were nothing, a mere insect.

*That will* not *happen again*, she told herself – and very quickly found a way. *I need a different body – one with a more pliable mind; one that won't fight me so much.*

*I have the perfect one.*

—◆•◆—

Somerville was now on his feet, prowling round the Cabinet Room like a tiger searching for its prey – and he sensed, somehow, that Poena was doing exactly the same.

Christina watched in silent fear, feeling the same strange presence in the room without knowing exactly what it was. She wanted to do something to defend herself, but didn't know *what*.

*Whatever it is*, she thought, *I don't want* –

—◆•◆—

Her last conscious thought was knocked away as Poena slammed into her consciousness and began feeding.

*There is much you can teach me*, Poena told her, *and you can begin by telling me all you know about Lucifer.*

# Broadstairs High Street – Present Day

Nausea swept through Lauren's spiritual body. She lost control of her momentum and would have been swept away into the vastness of space had a wispy hand not caught her spectral wrist and steadied her. After a dizzying moment, she realised that it was Rachael who had saved her. Lauren drew strength from her friend's firm grip, although it took her a moment to realise that Rachael herself was shimmering in front of her.

"Don't lose your form!" Rachael said urgently. "If you do that, you won't be able to re-establish it for a *long* time!"

With a sudden rush, the nausea disappeared as though it had never been there.

"What the hell was *that?*" she asked.

"Spirits," Rachael replied. "They were feeding."

Lauren shivered involuntarily. Fear shuddered through her every time she thought about the older spirits.

*And I can't help wondering if I'll end up like that one day.* She shivered. *I don't even want to think about it.*

She noticed that Rachael had gone quiet. "What is it?" she asked. "What's wrong?"

"I can remember … something," Rachael murmured. "How that soul died, ripped out of the physical plane – it feels … familiar. I just … I just don't know why."

Lauren watched her friend carefully, but didn't say anything. Rachael was clearly distressed, and she needed a moment to work out what she was feeling.

They were hidden away on Earth, trying to stay out of sight until they knew what to do, and the world suddenly felt very big and very lonely – and very silent. Rachel wrapped her arms around herself in comfort, but they dropped away as she remembered that they were mere composites – *memories* – of her real arms, now left far behind her on a world far below them.

"Can you remember how you died?" she asked.

Lauren frowned, another reflex from her days in a physical body; if she didn't concentrate, she wasn't even aware she was doing it.

"Not clearly," she replied slowly. "Rachael, it was you that told me about this, remember? It's rare that you remember your own death. I remember … images, brief sparks of memory, mostly because of Beelzebub." She smiled, wanly. "It seems that angels have far better memories than we do."

Rachael's mouth turned up automatically at the humour, but the smile didn't touch her eyes. "When the spirits fed, it brought back a half-memory," she said. "For a second, it was like I could almost remember how I died – as if they were connected somehow. I wish I could explain it."

She took in a breath, then expelled it. "Something's happening. The older spirits are angry about something."

"They're always angry."

"More than usual, I mean."

Lauren set her jaw determinedly. If her brother had seen the look in her eye, he would have hidden under a table and refused to argue with her. "How do we deal with this?"

Rachael blinked. "By staying as far away as possible from any spirit."

Lauren considered this option, then shook her head. "No."

Rachael chuckled nervously. "What?" she asked in agitation. "Lauren, these are spirits! You don't get involved with them. They're dangerous. Whatever they're involved with, I don't want any part of it!"

"We're *already* involved, Rachael," Lauren said sharply. "Some of them are looking for Beelzebub – and I doubt very much they'll just stop with her."

Rachael opened her mouth to argue, then shut it again as she realised that she couldn't. She and Lauren were tainted by association with Beelzebub, so the spirits would undoubtedly hunt them down and feed on them as well.

*I admire Lauren's courage*, she thought. *I wish it had occurred to me to be as brave.*

"What do you suggest we do?" she asked her friend.

Lauren shrugged. "It's Beelzebub's life on the line," she said. "Let's ask her."

Beelzebub was hovering just above the ground, a short distance away. They were in Broadstairs, a town not far from Ramsgate and Customs House where they had first arrived. They were all on the long promenade, which looked down over a chalky cliff to the beach and sea below – it was a sight that an angel didn't see very often, and she was clearly savouring it.

"Beelzebub?" Lauren prompted. "I was asking –"

"I heard you," she said quietly. She turned round to face the two spirits. She was a head taller than either of them, but she seemed smaller for a moment as she was lost in thought.

"Poena is on Earth," she said. "As are we. This … could be fortuitous, as she must not be allowed to rain down destruction on this world. We cannot avoid her any longer. It is time to fight."

Rachael smiled. "It's good to fight every now and then … when the cause is just."

Lauren raised an eyebrow in curiosity. "Would you consider this a just cause?"

"I would." The tension of a moment ago had dissipated, although Rachael still felt nervous; she knew that Lauren was right; they couldn't just stand by.

"Let's go help Paul and my brother," she said. "I think they're going to need it."

# Heaven – The Distant Past

It was a strange feeling for Lucifer, to know that he'd just had a conversation with Poena after so many years of war and hatred. He had fought in the war alongside the Almighty, Satan, Beelzebub, Michael and Micah for so long that he had almost forgotten what it was like to be at peace; even before the conflict had started, angels and spirits had lived in a state of cold war for quite some time.

*Now I am allying myself with my sworn enemy*, he thought. *How can I trust her?*

He paused by the large, arched doors to the Ruling Chamber, and then it came to him. *How can I not? My Father is not taking that final step. If it were just the spirits, then I doubt he would hesitate. But it is the* Seven Sisters … *they are important to all of us.*

It was an insane proposition, but one that he could see a kernel of logic in.

"Lucifer!"

He looked over his shoulder and saw Satan striding purposefully towards him, determination set on this face.

"Hello, my friend," he said, and held up a hand to forestall any conversation. "I cannot speak with you right now. I must see my father."

"No, Lucifer, you really must not."

Lucifer blinked in surprise, sure that he hadn't just heard his best friend cautioning him against speaking to his own father. He looked again at Satan, who paused by him in the large, arched corridor, and scowled at him.

"Perhaps you would like to reconsider your last comment?" he prompted.

Satan shook his head, still looking determined and resolute. "No, my friend, I don't think I would. Lucifer, what are you planning to suggest to the Almighty?"

Lucifer glanced left and right, to make sure there was no-one around to listen in, then turned back to his friend. "What do you think I am planning to say to him?" he asked.

"All I know is that it's to do with the Seven Sisters."

Lucifer was surprised. He hadn't breathed a word to anyone, and yet here was Satan, guessing his thoughts.

"Satan …" he said slowly. "I am entitled to speak my mind, and give my opinions to the Almighty."

"But what if the thoughts aren't your own? What if someone else has thought them for you?"

Lucifer didn't know what to say; he knew that Poena wouldn't have spoken to anyone else.

"I know you, 'fer," Satan said, as if reading his friend's mind. "You wouldn't be coming here today without a firm idea of what to propose, and I can't believe that anything regarding the Seven Sisters came from you."

"Just let me put my idea before the Almighty," Lucifer retorted. "He will make up his own mind."

A new voice joined the conversation. "Not before you put it before Michael."

Lucifer and Satan looked towards the door; Beelzebub had managed to approach without either of them hearing her.

"This is a private discussion," Lucifer snapped. As soon as he'd said it, he regretted it, and made an apologetic face towards his friend.

"At this rate," Beelzebub went on, seemingly oblivious, "we will lose this war three battles down the line. Lucifer, you can't just take it straight to your father without discussing it with Michael first."

Lucifer sighed. He knew his friend was right. He had just hoped to speak to the Almighty before losing his nerve.

"Very well," he conceded. "I will seek an urgent appointment with him."

"Strange you should say that," Beelzebub replied. "The Almighty and Michael have emerged from their conference. Michael wants to speak to us. Now."

# Heaven – Present Day

Joseph had hoped Michael would return to the Observatory before the half-angel left for Earth. Instead, he had remained locked away in his quarters.

*I would never have thought Michael was a sulker*, he thought. *Still, I won't let him just sit there and pout. If I have to go to him, then so be it.*

"I've been expecting you, Satan."

Michael sounded tired, and Joseph wasn't entirely surprised. *It must be tough, to lead Heaven's army and, on this occasion, be overruled by a new leader.*

He stepped into Michael's quarters' hesitating after a couple of steps, he marvelled at the sparseness of the senior angel's surroundings. There were three reclining chairs around a small table to his right, and a large desk took up most of the space to his left. Three large windows ahead of him looked out onto the vastness of space.

A sudden chuckle caught Joseph's attention; Michael was sat in the lounge area, and he motioned the hybrid angel to join him – which Joseph did appreciatively.

"You always seem to think I should have more things."

"Am I that transparent?"

Michael shrugged. "No. I am just good at reading you."

"I still consider myself human, despite these … angelic memories."

"Joseph, you …" Michael shook his head. "You're more angelic than you realise. You may be half-human, but you are also half-angel. Satan is an equal part of you."

Joseph had struggled with that concept since he had left Earth behind – his angelic memories were still un-jumbling themselves and he often lost track of whether he was Joseph or Satan … or both.

*I hope that will resolve itself,* he thought. *I suspect I will become some sort of amalgam.*

Michael interrupted his thoughts "I know why you're here, Satan," he said. "You wish to find common ground before you go on your fool's errand."

"I wouldn't call it a fool's errand," Joseph retorted. He sat upright as he tried to suppress his annoyance. "I am trying to reason with someone in order to stop a war, another *pointless* war that will only cause more deaths."

Michael scowled. "You really believe that Poena is open to reason?" he asked. "Do you not remember what Lucifer and she wanted to do to the Seven Sisters, before he saw sense and she was imprisoned? She will not stop until either every single angel dies … or she does."

Joseph stood angrily; he had been about to snap at Michael, but had realised that an argument wasn't going to help matters. Michael was an older, more experienced angel than he was and, despite Joseph's plan being accepted over his, was still held in great regard by many angels.

To calm himself, he paced to the windows and looked out over the stunning vista of galaxies spiralling away beneath him.

*Absolutely beautiful,* he thought. *Look at all the stars burning out their lives in the depths of space. It's … awe-inspiring.*

"Michael ..." He sighed. "Things have changed in this realm. I can respect that, but ... I'm new here. Well, half of me is, anyway."

He turned and smiled – and was relieved to see Michael smiling back.

"So many things are possible now that we're a republic. The Almighty had his own opinions ... and now we can do whatever we wish."

"Very admirable," Michael replied wearily. "But we have kept the astral plane separate for a reason. They rose up against us, we fought them ... and we won, by the narrowest of margins. I know that they have been planning retribution ever since. Putting a human ... or a half-human ... into that situation would only inflame it."

"Short of going in there with a full battalion of angels," Joseph said, "what else would you suggest?"

"Nothing, because going on the offensive is the right thing to do." Michael stood and his wings ruffled. "Spirits need to understand that we are serious about ensuring the astral plane knows its place. We need to find out what is happening and save Beelzebub ... by force if necessary."

"Michael..." Joseph said hesitatingly. "Micah has given me the authority to approach Poena ... and Paul. For that to work, I need your agreement that you won't try and lead an invasion force until I have been given every opportunity to negotiate a peaceful settlement."

Michael didn't respond. The silence stretched on until Joseph wondered whether the senior angel had managed to fall asleep while standing upright.

*He looks tired*, Joseph thought. *Is he feeling old? Is that even possible with angels?*

"Do I have your word that you'll let me at least try?" he went on.

"I respect you, Satan," Michael replied, "more than you know. You have done well to integrate yourself back into Heaven since your return – and your willingness to abandon your previous life in order to learn about your angelic existence is commendable. I wish others were like you."

It took Joseph a moment to understand what Michael was getting at, but when he did, his face flushed red with annoyance.

"Paul and Lucifer made that agreement together," he said angrily. "They hadn't merged personalities like I had. They're still separate entities – and would prefer to remain that way."

"If you had been given the opportunity, would you have preferred that?"

"At the time," Joseph conceded, "yes. I would have remained separate. Now … I am content with my life."

"But your human side is still loyal to your humanity?" Michael countered. "Is that not why you are recruiting Paul for this errand? Because he is your friend?"

"I trust him!" Joseph snapped. "I will be recruiting Lucifer too, by default."

"A human cannot stop what is happening."

"What *is* happening, Michael? Are you in receipt of some secret knowledge that I'm not?"

"I once allowed Heaven to be taken over by Metatron. I will not allow another invasion, and if it means invading the astral plane first, then so be it!"

Joseph's swallowed at the sight of this powerful angel angry not just at those around him, but at himself. He harboured guilt over the Civil War that had wracked Heaven, between the forces of the Almighty and those of Lucifer, which had allowed Metatron – the Almighty's scribe – to take control of their realm.

"Michael, it wasn't your fault!" he retorted. "You are one of the most honourable people I know, but what you are suggesting is *wrong!*"

"And what you are suggesting is… human," Michael replied, disgust suddenly obvious in his voice. "I wonder if you have forgotten your angelic origins, Satan."

Those words were like a slap in the face to Joseph, who – as Michael himself had pointed out – had given up his earthly life in order learn more about his angelic past … and integrate his memories.

Michael seemed to sense that he had overstepped an invisible line. His anger had taken him beyond reasonableness and, despite their differences of opinion, he did like Satan / Joseph a lot.

"I … apologise," he said. "But I am convinced that I am right."

Joseph inclined his head. "As am I."

"Then we have nothing more to discuss," Michael went on, a level of ice present in his voice that hadn't been there a moment before.

Joseph set his jaw in an angry line. "Just remember, Michael, that Micah approved *my* plan, not yours."

Before Michael could respond, Joseph turned on his heels and walked purposefully out of the angel's quarters.

Michael watched him go. For a moment, he considered going after him, but realised that it would do no good. Their minds were both made up.

"And our paths will now diverge," he muttered. "I must make a choice."

# Paul's Flat, Broadstairs - Present Day

Paul and Kirby had returned to the real world abruptly and without warning; they both gasped in shock. The pair slumped down amongst the boxes in Paul's front room, and this time, Paul's spirit didn't disappear *through* the box.

Lucifer watched them both, understanding that they had each experienced something that was incredible and unique – even if it was just from his own memory. It was still odd, being temporarily in a human body, but it was refreshing to be awake again.

*However long it is for.*

He didn't like to consider what would happen when this crisis was over; he supposed that he would have to sleep again inside Paul's head. He accepted it with a weary resignation; while he wanted Paul to have a full life, now that he had awoken, he wanted to get on with living *his*.

*I can never tell Paul that,* he knew. *I will wait for my time, and know that my honour is intact as a result.*

Paul was trying to ignore the throbbing headache that had started; he couldn't entirely work out *how* he was having a headache, as his body was over on the other side of the room, but it was there nonetheless.

*There are some things I'll never understand.*

"Weird things keep happening to us, don't they?" he said.

"You're the one who's been displaced from his body."

Paul chuckled. "Let me know if you ever want to swap."

Kirby smiled, but didn't reply; he didn't know what to say. The stupid jealousy had risen again, and he tried to fight it.

*Stop it,* he told himself. *Would you* actually *want to leave your body?*

He couldn't stop a tiny part of his brain thinking; *At least that way I could know what it feels like. I always seem to be one step behind.*

Shifting uncomfortably in his chair, he forced himself to think differently; *I'm* here, *and I'm helping.* He looked over at Paul, who seemed to be in some discomfort.

"What's wrong?" he asked.

Paul shook his head. "Headache," he replied. "It won't shift. I don't know why –"

With that, he disappeared. There was no sign of him – except for his physical body, stood by the front room door.

Kirby sighed, and exchanged a weary glance with Lucifer.

⬤●⬤

Paul looked around at the white space surrounding him and sighed. "Not again," he snapped angrily, helpless fury bubbling up inside him. "Why the hell am I here?"

"Hell doesn't exist, Paul," came a now-familiar voice. "At least not in the way humanity thinks of it. I often think of this place as hell."

"Considering I don't know where I am, that's not much of a clue," Paul said testily. He was fed up of being brought to this empty, white void without his consent – and being spoken down to by this (admittedly beautiful) voice that he just couldn't pinpoint.

"Look," he said sharply, "I don't want to be at your beck and call all the time. I'm getting bored at not having a clue what's going on."

"Then perhaps I can enlighten you, Mr Finn. It's not as if you haven't travelled here before. I am sure Lucifer will be most … upset that he is not here as well."

"This isn't heaven," Paul said thoughtfully, "and if you're telling the truth, then this isn't hell either. It's … some kind of pocket dimension or something."

"Yes," the voice said. She sounded impressed that he had deduced that. "A few of us are still able to access it for … private meetings, even after all this time."

"You told me you weren't an angel."

"I'm not."

"Then what sort of spirit are you?" Paul decided he had nothing to lose and went on; "Are you Poena?"

The voice was silent for a while longer, and Paul began to wonder if she was still there. He wanted to ask, but decided against it.

She *brought* me *here*, he thought stubbornly. *I'll let her work for a change.*

"I wonder …"

"What?" Paul snapped.

"What part do you actually place in this conspiracy?" she asked. "How do you get the angels to listen to you? Or are you actually in league with Poena?"

"So you're *not* Poena." Now Paul was just plain intrigued. "Look, I just want a quiet life. I just want to live quietly with my girlfriend. I would be very willing to leave everything else behind."

"Well, you are part of this now," she replied. "You are part of this conspiracy."

"There is no conspiracy!" he exclaimed.

"I do not believe you."

Paul snorted in derision. "Then I don't know how I can prove it to you," he said. "You're the one that's kidnapped me, remember?"

The voice was silent again. It was clearly following a thought process, and quickly came to a conclusion.

"Find me," said the voice. "If you can find me … find my prison … then I will be more likely to listen to you. Whether I believe you is another matter."

* * *

"Welcome back, mate. Pleasant trip?"

"What?"

Paul blinked. He was back in his flat, in the same seat, as if he had never left. His body, under angelic power, was over on the other side of the room, and nothing else had changed.

"How long was I gone?"

Kirby shrugged. "A few seconds, that's all."

Paul was surprised; it had felt like a lot longer. All three encounters he had had in the white realm had been more than a few seconds; he had the memories to prove it.

"It is a realm where time and space do not factor," Lucifer mused. "Certain groups use as a private space, to avoid being overheard. Whoever took you was definitely not an angel."

"How do you know?" Paul asked. He'd already come to the same conclusion, but wanted to know why Lucifer was so sure.

"I would know," Lucifer said confidently. "I may be in a human body, but I still have a sense about certain things. They clearly do not wish me to be aware of your conversations with them."

Paul frowned. "Why?"

It was Kirby who answered. "Some sort of conspiracy within the spirit world?" he said. "If this kidnapper isn't an angel, then could it be Poena ... or another spirit, trying to gain human support?"

Lucifer nodded. "It is possible."

The two humans exchanged a glance.

"We need to get in contact with your sister and Lauren," Paul said. "They might know something – or be able to find out."

Kirby shook his head. "I can't contact her right now. I've been trying, but I keep failing. I wonder if she's still on Earth; our connection might only work *between* the realms."

Paul felt suddenly exhausted. He was getting tired of all this talk of conspiracies.

Kirby watched Paul stand and pace over to the bay windows. His friend was pensive and restless, and Kirby knew there wasn't anything he could say in comfort.

"Are you thinking about the spirits?" he asked.

Paul blinked, almost surprised by Kirby's question.

"No," he replied – then chuckled. "I was thinking about Christina."

He bit on a nail – or the replica of a nail that actually existed on his body – for a moment, and then stopped as he caught Kirby smirking at him.

"What?" he asked.

"You only bite your nail when there's something you don't want to say," Kirby said in amusement. "It's better if you say it, mate. You'll feel better, getting it off –"

"What if Christina doesn't *want* to come back?"

Paul had blurted the words out quickly in case he lost his courage, which Kirby couldn't blame him for.

*I'd have probably done the same*, he reasoned.

"Why else did she go?" Paul asked. "I can't work that one out, Kirby – why did she just leave and go with … *him?*"

Kirby frowned. "Because she was frightened and confused," he replied. "She'd just found out something pretty huge about your past, and she didn't know how to deal with it. She needed time to think … and Somerville was offering her that time."

Paul opened his mouth to speak, but Kirby cut in. "Stop beating yourself up about it," he said. "Christina loves you, mate. I see it in her eyes every time she looks at you, so don't ever forget that."

Paul was stupidly grateful for Kirby reminding of that simple fact. He swallowed and felt a surge of conflicting emotions swirl up inside of him; truthfully, he didn't know what to feel right now, and he averted his gaze as he tried to get his emotions back under control.

"You're pretty quiet over there, Lucifer."

Lucifer shrugged – that gesture, above all, was universal, it seemed.

"I do not understand human emotions that well," he conceded, "nor do I often speak on subjects that I am not an expert in."

Paul smiled; he found himself liking Lucifer the more he got to know him.

"Very wise," he replied. "I'd value your counsel on a subject you undoubtedly *are* expert on, though. Poena. I keep hearing her name."

Lucifer nodded. "Unsurprising," he said. "She was the senior spirit at the time of the war between spirits and angels. Poena was the primary advisor to the Seven Sisters, and a very ... dangerous entity."

"You knew her, didn't you?" Kirby asked.

Lucifer nodded, and his eyes looked into the middle distance for a moment as his mind was lost to nostalgia.

"Yes," he admitted. "Yes, I did ... and she was very beguiling at one time. Everyone has regrets, but there is one thing I regret with every fibre of my being."

"Falling in love with her?" Paul guessed.

Lucifer looked up, clearly surprised by Paul's question.

"Love?" he repeated. "No, not love. I was stupid and young ... and I listened to her. I believed what she said ... and have regretted it ever since."

Paul didn't ask anything else; Lucifer was clearly deep in thought, and uncomfortable with continuing.

*He'll tell me when he's ready.*

He shook his head and looked again at the detective sat on the opposite couch.

"Sounds to me like we need to do something about this," he said. "The Seekers of Truth have ruined things for everyone; they've torn through the barrier, and there's only a scar now keeping all these spirits swarming through and killing us."

Kirby rubbed his forehead. "I was thinking about calling in Special Forces, but I don't think they'll be quite enough somehow."

Paul grinned. "True, but we've got a human, an angel in a human body and an unwilling spirit. What more do we need?"

"Several thousand more of us?"

Paul laughed. "Sometimes three people can do more good than several thousand."

"You've clearly never been in Margate town centre on a Saturday night, pal," Kirby replied, abruptly remembering his old days in uniform. "But I take your point. We need to find out what's going on. At the very least, let's try and find my sister and Lauren. I'll feel better with them on our side."

Paul nodded. "Agreed," he replied. "Now all we need to find out is where they've gone."

"I know just the place to start."

# Ramsgate Harbour – Present Day

Ramsgate Harbour was sparkling in the afternoon sun. The blue water, interspersed with yachts and cruisers of all shapes and sizes, glittered as the sun slowly moved over the yardarm and began its slow descent down towards the horizon.

As it was a Saturday, the harbour was busy – the string of smart, affluent bars along the marina attracted a lot of people. Customs House was situated at the end opposite a museum and was a busy thoroughfare for shoppers, drinkers and people out for a stroll to enjoy the sunshine. In many ways, it was a typical summer afternoon – except for the fact that an angel was walking amongst them.

Not that anyone realised that an angel was there, of course – Joseph knew that he had to be far more circumspect than that. He almost hadn't been; he was so used by now to his wings – and begun to lose his inhibitions regarding clothing – that his first attempt to travel to Earth had quickly been aborted.

He had quickly created some clothes out of the ether – and it had taken him a while to realise that he created facsimiles of the jeans and shirt he had been wearing when he had died.

*I could have chosen anything*, he thought. *A smart suit or something.*

Before that thought could change into deed, he quickly chastised himself. *Then you'd look like a prat and Paul would just laugh at you.*

As he walked along the marina, he felt nervous energy churn in the pit of his stomach. He was worried about how Paul would react to seeing him again after … *How long is it now?* he wondered. *It must be years.*

Joseph hadn't given any active thought as to his starting point; he had just ended up here, at the harbour. He wasn't entirely surprised – after all, he had spent many happy evenings here, mostly with Paul, sat outside the Belgium Bar whenever the weather allowed it, as they had put the world to rights.

Something else nagged at the corner of his brain, however, and he realised that hadn't been the sole reason for his subconscious bringing him here. He paused on the opposite side of the road to red-brick building of Customs House. Something about it made him feel uncomfortable. He stood there for a moment, trying to analyse what it was that bothered him so much.

*Perhaps I'm wrong*, he thought. *My senses are still … adjusting.*

He turned to go, but something caught his eye; two people had just walked out of Customs House. In itself, that was nothing unusual– except that, for a moment, it had looked like there were *three* people leaving.

Joseph knew he wasn't mistaken; his angelic eyes had perfect vision and he was confident he'd not been confused.

A male had exited first, and he was looking both fearful and angry at the same time. He was walking ahead of the female, who seemed like she was pursing him. He had made it a metre or so away from the building when the female caught up with him and grabbed him by the arm.

He looked as if he'd be struck by an electric shock; he jerked backwards, trying to yank her hand off him, but she remained firm.

Joseph watched the interaction carefully, curious to know what the argument was about. He was curious about something else as well. He squinted and turned his head to one side.

*Come on*, he thought. *Where are you? I know you're there.*

Then he saw it. He tried – and failed – to suppress an audible gasp.

"No!" he whispered in exclamation. "It's not –"

He stopped himself from saying "possible", because it clearly was. Poena had done it – she had actually done it – managed to break through the barrier to Earth and take over a human body.

Joseph found himself frozen to the spot. He didn't know how to react as a thousand thoughts ran through his mind.

Poena's words, whatever she was saying to the man, died in her throat as she seemed to realise that something wasn't right. The man looked at her in surprise, and tried to distract her with a question. He forced her hand off his arm and asked the same question again.

Joseph saw Poena's face contort in anger, and she turned back to face the man next to her.

*No!* Joseph thought urgently, and took a step forward – and then hesitated. That hesitation was all Poena needed to do her job; a hand snapped forward and grabbed the man's face. He convulsed for a moment, as if in an epileptic fit; Poena took her hand away, and he collapsed to the floor. A couple of seconds later, Joseph watched helplessly as the man's spirit floated up, away from his body.

Ignoring the spirit, and the cries of alarm from nearby people that had seen him collapse, Poena's eyes began roving along the road, resting on each individual lining the pavement before moving on to the next. Joseph was seized with a sudden – and certain – knowledge that she would recognise who he was as soon as she fixed her eyes on him.

*I can't be here!* he thought. *My god, she's mad – I need Lucifer's help on this, before it degenerates into open warfare.*

With more questions than he arrived with, Joseph vanished.

⬥•⬥

*What is an angel doing here on Earth?*

Ignoring the swelling crowd of people moving around Somerville's slumped body, Poena – looking out through Christina's eyes – coolly looked up and down the street until she was sure that the angel was gone.

*I knew about the imprisoned angels,* she thought. *Everyone knows about* them, *but why is an angel here? Do they know about me already?*

She would have thought it impossible that they could have learnt about her actions quite so soon, but clearly some word had already got out.

*Perhaps there* is *a conspiracy after all,* she speculated. *Angels and humans, working together to defeat the spirit world. I wouldn't put it past Lucifer after the war; he is ashamed that he surrendered to his fear at the last minute, and has turned to humans to help him … do what?*

*There is no conspiracy!*

Poena looked around – and up – to where Somerville's soul was floating above his now-deceased body.

"Go away, you insignificant being," she said. "You are nobody."

*I am leader of the Seekers of Truth, and I managed to access your realm – something that you needed an* angel *to do for you to travel to Earth!*

Poena paused for a moment, as if searching deep in her memory for something, then smirked as it came to her. "The Seekers of Truth. How quaint." She narrowed her eyes. "They are nothing – especially now I have killed their leader."

Turning on her heel she strode off along the marina. She was going to find Lucifer and this other angel, and she was going to kill them herself.

# Ramsgate Harbour – Present Day

Lauren coalesced again and drew in a breath. She knew she didn't need to, but it was a force of habit; rematerialising always made her ache somehow, and it didn't get any easier.

"Where are we?"

She looked over her shoulder and saw Beelzebub stood behind her, with Rachael next to her.

*Good,* she thought, *at least we're still all together.*

Rachael was looking around at their surroundings, a stupid grin on her face.

"I didn't think I'd ever see this place again," she said.

Curious, Lauren took a moment to take in where they were – and couldn't help but laugh.

"My brother and Paul used to come here every week for a drink for … well, as long as I can remember."

Without realising it, they had materialised very close to where Joseph had recently been. They all noticed the mass of bystanders crowding the pavement outside Customs House.

"What's going on over there?" Lauren asked.

Rachael shrugged. "There's only one way to find out."

She crossed the road and quickly blended in; Lauren marvelled how "normal" she looked amongst the other humans.

"You'd never think we were spirits," she muttered.

"Do not get used to the feeling," Beelzebub said shortly. "When this is all over, you will be expected to return to the astral plane."

Lauren frowned. "What is *wrong* with you?"

"Someone died here."

Lauren's retort died in her throat as she processed Beelzebub's coolly-delivered statement. Beelzebub didn't seem to notice her one-time host's discomfort; instead, she turned to face Rachael, who had returned to the group.

"It's Somerville," she said, looking ashen. "He's –"

"Dead?"

Rachael blinked in surprise, her grief momentarily forgotten. "How did you know?"

Lauren's eyes slid across to Beelzebub, and Rachael nodded in understanding.

"How did this happen?" she asked. "I knew Somerville for years, and now he's just dead – and I can't see his spirit anywhere."

"Poena killed him," Beelzebub said bluntly. "I can feel her energy from here – it is … *distinctive*." She paused, put her head to one side, and stared into the middle distance for a moment. "Also, your brother was here."

"My … brother?" Lauren repeated, her voice thick with emotion. "He was here, on Earth?"

Beelzebub nodded. She was glad that she had gotten to the bottom of what she had been sensing, but it just worried her even more; what was Satan, an old friend of hers that she loved and trusted beyond words, doing here on Earth?

"We need to find him," Lauren said, clearly thinking the same as Beelzebub, "and we need Paul and Kirby as well.

Maybe the six of us can stop Poena before she kills anyone else."

Beelzebub didn't say anything else; she didn't want to let her companions down, but knew it wouldn't be as easy as they thought it would be.

"Then we must keep looking," she said carefully. "Only then can we agree on a course of action."

# Ramsgate Harbour – Present Day

"I've only ever wanted a quiet life, you know."

"So you keep saying. Now shut up; I'm trying to concentrate. Keep an eye out for police."

"Police that *aren't* you, I assume?"

Paul's sarcasm didn't register to Kirby; the detective continued his work instead. Realising that he wouldn't get anywhere while his friend was so lost in concentration, Paul shrugged and looked up and down the street.

"Right," he muttered. "I'll just wait somewhere else until you're done."

Dusk was falling in Ramsgate and Paul forced himself to stop hovering nervously over Kirby's shoulder. He hopped off the front step of Customs House and looked out over the beautiful vista of the Marina. Thankfully, there weren't too many people around to see Kirby trying to break into the building, but Paul still didn't fancy trying to explain what they were doing.

"Come on, come on," he muttered.

"Humans are so impatient."

Paul scowled at the angel standing next to him, but tried to change the subject. He had a feeling that there would be no point in trying to argue with an angel.

"I wonder what that ambulance was here for," he said.

"I do not know," Lucifer replied carefully. "Since I did not see inside the vehicle, I do not know who was injured."

Paul couldn't help himself this time. "Haven't you ever heard of small talk?" he snapped.

"What is the point?" Lucifer asked. "They are words without meaning."

Paul rolled his eyes and glanced over his shoulder at Kirby, silently urging him to unlock the door.

"You must allow Kirby the time to master his task."

"We don't think in millions of years like you do," Paul retorted, stomping his feet moodily on the pavement. "We do things differently down here."

"So I see."

Paul bit back his response; he had almost decided to drop it when Lucifer spoke again.

"A thought for you to consider."

"What?"

"The being that took you on your out-of-body experience?"

"Yes?"

"How powerful do you imagine they have to be to wake me up, put me in control of your body, and keep you on Earth as a separate spirit? That is something beyond the power of any angel except the Almighty."

Paul opened his mouth to reply, but found he couldn't think of anything to say. The thought frightened him, if he were honest, and there was nothing he could say to make himself feel better.

"Paul?"

He looked back over his shoulder, half-glad that he had something else to think about. Before Lucifer had voiced it, it hadn't occurred to him at all. Now, however, it was all he could think about.

Kirby stood in front of a now-open door, beaming proudly, and Paul fought to concentrate on here and now; Lucifer's question would be left to fester for some other time.

"All those years mingling with convicts," Kirby said with a laugh. "I knew it would pay off."

"Yeah…" Paul said distantly. A different thought broke through his consciousness. "Mate…"

Kirby's smile disappeared as his friend didn't react in the way he had expected. "What?" he demanded.

"Didn't McKenzie turn off a burglar alarm when we came in earlier?"

———•◆•———

Five minutes later, using what Lucifer described as "brute force and ignorance," the burglar alarm had been disarmed. Kirby was examining the remains of the device scattered over the floor, while Paul made one final check outside and then closed the door behind them.

"That went better than expected," he said.

Kirby glanced up at him and raised an eyebrow.

"I still don't see why you couldn't have at least tried to manipulate the lock from the inside."

"I can't even sit on a sofa without Lucifer's help," Paul retorted. "I think a key is a bit out of my reach at the moment."

"So what do we do now?"

Paul shrugged. "We … look around," he said. "We see what the Seekers know … and we find a way to let Lauren and Rachael know where we are."

"Right," Kirby said decisively.

"Do you actually know what you're looking for?" Paul asked.

To his credit, Kirby looked genuinely shocked and appalled by Paul's question. "I am an officer of the law," he intoned, "and my sister was a Seeker of Truth."

He turned away and looked around the large foyer, seemingly unsure about which way to go.

"You haven't got the foggiest, have you?" Paul asked.

Kirby hesitated. "I'll tell you one thing," he said.

"What?"

"We don't need to go through that door."

Paul followed Kirby's pointed finger and frowned. "I should hope not," he replied. "That's where we were held captive this morning."

—●●—

After a few wrong turns, they found themselves at the entrance to the basement.

"Look, Kirby. Are you sure about this?" Paul was terrified of being caught; he kept looking over his shoulder every few seconds, convinced that someone would discover them any moment. The thought that he was a spirit and wouldn't fit any handcuffs didn't seem to occur to him, and Kirby knew that this wasn't the time to have that conversation.

"We're here now," the detective replied. "Do you have any better ideas?"

Paul had spent the last twenty minutes trying to think of one, but had failed miserably. He wanted to do ... *something* to track down his friends.

*But what?* he asked himself, trying – and failing – to come up with an idea that would work.

He sighed; right now, there didn't seem to be *any* good ideas ... so Kirby's plan was the only one they had.

He indicated to Kirby that they should go on. As they descended the stairs, Paul felt a strange emotion from Lucifer.

"Lucifer..." he said slowly. "What's wrong? How can I feel your emotions?"

"We still have a connection," the angel intoned from behind him. "We shared a mind for your entire life. While we are both still connected to it, there is still a residual link to one another's feelings."

Kirby paused on a lower step and glanced behind him. "What's wrong?" he whispered.

"I am trapped inside a human body," Lucifer said softly. "It is taking me time to understand what I can sense, but something is wrong. I will tell you when I know what it is."

Paul didn't have the chance to question the angel further because Kirby reached the bottom step. The only light came from the small flashlight the detective was holding in his hand – he hadn't wanted to tempt fate by turning on the mains on the ground floor when the sets of doors that they had broken into were frosted glass.

Down here, however, was a different story. It was pitch black, and Paul was confident that they could get away with more light than the thin strip emanating from Kirby's torch.

*And in any case,* he thought, *I'm not a huge fan of the dark.*

"I've found a light switch," Kirby said.

Paul released a sigh of relief; the sigh caught in his breath as the lights flicked on and he saw where they were. It was a long, low-ceilinged room with six hospital beds near to the staircase, each with a computer monitor and a table with various pieces of medical equipment on them.

Further down, past the beds, there were four desks, surrounded on the outside walls by filing cabinets and microfiches. The low hum of the desktop computers told Paul that they were still on, which intrigued him. Looking over at Kirby, he could tell that his friend felt the same.

"This can't be a nurses' area," Paul said. "Is this how the Seekers contacted the spirit world?"

Kirby shrugged. "Rachael never really talked about her work with the Seekers," he confessed. "Their work was meant to be completely secret. She told me the odd bit here and there, but not much. It's possible this is where they … astral planed, or whatever they called it."

Both were silent for a moment, taking in the scene before them. Paul glanced up the stairs again, still worried that they were going to get caught.

"We need to start looking," he urged the detective. "I want to find anything on Christina."

Kirby nodded, tucked the torch back in his trouser pocket and navigated his way through the beds towards the filing cabinets. Paul glanced around once more, then moved to follow him.

Lucifer swallowed hard. He realised what it was that was bothering him.

"Terrible things have happened here."

Before Paul or Kirby could ask, Lucifer clarified; "People have died here."

Paul had never heard the angel sound so disgusted, and it worried him to hear it now, in this strange room in the basement of a place where his girlfriend might well have visited – in the past or recently.

Lucifer sensed Paul's question before he had a chance to ask it.

"I do not know *who* died here – merely that people *have*. I cannot be more precise than that."

Paul felt sick at the thought. His knees threatened to buckle at the mere thought of Christina – or anyone – losing their lives in this place.

"I need to find Christina," he whispered. Turning to face Kirby, he couldn't control the well of panic in his voice as he asked, "Seekers have died in this building. What if it was her?"

Kirby shook his head, and Paul couldn't tell whether it was from anger or sadness.

"Don't torment yourself," he told his friend. "Whatever Lucifer sensed … push it to the back of your mind. Let the angels think about the bigger picture. You need to think about the here and now. We need to find out what the Seekers are up to – and what they want with your girlfriend."

Paul took a steadying – and unnecessary – breath, and nodded. He was grateful to his friend for helping to calm him down.

"Is that your professional opinion, Detective Kirby?" he asked with a chuckle.

"No, that's my opinion as an amateur psychologist." Kirby smiled. "Come on, mate. We've got work to do."

Paul looked round the room. Filing cabinets and computers filled this half of the space, and it was a daunting prospect to consider how much they had to trawl through.

*A needle in a hay stack,* he thought. *But that doesn't mean we shouldn't try.*

He frowned. "There's something we've not considered."

Kirby frowned. "What?"

"I'm a spirit," Paul replied. "I'm not going to be able to pick anything up."

"Damn," Kirby muttered. "I hadn't thought of that."

Paul had already thought of an answer, however, and Lucifer tensed as the human turned to face him.

"Time to help out, Lucifer," he said. "How would you like to be my secretary?"

# Heaven – Present Day

Michael still hadn't left his quarters. Micah found himself wondering if something more serious had happened to the senior angel, but quickly dismissed it. There were ways of knowing if an angel had been badly injured; even a newly-re-awoken angel such as himself would be able to tell.

*So he really* is *sulking?* he thought. *I thought better of him than that.*

The ruler of Heaven was back in the Ruling Chamber, sat in his usual spot at the bottom of the stairs that led to the throne.

He was surprised at Michael; he and the senior angel had always been close, and he had always been supportive of Micah ever since he had ascended to the presidency.

*Even though it must have been difficult for him*, he thought. *A younger angel being elected to the most senior position in Heaven. He said he didn't want the position for himself, but still … I wonder if I wouldn't feel at least a little jealous if our situations were reversed.*

He tapped an idle finger against the white step as it continued to reflect the galactic light shining in through the high windows behind the throne. Being the first democratic leader of the angelic realm was never going to be easy, he knew that, but right now it felt overwhelming.

*I've sent a half-angel down to Earth against my better judgement to get him to negotiate with an ancient spirit that loathes Heaven and all who live within it, and I've got the leader of my armies skulking away in his quarters refusing to come out because he disagrees with my decision.*

He sighed and stood up, letting his huge wings gently unfurl and stretch as he did so. It had been quite a while since he had been able to fly properly; to stretch his wings and forget the stresses of his job.

*And it will be a while before I can do so again*, he thought. *I need to resolve this situation with Michael. He cannot just wallow in his quarters until this is all over. I need his counsel.*

Deciding to swallow his own pride and be the better angel, he left the Ruling Chamber at a fast stride. *I need to speak with him now, before my stubbornness returns and we continue ignoring each other forever more.*

—•—

It wasn't long before Micah stood at the doorway to Michael's quarters – and something didn't feel right. Angels were sensitive to the echo of strong, recent emotions. An argument had happened recently in Michael's quarters.

Micah knew instantly. *Joseph, what did you do?* he wondered. *Did you come here, and try to convince Michael of your plan? You foolish angel.*

Before he could even announce himself, the door to Michael's quarters opened. Micah stepped in – and swallowed as a wash of emotions flooded over him. Anger, embarrassment, humiliation – all a hundred times stronger than any human could ever experience.

Michael's quarters were as immaculate – and Spartan – as always, but Michael himself was nowhere to be seen.

"Michael?" the first amongst equals asked out loud, knowing it was stupid, but doing it anyway to satisfy his own curiosity.

Feeling a sudden surge of irritation at how events were running away from him, he strode over to the window and tried to draw strength – and calm – from the wonders of the cosmos.

Instead, his head reeled as his eyes rested on a figure in the distance, flying away from the heavenly citadel as fast as his wings would carry him.

"Where are you going, Michael?" Micah muttered under his breath. "And why do I feel so suspicious about whatever you are planning to do?"

He had to get word to Joseph; he spun on his heel and strode purposefully out of Michael's quarters to the Celestial Observatory.

# Astral Plane – Present Day

The spirits sensed their leader, although it hadn't been as they had expected. She had opened the barrier for them, and even provided them with a human spirit to feast on and whet their appetite, but then the barrier had shut before they could travel through … and they had felt their leader's pain.

They were confused … and frightened. They hadn't the strength to breach the barrier individually, and had been driven so insane over the centuries they weren't capable of rational, united thought. They might have forced a breach if they had worked together – but the thought of such united action wouldn't have occurred to them in the first place.

Fear and doubt hardly ever penetrated their deep, dark anger, but both emotions did so now; they wanted to feast on humanity, and having to wait made them more agitated than Poena could have imagined.

—•—

In the meantime, Alcyone could feel the spirits and their chaotic, jumbled emotions.

*There are many more of them than I remember*, she thought. *Their numbers have grown – as have their desires. They swarm like flies*

*– oh, Poena, have you begun your games again, just like you did in the past?*

A thought began to float round her vast mind. It was one that, at first, frightened her. But a being such as Alcyone didn't remain frightened for long – and instead, a terrible certainty flooded over her.

# Broadstairs High Street – Present Day

"Things have changed," Joseph muttered angrily. "They have no right to change."

He was stood outside the flat where Paul had once lived, above a shop in the high street – except that Paul was no longer there; he could *feel* it. Sighing, he gave in.

*I'd hoped that I could do this with good old-fashioned human ingenuity*, he thought. *But I haven't got time for that.*

He felt ill at ease; he would never admit it, but he was worried that Michael would do something thoughtless. Despite his millennia of experience in advising Heaven, Michael had been angry at being overruled – Joseph had seen that in the older angel.

*I need to get this done before Michael decides to try and prove us … me … wrong.*

It was now early evening and dusk was falling. It was the time of day when workers had gone home but the evening crowd hadn't come out in force – so Joseph could savour the relative solitude.

Despite the approaching cover of darkness, Joseph waited until he stepped into the doorway of the shop underneath Paul's old flat before he closed his eyes.

*Just because there's very few people around doesn't mean that I want someone to see me. I'm still human enough to know how people can get around folks acting weirdly.*

He stretched out his mind and searched for his friend. His human side was again disappointed that he was having to rely on his angelic nature for this. He wanted to prove that it was possible to merge the two sides together into something that was better – instead, he felt like because of his increasing reliance on his angelic side, he was slowly forgetting what is was like to be human.

It didn't take Joseph long to get a sense of where his friend had moved to; Paul's emotions had imprinted themselves on a new residence, somewhere nearby – *and not long ago, if I'm any judge,* Joseph thought. *I hope I can stay to get the tour.*

It was a special talent that Satan possessed, and one that Joseph had needed to relearn when he had joined with the angel. Being able to track a person's movements based on emotions was a useful tool, he had to admit. It didn't take him long to track Paul down – and he laughed as soon as he realised where his old friend was. A couple walking past the shop front, who hadn't seen him hiding in the doorway, jumped and quickened their step as they heard his laughter.

"I've just bloody come from there," he muttered. "If you're at the Belgium Bar, then I hope you've brought enough money for a round."

---

Rachael and Lauren had made themselves as transparent as possible without completely dispensing of their bodies, and floated above the shops that lined each side of the high street.

Beelzebub was searching nearby, but the two human spirits weren't inclined to summon her – they were worried that Poena would be more likely to detect her than them. A shiver ran down Lauren's back as she realised who was inside the human body they were observing on the ground.

"What's Poena done with the human soul?" she asked in a hoarse whisper; she didn't want to take any chances about being detected.

"Killed it, I imagine," Rachael said in a flat tone.

Neither of them said anything more. Someone was dead at Poena's hand – that went beyond words.

Rachael was scowling at the consciousness that lingered near Poena; it looked familiar, although she was finding it difficult to work out why, as it was struggling to sustain its shape.

*Unsurprising,* she thought. *Not many spirits can manage that.*

She had to concede some respect to the spirit, however; the fact that it was fighting to regain its shape, especially after such a violent event as death, was impressive. While some let their forms fade away, other spirits, such as Lauren and Rachael, deliberately kept theirs as a reminder of their previous lives.

The spirit's face coalesced – and she recognised it instantly.

"Evan Somerville," she muttered.

"I don't really want to stay around here anymore," Lauren said urgently. "Let's go and find the others."

Rachael couldn't take her eyes off Somerville, her one-time director and friend. Something had hit her when she had seen his dead body lying on the floor at Customs House, although she couldn't fully identify the emotion.

*I should be sad*, she thought, *that he's lost his life – and I should feel happy again that I've seen a part of him is alive.*

But she wasn't feeling either emotion – at least, in the order that she thought she should be feeling them, and it disturbed her.

"Rachael!" Lauren said, this time more urgently, and Rachael's attention immediately snapped back to her friend.

"Sorry," she said quietly. "You're right, of course. We should go."

Deliberately not looking back at the scene below them, Rachael grabbed hold of Lauren's transparent wrist – and they both disappeared.

❧

Poena looked up a moment too late – and saw … something she had not expected. She scowled at the sky, and Somerville watched her eyes scour the clouds for something.

He wasn't sure why he had followed her, if he were honest. She had killed him, and his soul had been ripped from his body. He'd had to act quickly, as he'd been confident that she would otherwise do the same to him as she had done to McKenzie – and without his own consciousness to fight back, there would be nothing to stop Poena keeping the breach open until the spirits poured through.

*I need to stop this*, he thought – and so had followed her, to try and see if there was anything that he could do. Ironically, she had just ignored him all the way here, which had briefly dented his self-confidence. She clearly didn't see him as a threat at all.

"It'll be raining soon," he said, "judging by those clouds. You may not be concerned about your physical body, but that won't stop the rain soaking you."

Poena continued staring intently at the quickly-darkening sky.

"They are not clouds."

Somerville frowned. "What?"

Poena moved her host's head to look round at the spirit, and he shivered. Where before he had seen Christina looking at him with a mixture of curiosity, fear and anger, now all he saw was contempt for this world – and him.

A thin smile crossed Christina's lips, one that would never have appeared there if she were still in control of her body. She looked up again towards the sky. "If you think those are clouds, then you are very much mistaken."

Somerville was confused – although he wouldn't admit it. He looked up at the sky himself and, squinting hard, tried to understand what Poena was talking about.

The light was fading fast – much faster than it should have been on a midsummer's night. He turned his head this way and that for a few minutes and peered as carefully as he could into the oncoming darkness.

For a second – just a single second – he caught sight of something moving within the gloom. It was gone as quickly as it arrived, and it took his brain a few seconds to catch up and realise what it was. When he did, he gasped in shock.

"You can see them now that you are a spirit," Poena said. "If you were still human, then you would fail to see beyond this realm. You should be grateful that I have given you that freedom."

Somerville's anger caught in his throat. He was disgusted by Poena's arrogance and confidence in the murder she had committed – and yet she still believed that she had done a good deed by "freeing" his spirit permanently from his body. The menacing smile on Christina's face didn't suit her gentle features.

"They're …" He hesitated, almost reluctant to say the word. "… angels?"

Poena nodded once, jerkily, and turned away again.

"Angels," she said with disgust. "I knew it. Humanity and the angelic realm have been conspiring against us … but for how long? Have you been a part of this, you and your merry band of Seekers?"

Somerville had taken a step back out of shock at the level of pure malice and hatred in her eyes. He had to remind himself that she had killed him in cold blood, and that he was with her because he sought vengeance.

*I am a leader of men*, he told himself. *I will not have this … being intimidate me.*

"You have no clue at all what you are talking about. There is no conspiracy."

"A massing battalion of angels may well disagree with that statement."

"Why are they here?" he demanded. "What do they want from us?"

Poena shook Christina's head; whether she was angry or disappointed with Somerville, he couldn't tell.

"Why must everything be about you and your species?" she said in disgust. "There are other realms out there. Those angels are massing for the astral plane … for my realm … and are doing so while I am here on Earth."

She looked suddenly uncomfortable. She rubbed a hand across her face and blinked her eyes, as if trying to clear a particularly uncomfortable headache. Somerville couldn't help but smile as he realised what was happening.

*Christina!*

The one-time Seeker was fighting back against the intruder in her brain, and clearly causing Poena some discomfort. Wanting to help her, he stepped forward and thrust an arm out towards her head to try and get into her thoughts and support Christina.

Before he could connect his spiritual form with her, however, Poena lashed out and somehow connected with Somerville, her open palm slamming into his chest. He stumbled backwards; he was still floating slightly above the ground – as a spirit, he couldn't easily connect with the pavement – but he was somehow able to slow his momentum to a gradual stop.

"Fight her, Christina!" he yelled, confident that she would hear him on some level.

Poena staggered backwards, clutching at her head. Her face contorted in agony for a moment – and then, abruptly, her features cleared and calmed again.

Somerville knew, with a sinking certainty, who had won the battle – the hatred and anger was radiating with every movement and expression.

"I'm so sorry," he whispered – and truly meant it.

Poena looked back up at the sky again – and then directly at Somerville. This time, he refused to be intimidated by her, and stood up and squared his shoulders.

"It's time to return to where I came from," she said. "I need to prepare. This was not the deal. The angels have reneged on their agreement, such as it was, so now I must lead my spirits into war and protect my realm."

"Let me come with you," he urged. "I can help broker a deal – perhaps I can stop this from happening."

Deep in the pit of his soul, Somerville knew that this was wrong – the astral and heavenly realms were meant to be peaceful and spiritual, not divisive and at war. Poena, looking out through Christina's eyes, burst out laughing.

"You think you can do a … deal?" she snapped, almost spitting out the last word in disgust. "You? You belong to a human organisation that does nothing but pry … and you are dead. You are a spirit … if you wanted, you could join my army?"

Somerville's top lip curled up, and he shook his head angrily. "I would never join an army led by you."

"You arrogant humans with your delusions of grandeur," Poena snapped back. "You disgust me – all of you. You were the cause of the rip between our realms in the first place; the blame for all of this falls squarely at your feet."

Somerville refused to accept that criticism, and he balled his fists together, wanting nothing better than to wipe the smugness from her face.

Ignoring – or not seeing – Somerville's anger, Poena went on, "I promise you one thing, Evan," she said. "When this is over, and we have beaten the angels back to where they belong, we will turn on you and your kind next … and we will show you all what happens when you conspire against us."

Christina's eyes suddenly rolled into the back of her head – and Somerville knew that Poena had somehow departed back to the astral plane.

As he knelt down to examine Christina for any signs of life, he felt a passionate anger bubbling away inside him. All his life, he had fought for contact between the two realms; for a deeper level of understanding which could only lead to human enlightenment. But now that dream was lying in tatters – and Poena had the nerve to call humans arrogant, even as she instantly dismissed his species and made plans for the future of the human race.

"I will not allow this to happen," he told himself. "I simply will not."

# Heaven – Present Day

It was unheard of for an angel to fly through the chambers and corridors of Heaven's main concourse – it was considered impolite in a place where angels, with untold millennia of existence behind and in front of them, debated, discussed and thought.

Today, however, was different – Micah was willing to be impolite. His wings beat hard as he weaved his way through the wide and high angelic corridors from Michael's quarters through to the very top of the building, above the Ruling Chamber and out through the aperture at the very top.

He was still out of practice at flying after nearly 2,000 years without wings, so had to pause for a moment and recover his energy; he took the opportunity to absorb the sights around him. The Heavenly concourse was enclosed by a large domed roof, which centred on the Ruling Chamber underneath it, but with eight large levels surrounding it – and the Celestial Observatory around the edge, looking out into space.

Before he had managed to contact Joseph down on Earth, he had seen something outside the citadel that had worried him. To make sure his eyes weren't deceiving him, the Observatory would not be enough. The screens had only offered the smallest slice of the outside view, but it had been enough for Micah to see angels, massing against the inky blackness of the cosmos, blotting out the stars one by one.

He looked around and tried to catch sight of Michael, but he was just one angel among 144,000 – a full battalion, armed and ready to fight against the astral plane, which was both far away and incredibly close at the same time.

*"MICHAEL!"*

His voice carried across the cosmos, reverberating off celestial bodies in a way that mere mortals could not understand. Micah listened for a response, but none came.

*Where are you?* he thought to himself, as he watched the angelic battalion before him. *Come on, you coward, face me!*

But Michael did not appear – and so Micah went searching for him.

*This is my priority now,* he thought. *I don't care how long it takes; I will find him and make him answer for what he is doing.*

# Seekers of Truth HQ, Ramsgate – Present Day

Kirby had given up trying to be tidy; under Paul's direction, they had continued to search for clues in the basement, and so paperwork was now scattered across the floor. He was sat cross-legged, trying to focus on the pile immediately in front of him.

Paul was floating a couple of inches above the ground, looking frustrated that he wasn't able to practically help. "Well done for pretending we were never here," he said. "Have you ever heard of the word 'subtle'?"

"Don't start," Kirby mumbled. He put down one sheaf of papers and picked up another, rifling through to see if anything caught his eye. "I just wish I knew what we looking for."

It was Lucifer who answered, from where he stood near the hospital beds.

"Any clues as to how Somerville was able to breach the barrier," he said. "If we can find that, we may be able to prove to Poena … and whoever you met in the other realm … that there is no conspiracy."

Paul nodded. He hesitated for a moment as a thought occurred to him.

"What if there *was* a conspiracy?" he asked.

Lucifer paused in his examination of the beds, but didn't look round.

"What if Somerville was conspiring with someone?" Paul prompted. "Human, spirit, I don't know, but what if that *did* happen?"

Kirby sighed. "Then we're in deep shit."

Needing to stretch his legs, the detective stood and walked over to the computers, hoping he might be able to crack the passwords. Paul watched his friend cross the room, and reflected on a second goal he had whilst they were here.

*A clue as to where the hell Christina is now would be nice*, he thought angrily.

He felt helpless, unable to help his girlfriend, find the spirits of his friends or even find a clue as to what the Seekers were truly planning.

"Dammit!"

Paul was caught off-guard by Kirby's exclamation. The detective slammed his fists on the desk and pushed himself away from the computer.

"What?" Paul asked.

Kirby shook his head. "I can't get access," he said moodily. "There's no way I know enough to bypass the system. Whoever designed it is very good at their job."

Paul's shoulders sagged. He'd been pinning his hopes on Kirby, a self-confessed computer geek, to get access to the network. He stood and walked towards the computers, wanting to offer help.

A new – unexpected – voice joined the conversation. "Want me to try?"

Paul and Kirby spun round; their hearts leapt into their throats as they realised they had been found. Paul's eyes widened as he saw who their discoverer was; his legs almost buckled under him, and it took all his strength to remain standing.

"No…" he croaked.

Joseph made an apologetic face. "I didn't mean to startle you."

"I'd say you've failed on that score," Kirby deadpanned.

He looked at both Paul and Lucifer, their identical faces – one physical, one spiritual – registering equal amounts of shock. Kirby had never known Joseph that well, having been reborn as an angel/human hybrid shortly after meeting the detective. He had got to know Paul well in the past two years, and so had learnt about the depth of the friendship he had with the other man – and how upset he had been at believing that he would never see him again.

*Lucifer's known Satan for even longer,* he thought. *A* lot *longer. I can't imagine how that must feel.*

"Someone say something," he said, weakly trying humour to break them out of their emotions. "I'm not good at…"

His voice trailed off. Paul scrubbed his spiritual face with the back of his hand; his eyes were glazed for a moment as he tried to gather his emotions.

"I thought I'd never see you again," he said, his voice thickly.

Joseph didn't reply, and it wasn't until Paul finally found the courage to look around that he realised why. Tears were rolling freely down his friend's face, and he didn't look ashamed at having them.

"Satan."

Joseph looked round at Lucifer's single word, and he smiled.

"Hello, old friend," he said – and didn't need to say anything else. There was so much emotion in just those three words. A frown suddenly creased his features. "I don't recall you looking like Paul when we last met." His eyes flickered between Lucifer, still resident in Paul's body, and Paul's spirit, a short distance away. "It looks like I've missed a lot."

A wave of emotions hit him. He had expected it, as he'd had time to prepare for this meeting, but sorrow and happiness gnawed at him just the same.

A hand gripped him hard on his left arm, and he looked up. It was Paul's face before him, and he had to blink a couple of times before he realised that it was Paul himself, in his spirit form, rather than Lucifer.

"Good to see you, my friend," Joseph said with a sudden smile. He saw no reason to beat around the bush. "Heaven needs your help." He glanced over at Lucifer and Kirby. "Well, everyone's help, to be honest."

Paul nodded. "It's about Poena, isn't it?"

"… Yes," Joseph said, surprised by the swift answer. "You know about her?"

Paul glanced at Lucifer.

"Of course," Joseph said. "Then you'll know that we have an uphill battle on our hands."

"In more ways than one," Kirby chimed in. "The spirits are massing on the other side of the barrier between their world and ours. They want to feast on humanity."

Joseph's eyebrows almost climbed into his hairline. "Is there anything left that I need to tell you?" he said with a wry smile. "You're all as well-informed as I am."

"I suspect we are slightly more informed, old friend," Lucifer said. "I believe that Paul has been taken into a side dimension on a number of occasions now … by one of the Seven Sisters."

Paul's eyes widened, and he spun to face the angel now inhabiting his body.

"You knew who was taking me out of my body?" he asked incredulously. "You knew, and you didn't tell me?"

Lucifer shook his head. "I only suspected something after your most recent … adventure, when you were returned outside of your body, and I woke up as a result."

Joseph's forehead creased in a deep frown. "Lucifer, did you go as well?"

"No," the angel replied. "The being was strong enough to remove Paul from his body without even waking me on the first occasion. Only a Sister would be strong enough to do that."

Joseph nodded sharply, and looked even more pensive than before. "I don't understand everything about the Seven Sisters as yet," he confessed, "but I know they are ancient … and that they fought against us in the war."

Paul glanced at Kirby and rolled his eyes. "If you have a clue about what the hell is going on, then you're a better man than me."

"The situation is clearly more urgent than I realised," Joseph said. "If Poena and the Seven Sisters are awake, then Michael might have been right all along. Perhaps a battalion of angels is the right answer."

"War is not the answer," Lucifer said firmly. "I thought it was all those millennia ago. I was wrong."

Joseph gritted his teeth. "Then we not only need to stop Poena from doing anything stupid," he said, "but we need to stop Michael doing the same."

# Heaven – Present Day

Michael was calm. His unruffled appearance would have been a surprise to most that had seen him during previous preparations for war. The closer a battle approached, the more his passion came to the surface and he imbued his troops with the same energy.

Now, however, his anger had subsided and solidified into cold, hard determination as he contemplated the impending battle. It had been waiting to begin for millennia, and this was just the starting point, with the astral plane deserving everything they had coming to them. They had invoked the Seven Sisters during the last war, and angels had died had as a result.

*Angels should* never *die*, he thought, *and the republic needs to make the spirits understand that. I know this, even if the rest of the Council don't seem to.*

He savoured the feelings of flying free in the depths of space, outside the confines of the Heavenly Chambers that sometimes felt claustrophobic, despite its vast size.

The Heavenly Dominion was as vast as the universe itself, and angels travelled the length and breadth of it as they wished, but their home, the nexus of their existence, was the Heavenly Chamber, where the Almighty had ruled from and now the Council of Twelve ruled in his place. Turrets and high-ceilinged buildings rose from ground level – although ground level was a misnomer in this instance, as the entire vast structure, built to house angels and their tall, broad frames and their equally broad wings, floated in the Heavenly realm, in the depths of space.

Michael had lived his entire life in Heaven, which had had a broader meaning back in the days of his youth, when the astral plane and the angelic realm had been one. That was before the ancient War, of course, between the two realms, which Michael had willingly fought in.

*I fought because it was the right thing to do,* he thought, *and the barrier always kept us safe. Now…*

He paused, because he didn't know how to phrase his thoughts, even to himself. So much was going through his mind right now. The barriers *had* been breached, he could feel it. Not every angel was attuned to changes in the barrier as he was, so he knew most of his angelic army hadn't yet been able to conclude the same.

*There is no going back,* he told himself. *This is necessary. They will understand … in time. I am doing this for them.*

He looked back at his army, massing against the backdrop of space. Their presence, Michael knew, would be felt everywhere there was life – including Earth, where Joseph was currently on his fool's errand.

*Paul cannot help,* he thought with absolute certainty, *and if Lucifer were free and with me now, he would agree with what I am doing. The time has come – and let history be our judge.*

# Outside Customs
# House – Present Day

"They look like thunder clouds to me."

"Look again, Paul," Lucifer prompted him.

Paul took the angel's advice and squinted hard against the sky, trying to get his eyes to see what Lucifer and Joseph could clearly see already. The skies were darker than they should be for an early summer's evening, certainly, but summer rain wasn't exactly unheard of.

"Paul…" Kirby was squinting up at the sky like Paul was, and his face was a mask of shock.

"Oh my god," Kirby whispered. He clutched a hand to his chest. "I see it."

Paul frowned. *See what?* he wondered. Kirby had a natural psychic ability that Paul lacked, so he wasn't surprised that his detective friend had seen it first, but Paul had been hoping that Lucifer's residence inside his head would have helped him –

"Oh, bloody hell."

His brain overloaded as he processed the enormity of what he was seeing, and he briefly lost the ability of cogent speech.

"Angels…" he muttered. "The clouds are all angels."

Out of the corner of his eye, he saw Lucifer stir and look at the host of angels with deep emotion. He was clearly moved by the sight of people he had lived amongst for tens of millennia gathered right above their heads.

"How is that even possible?" Paul asked out loud to no-one in particular. "I thought the heavenly realm was completely separate to ours."

"It is," Joseph replied behind him.

Paul's forehead creased with confusion. "So how…"

"There are such a large number of angels in close proximity, their presence is showing even across the barriers separating our realms. If the pressure continues to grow with an increasing number of angels, they will have to open an access point."

Kirby snorted with black humour. "You mean 'in case of emergency, break here', that sort of thing?"

His smile faltered in the face of blank stares from both angels. Clearing his throat, he noticed something that would help him change the subject – and satisfy his curiosity at the same time.

"Why isn't everyone else noticing the angels like we are?"

Paul followed Kirby's gaze and looked around him – and realised that his friend was right. It was just before six on a Saturday evening, and the pubs and restaurants further along the marina were filling up. It had been a clear, sunny day up until now, and shouldn't have become dark for another couple of hours. Even if this had been a normal summer storm, the darkness would have at least drawn *some* comments from the locals.

The people along the seafront, however, didn't seem overly concerned. Once or twice, Paul saw the odd individual glance up at the sky, shake their heads in weary resignation, and then resume their conversation. No-one at all seemed to notice the angelic presence.

"How can they not see what's up there?" Paul asked in confusion. "It's right there in front of their faces!"

"Spirits see it automatically," Lucifer said calmly. "As do angels."

Kirby was intrigued. "What about me?" he asked.

Joseph smiled. "If I'm right, you and your sister are psychically attuned. The vast majority of humans are less psychic than ... a whale."

A surge of guilt ran though Kirby. He hadn't tried to contact his sister since that morning. Logically, of course, he understood why his sister hadn't awoken him earlier; a time lock was incredibly complicated, and there hadn't been enough leeway to try. The logical part of his mind understood that – but the emotional part refused to.

*I'd give anything to see her again.* The rebellious thought came unbidden. *We were so close, and she didn't even try.*

"Kirby!"

Kirby blinked and looked round at Paul, who was looking at him with a mixture of concern and amusement.

"You okay, mate?" he asked. "You were somewhere else then."

Kirby cleared his throat and hoped his features didn't betray the mixture of feelings he was experiencing.

"Yeah, sorry," he muttered. "Just thinking about …. you know, all this."

If Paul guessed anything, he certainly didn't let on. He smiled and looked back up at the assembling host of angels.

"It's ... incredible."

"So what do we do now?" Kirby asked. "Joseph, does this have anything to do with your return to Earth?

"Yes and no," he conceded. He briefly relayed the conversations he'd had with Micah and Michael before he had come back.

Lucifer shook his head. "I would never have thought that Michael would have been so stubborn and unwilling to listen to reason. He is forcing us into a war that we might not even need to have."

Joseph nodded. "The barrier between humanity and the spirits is weak, all because of the Seeker breaking through, but we could still resolve it peacefully. It's one isolated human travelling through, after all."

Paul and Kirby exchanged a nervous glance. Joseph almost didn't pick up on it, but something about their body language told him it was something important.

"What's wrong?" he asked.

"Not just humans, Joseph," Paul replied.

"Paul, I already know about Poena breaking the barrier —"

"No," Paul retorted, shaking his head. "I'm not talking about Poena. I'm talking about Lauren … and Kirby's sister."

Joseph looked between his old friend and Kirby, not following the conversation. Lucifer stepped in.

"They are both spirits, Satan," he said, "and, with Beelzebub's help, they breached the barrier. They are all *here*, on Earth … and it's entirely possible that Poena followed them through."

Joseph didn't hesitate. "Then we've lost," he said immediately. "If Poena knows about their presence on Earth … and maybe even mine … then she has no reason to negotiate with us. We are going to war, and there's nothing we can do to stop it."

# A Hidden Dimension – Present Day

Alcyone could see out now, beyond the narrow confines of her sleeping chamber – *No,* she reminded herself. *My prison. I must always remember this place for what it truly is. Just because my sisters and I chose to come here doesn't make it any less of a place of incarceration. The angels are still our guards, even if they won't admit it.*

Her field of vision had expanded to the other realms and, although she couldn't see everything yet, the massing angels were plain enough.

*Are they coming for my sisters and I?* she wondered. *Is the battalion for us ... or for the spirit world?*

She needed to act – she was certain of that now. It was time to do something – and so she sought out those she needed to put her plan into action.

# Heaven – Present Day

*W*e have no more time.

It was an uncomfortable realisation for an angel; to know that there was no time left so quickly, and that a decision *had* to be made.

*But that is where I find myself,* he thought reluctantly. *I had hoped Joseph would have longer for his task, but Michael has taken matters into his own hands.*

He was back in the Ruling Chamber, unable to watch the preparations for war any longer. He knew that as soon as they were ready, Michael would lead them into the astral plane and try to destroy everything there – because the spirits would retaliate against the battalion, and it would be a devastating end to one side or the other.

*He has become blinded by anger … the Sisters sided against us, and he is terrified that they will do so again. He wants to act before they wake.*

Micah did not want to fight the astral plane; he had never sought out war, especially wars that seemed worthless. He could only imagine one outcome: destruction.

*And I worry about humanity being brought into the war by the spirits,* he thought. *When so many of our best angels are still asleep inside the heads of humans, we cannot defend our realm indefinitely – especially if they increase their ranks from amongst humanity.*

He had formulated a desperate plan to stop the preparation for war, but negotiation was an all-or-nothing scenario right now and relied on everyone being in the same place to talk. He could possibly bring them all together, but it was a skill he hadn't used in a long time. *I do not honestly know if I can still do it … and there's a chance I may kill someone as a result.*

He looked up at the empty throne on the dais, and swallowed hard as he remembered all that he and his fellow angels had fought for in that chair's name; free will being the one thing that they had craved … and now had.

"May I be forgiven for what I am about to do," he said quietly.

He focused on the people he needed to negotiate with; trying to push his emotions to one side, he began to summon various people – and hoped for the best.

# Broadstairs – Present Day

Lauren felt sick with worry, as if they had failed already.

"We've looked everywhere," she groaned. "How can we have lost Paul and the others?"

"It is not a precise science," Beelzebub said, irritation in her voice as she continued to mentally search the physical plane.

Rachael raised an eyebrow. "Are you saying that the majority of what you're doing is guesswork?"

Beelzebub paused to give Rachael a withering glance. Rachael swallowed and smiled an apology, then glanced up at the sky to change the subject.

"Will Michael really do it, do you think?" she asked. "Will he invade the astral plane?"

"If he believes it the only way to win against Poena, then yes," the angel replied.

Lauren looked up as well, still nervous at the sight of so many angels pressing against their realm.

"How long before they break through?" she asked.

"I … do not know," Beelzebub conceded reluctantly.

Lauren was surprised; it was unusual for Beelzebub to sound uncertain – or worried, and she sounded both at the moment. Her need to find Paul only deepened.

She was about to offer encouragement to Beelzebub, but the words died in her mouth as her head snapped back and she screamed in agony.

<hr>

Half-way across town, Paul, Kirby, Lucifer and Joseph were lost in deep thought, trying to come up with an alternative to the war.

"We can't just give up," Paul said urgently. "We have to try and talk Poena and Michael down."

Lucifer shook his head. "You do not know Michael as Satan and I do," he said. "He will not negotiate with Poena, nor she with him. Not now that we have reached this point and have an army gathering before our very eyes."

Joseph nodded, and opened his mouth to agree – but no words came out. His eyes widened in agony – and he disappeared, before anyone else could react. Then, Lucifer's face contorted into a similar frieze. He grasped the sides of his head, clearly in savage pain – and then his temporary human body went slack and collapsed to the floor.

Kirby caught Paul's abandoned body before it hit the pavement. The detective checked for a pulse, and nodded in relief. The body was still alive, which meant that Paul – he looked up, and then looked around, but couldn't find Paul anywhere. He, too, had disappeared, leaving Kirby alone. Again.

He could hear shouts of alarm from across the street, coming from the direction of the various pubs. He saw people starting to run across the road towards them, but it no longer mattered – Paul and Joseph had disappeared, and Lucifer had left Paul's body. None of this was coincidence, but it did send a shiver up his spine.

"Is this you, Michael?" he muttered as he looked up to the sky. "Is this your doing?"

# A Hidden Dimension – Present Day

Everything was white. Not off-white, or a bit white, but pure, unadulterated white in every direction. The pairs of eyes that were present in this strange, bright space couldn't focus on … well, anything, and couldn't even tell if they were the only sets of eyes in the space.

"Why have you brought me here again?" Paul's voice rang out around the all-encompassing whiteness.

"Paul?"

"Joseph?"

A third voice chimed in; "No … this isn't possible."

The silence returned, and this time there was a deeper, more sonorous quality to it as the owners of the voices processed what they had heard.

Paul, Joseph and Lauren had been reunited.

It was a strange thing, observing the trio's range of emotions from a distance. Micah wanted to step in immediately and discuss their options, but something had seeped through from his two millennia of being trapped inside a succession of human minds.

*They won't focus if I interrupt now.*

In truth, he knew that he wouldn't either. Lucifer, Satan and Beelzebub had all returned as well, and he was joyously happy to see them.

*Their eyes will adjust,* he knew, *and they will need a few minutes to emotionally recover. I just hope we can spare it. Michael's forces continue to grow. All is changing far too quickly. I wish we'd made better choices all those years ago; we would not be in this position now.*

◆ ◆

Micah had been right – Paul, Joseph and Lauren's eyes had begun to adjust to the pure whiteness of the realm; outlines and figures had begun to coalesce – and brother, sister and friend were reunited.

Paul was the first to see Micah, and he did a double-take through tear-misted eyes.

"Who –" Paul began, but Satan – *Joseph*, Micah reminded himself – hushed him with a glance.

"This is Micah," Joseph said. "He is first amongst equals in the Heavenly Republic – and leader of the Council of Twelve."

Paul nodded at Micah, and Micah returned the acknowledgement.

Lauren stood close to her brother, as though worried he might disappear at any moment, looking almost frightened, and Micah saw her eyes flick around the white realm before she looked back at the angel.

"I am not here to cause you harm," he said. "It was I that brought you all here."

"Have you been bringing me here all these times?" Paul demanded. "Lucifer thought it might be one of the Seven

Sisters, but if it was you, then I have to tell you that it wasn't very funny."

Micah looked thrown for a moment; he had clearly not been expecting that.

"I have never brought you here before, Paul. You … have been here recently?"

"Yes."

Micah looked at Lucifer.

"You suspect the involvement of the Seven Sisters?"

Lucifer nodded. "I do."

"That is … concerning," Micah said thoughtfully "I had hoped the Seven Sisters would remain asleep for longer."

Lucifer gave a half-smile. "I hoped they would remain asleep forever, given their opinions of me."

Micah returned the smile. "It is good to have you back, my friend."

"It is good to be back."

Paul looked around that this strange, white place that he vaguely recognised. His curiosity must have shown on his face as Micah raised an eyebrow and caught Paul's eye. "You have been here before. Two years ago, by your human reckoning. Michael and Gabriel brought you here."

"And someone else brought me here today," Paul replied. "I've seen Heaven, Micah, and I have to say that this is by far the most boring part of it."

Micah shook his head, his mane of brown hair ruffling as he did so. "No," he replied. "This dimension is outside of the three planes of existence you are aware of. It is a place known only to a select few people, even now. It was where we planned and executed the Civil War."

Paul listened to Micah carefully, and there was no hint of anger or sorrow in his voice as he said that. He had carefully remained neutral as he hinted at the events that had led to so many angels being imprisoned inside human minds.

"Why have you brought us here?" he asked. "I don't know if you've noticed, but there's quite a lot going on."

Micah gave him a long, hard stare, which made Paul almost tremble under the weight of it. He'd been rather glib – he knew that – and had forgotten where he was for a moment.

"I'm … I'm sorry," he muttered. "I wasn't thinking. I'm not usually that rude."

"You are reunited with your friends," Micah said. "Yes, I understand – because I am as well."

He glanced at Joseph, who smiled back at him. "I am fortunate to have already been reunited with one, and I have valued his counsel highly, but it is … exciting to be so close to my other old friends as well."

Paul nodded; he could understand that. He caught Joseph's eye, and they exchanged a stupid grin. He caught Lauren rolling her eyes at them both. For a moment, it was just like old times and his stomach rolled with several different emotions at seeing them both in front of him again.

Joseph looked away for a moment, his eyes brimming with tears at the reality of standing next to his sister and best friend after so long. He cleared his throat and spoke to Micah. "You could have just summoned me in the normal way," he said reproachfully. "Bringing us all here using your force of will hurt."

Micah inclined his head in apology. "I am sorry," he replied. "I needed counsel, and you three … six … are all people whose advice I would respect beyond measure. My mind might well have been coloured by my emotions in this instant."

Beelzebub, intently serious, looked at Micah. "I assume we are all here to talk about the impending war?"

Micah nodded. "Michael has his heart set on it," he said.

"So does Poena," Beelzebub noted. "She has taken over a human form, clearly trying to learn human weakness before she unleashes the spirits upon them."

"With the angels so obviously congregating, will that now be her first priority?" Lauren asked. "Won't she want to…"

"Get back to the astral plane?" Lucifer asked. "Yes, absolutely. Her human … exploration will seem less important to her than the defence of the realm she sees as hers."

"Who was the human?"

Everyone's eyes turned to Paul, who had been the one to ask the question. He kept his eyes firmly fixed on Beelzebub, who seemed nonplussed by his intense focus.

"I do not know the human woman's name," she said, "but I can describe her for you."

As soon as Beelzebub did so, Paul knew it was Christina that Poena had taken over – he knew it beyond a shadow of a doubt.

Joseph gripped his arm, and they felt a brief shiver of shock as their two outlines touched.

"Paul, I saw her possessed," he said in alarm, "but I had no idea it was your girlfriend. I'm sorry, but…"

"It's okay," he said, "you weren't to know."

"No, Paul, that's not it," Joseph interjected, shaking his head emphatically. "I was going to say that I saw Poena, while using Christina's body, kill a man."

While Paul reeled from that shock, Lauren added; "It was Evan Somerville," she said. "Poena killed the leader of the Seekers, but his spirit is still alive."

Paul wanted to be sick; so much was happening, he felt overwhelmed.

"Is Christina dead?" he asked in a hoarse whisper.

Joseph hesitated – and Paul had to fight hard to restrain the tears from flowing again.

"I don't know!" Joseph said quickly, realising that he had made a mistake by pausing for breath. "Paul, I'm telling you the truth – I genuinely don't know. I hope she's still alive, I really do."

Paul nodded, and took a moment to compose himself. He knew that this wasn't doing himself – or anyone else – any good. He took in a deep breath – despite the fact he knew he didn't actually need it in his current position – and looked again at Micah. Paul knew that he understood the human's emotions – and the need to focus on the bigger picture.

*I need to keep busy until I can get some answers.*

"How long before Michael leads his battalion into war?" he asked.

Micah shook his head. "I do not know," he admitted. "If I know Michael, then he will want guarantee of success, and that will involve a full battalion of angels – 144,000 of them. He is angry, but he is not stupid. He will wait until they have all come together before he attacks."

Paul relaxed slightly. "So we could be talking about a few days here." He glanced at Joseph and Lauren. "We've got some time."

"A few days?" Micah repeated in surprise. "No, Paul, we're looking at no more than a couple of hours at most."

A gloomy silence followed; Paul knew they were all trying – and failing – to think of plans that could be put into place immediately.

"This is insane," Paul muttered.

Lauren nodded in agreement. "More than insane," she replied. "Utterly bloody bonkers. I thought Michael was always the most level-headed out of all of them."

She glanced at Micah. "No offence."

Micah was nonplussed, mostly because he didn't entirely understand what Lauren was talking about. "None taken."

"In any case," Lauren went on, "this won't be confined to the two realms, will it? It'll impact Earth eventually, because it won't be over quite as quickly as Michael wants. The spirits will fight back … and then will be emboldened to attack Earth if they win."

Joseph released a breath, knowing that his sister was right. He crossed his arms over his chest and tensed up as he thought of the chaos this war would cause.

"This will change everything," he said. "Paul, Kirby's down there."

Paul nodded. He hated the thought of his friend being caught in the crossfire, especially as he had stood loyally by over the past two years as Paul had recovered from the loss of his oldest friends.

*I don't tell him enough how much I appreciate that.*

A thought occurred to him; "Why can't you lead the remaining angels against Michael?" he asked. "Surely there are more angels who don't want this than there are angels that do?"

Micah's face told him that it hadn't been a good question to ask. His eyes opened in shock, as did Lucifer's, and even

Joseph – now aware of so much more as a half-angel hybrid – looked uncomfortable at the thought.

"You must understand," Micah said slowly, "none of us have much appetite for another civil war. Some angels are answering Michael's call, because it's against the astral plane ... but to fight our brother angels again is something we cannot face."

"Then we've got to find a way to solve this ourselves," Paul said. "We can't let this disintegrate into open warfare. We've got to stop Poena ... and Michael."

# Customs House – Present Day

Evan Somerville's rage consumed him. He had been embarrassed and humiliated by Poena, who had travelled here and seemed hell-bent on doing nothing but seeing conspiracies where there were none – and if her parting comment was anything to go by, this certainly wasn't the end of their encounters.

*I certainly hope not*, he thought. *I've got a lot of unfinished business with her. If anything, I am stronger now than I have ever been.*

His thoughts were channelled on one thing and one thing alone: revenge. He had forgotten all about Christina already, leaving her to the elements and the paramedics.

Paul, on the other hand, intrigued him. There was something about him that fascinated the Seeker. His travels to Heaven, his seeming lack of ambition at exploring the cosmos with his obvious talent, and his ability to be tied up in the middle of all these cosmos-changing events.

*I need him on my side.*

He had reached Customs House in double-quick time – a walk like that would normally take 45 minutes to an hour, but now that he was unencumbered with a body, he had reached the Seekers' headquarters in just a few minutes.

He paused on the corner that led down to the marina and Customs House. It was now 7 p.m., and he could see the evening revellers filling the promenade's pubs properly now – they were still sober, as the evening was early, but Somerville knew that would change over the next few hours.

He walked calmly down the marina towards Customs House. Most people didn't even notice him; being a spirit, he was fairly transparent. Anyone who saw a vague movement out of the corner of their eye quickly dismissed it as a trick of the light. All that did, however, was make Somerville angrier towards humanity in general.

*I plan to protect all these people from Poena, and they are not even the slightest bit attuned to the mysteries that are out there. If Rachael were here, she would understand me.*

He sighed, and corrected himself. *Rachael betrayed me*, he reminded himself. *She tried to take it all away from me … and she had to pay the price as a result.*

He missed a step as he saw an ambulance sitting in front of Customs House, its blue lights flashing urgently as it prepared to whisk its inhabitant to hospital. Seeing the paramedics had helped a thought pierce his angry cloud – the image of Christina lying in the road, unconscious or dead. He hadn't thought to check.

With a sudden surge of compassion that surprised him, he suddenly hoped that she would be alright.

His empathy was short-lived however, as soon as he spotted someone that distracted his thoughts.

The friend of Paul's who had visited Customs House earlier that day was stood outside the building, talking animatedly to another paramedic.

Somerville began to wonder how he could turn this situation to his advantage. Deciding to take the bull by the horns, he strode over to the duo in time for him to hear the man – *Kirby*, he realised abruptly. *Rachael's brother – my word, they look alike* – saying sharply, "You don't understand! I've got to follow my friend! Please!"

The paramedic held up his hands to placate Kirby. "Okay, okay," he acceded. "Jump in. I'll radio Control and let them know –"

"Excuse me? Mr Kirby?"

Kirby looked round at the voice – and started. Looking back at him, with a smile on his face that didn't touch his eyes, was Evan Somerville.

*But you're dead!*

He stopped himself from saying that out loud, because of the paramedic stood behind him. He couldn't guarantee that he wasn't the only person that could see Somerville right now, and he didn't need to have any accusations of "seeing things" flying his way. Without thinking, his eyes flicked up to the gathering darkness in the skies and then back to Somerville – he couldn't help but wonder if Somerville was somehow involved with their presence.

"Are you alright, Mr Kirby?" the paramedic asked. He sounded curious – and it was obvious to Kirby that he couldn't see Somerville.

Kirby nodded, his eyes never leaving Somerville's face. "I'm fine, thank you," he said without turning round. "I … thought I heard something, that's all."

The paramedic shrugged. "Not at all," he said. "We need to leave now."

Without being conscious of it, Kirby had clenched his fists. He was terrified for Paul, Joseph and Lucifer, as he couldn't explain what had happened to them – except that Paul's body had a strange, lifeless quality to it that sent a chill through Kirby's spine. Now, he had to deal with the spirit of the man who his sister had worked closely with for so many years – and had tried to poison Christina's mind against his friend earlier that day.

Nodding his acquiescence, Kirby turned towards the ambulance car, glad he could excuse himself from the situation. His hand froze on the door handle, however, when Somerville shouted, "We're a lot alike, you and I, Mr Kirby!"

The tumult of emotions that Kirby was barely keeping restrained suddenly erupted.

"We're alike?" he snapped, looking over his shoulder at the spirit. "Do you actually believe that, or is that just another lie you're spouting?"

Somerville's face turned serious from the faux-smile he had plastered on a moment before.

"Whether you wish to believe me or not, it's the truth, Kirby," he retorted. "Your sister spoke about you often, and I know you have a gift like me. We can both see what's really there."

His eyes looked to the sky for a moment and then back again to Kirby, who immediately understood the inference.

*You can see the battalion*, he realised.

The paramedic had moved to the driver's side of the car, but had now paused and was watching Kirby with concern.

"Mr Kirby," he said, interrupting his train of thought, "who are you talking to?"

Kirby was frozen to the spot as he met Somerville's eyes. *He knows I've got the ability*, he thought. *He knows I'm like my sister.*

"Mr Kirby," the paramedic insisted, "what's the problem?"

Kirby swallowed. Somerville was a canny operator. He obviously had an ulterior motive for wanting Kirby to go with him, and the detective wanted desperately to know what that was.

A part of him was appalled that he was even considering staying behind to learn what Somerville was thinking, but then a subversive part of his mind spoke up. *Paul's gone and left you again to go who-knows-where. His body was just that – a body ... and I'm left here on Earth ... again ... to do what? Twiddle my thumbs like last time? Sod that.*

He made up his mind. Turning to the paramedic, he shook his head. "I'm fine," he said. "Honestly. Thanks for the offer of the lift, but ... I'm staying."

"What about your friend?"

Kirby paused for a moment before he replied, "He won't miss me. I'm staying."

Somerville fought hard to suppress a smile; people were so easy to manipulate.

—•—

The spirit of Rachael Kirby didn't know what to do. Lauren and Beelzebub had disappeared without any warning, and she was all alone.

*I can't deal with this by myself*, she thought. *I need to talk to someone – and I need help.*

There was one person who came to mind, and she knew immediately that it was the right decision. Before she could consciously think of his location, a particular building came to the forefront of her consciousness. While it surprised her, she decided to wait before making any judgements.

She needed to see her brother – and would travel to wherever he was, no matter how nervous it made her feel.

# A Hidden Dimension – Present Day

*Why can't I bring Paul back to me?*

She knew that she hadn't dreamt their previous conversations. While she was still groggy from waking up so suddenly, she could see Paul in her mind's eye, standing in front of her as she interrogated him.

*So why will he not come back to me again?*

There was only one logical explanation: he was no longer in the physical plane.

*Has he allied himself with Poena or Lucifer?* she wondered. *Or has he realised what I wish him to do – and he has already made a start?*

She stretched – and it felt good, after being imprisoned for so long.

*It's time to leave my prison, once and for all. Paul will undoubtedly need my help ... and the angels and spirits need to learn what I am willing to do.*

# Heaven – Present Day

S oon, the invasion would begin. The angelic army was almost complete.

Michael looked out across the heavenly vista and felt proud that so many angels had responded to his call. In his mind, their willingness to fight told him he was doing the right thing.

He couldn't help but feel a small degree of sadness that Micah and Satan hadn't seen the logic of his argument. He would have been quite content to remain as commander of the Heavenly armies forevermore, however it was ruled, but it had become clear to him some time ago that the Republic was already a failure.

*We cannot rule by committee*, he told himself. *That is not how Heaven operates. The Almighty knew this – I just wish I had seen it as well.*

He knew the Almighty would be beyond reach now – He had decided to travel to realms normal angels couldn't access, to explore new possibilities away from the realm he had once ruled.

*We will need a new ruler, when this is all over.* He sighed, a heaviness weighing on him. *I will have to step up and do that myself, as no-one else seems worthy.*

Democracy had come to Heaven … and failed.

*I will restore the kingdom to its rightful place amongst the stars. The spirits cannot be trusted. I trusted them once, and look where it ended. Betrayal.*

*The lights are starting to turn off,* he thought, watching the stars gradually wink out under the weight of angelic bodies. *In Heaven as well as in the astral plane.*

He wondered if Paul and Lucifer were able to see their preparations from Earth, and what they would think of his plan.

*Lucifer would agree with me,* he told himself. *He wouldn't want to see Heaven weak.*

His second-in-command, Halamiel, appeared by his right shoulder. The two angels had fought together in the first angelic campaign against the astral plane all those millennia ago, and Michael was glad she was by his side again – it felt right.

"Are you sure Micah won't raise up the rest of the angelic forces against you?" she asked. "It's what I would do … if I were in Micah's place, and I thank the heavens I am not."

"No," he replied. "Micah won't do it, my friend. He doesn't want more war."

Halamiel looked round at the angels. "Then he won't like this very much, will he?"

Michael chuckled. "No," he replied. "No, I can't imagine he will. However, we must continue – this is the right thing to do. I know it."

"I believe you," Halamiel replied. "You have my loyalty, Michael. Always."

"Thank you, old friend." Michael was truly gratified to know his friends were there for him. He knew that the time was almost upon them, when the world of spirits would be brought under heavenly control once and for all … and after that, Heaven would be brought under *his* control.

*If others will not have the courage to do it, then I shall have to do it myself.*

# Astral Plane - Present Day

aul felt sick to his stomach; having experienced his second fast shift of the day, nausea was threatening to take very decisive action.

*Although how it's possible without a stomach, I don't know.*

He kept his eyes squeezed shut as his senses settled down. He had never been a big drinker, but the couple of times as a teenager he had got very drunk and felt a similar level of nausea, he found that closing his eyes and focusing on the darkness behind his eyelids helped reduce the after effects.

*Here's hoping it works again*, he thought.

A groan to his left told him that he wasn't alone; at the very least, Lauren was with him.

"That didn't feel so good," she muttered.

Paul couldn't suppress a smile. *Poetic justice*, he thought.

He and Kirby had experienced two such shifts today; once done by Beelzebub, the second – just now – by Micah. Lauren now knew how her two human friends felt, and Paul wouldn't ever let her forget it.

As the nausea lessened, he tried to process his surroundings. Other than Lauren's voice, there was calm silence all around them. He was standing on a thick carpet, and the –

*Wait. Carpet? I thought I was going to the astral plane?*

He opened his eyes, alarmed by the change in location.

*Has someone interfered with our journey?* he wondered. *Where have they taken us?*

Their new surroundings faded into the background as Paul's eyes focused on the being in front of him.

"Lucifer," he said, very aware of the surprise in his voice. "You look … angelic."

He glanced around. "If we're back on Earth, how are you doing this? You were linked to…"

His voice tailed off as he saw Lauren just off to his left, looking bemused, and, next to her stood a female angel looking as solid as Lucifer. With short brown hair, green eyes and a wicked smile, she would have looked like Lauren's sister … if it hadn't been for the pair of large wings on her back. There was no hint of spirit about her – she was as solid as Micah had been.

"Beelzebub?"

The female angel inclined her head, smiling for the first time that day.

"I seem to have retrieved my physical form," she said in a deep, husky voice that made Paul clear this throat and think of cold showers. "Do I look how you would expect an angel to look?"

"You look very … er, angelic," Paul said weakly.

He realised that he was seeing Lucifer and Beelzebub as their true selves for the first time. Earlier that morning, when the tall, lean angel-spirit Beelzebub had appeared before him, she had looked as transparent as Lauren, who was also looking far more solid than he expected a spirit to look – and who didn't currently seem to understand what was happening any more than he did.

*Glad I'm not the only one.*

He looked around in desperation and breathed a sigh of relief as he saw Joseph. Strangely, given that his best friend had his own set of feathered wings and had only reappeared to him for the first time today in two years, he was the most normal thing in Paul's worldview right now.

"Joseph!" he exclaimed. "What the hell is going on?"

Joseph frowned, looking confused. "Did you black out on the way here?" he asked. "Don't you remember what Micah said?"

Paul laughed – he couldn't help it. He had missed Joseph's innocent confusion, as well as the big sisterly concern written over Lauren's face, despite the fact she was the youngest of all three of them.

The five of them were stood in a large, open hallway, with an opulent staircase in front of them that split halfway up so that people could go either left or right to the first and second landings. Behind them, on their level, was a huge front door, almost as wide as it was tall. Two open archways to his right led into two separate living rooms.

*Would one of them be a drawing room?* he wondered – then thought, *Does it really matter?*

To his left were two closed doors. Paul was instantly curious about what was behind them; he hated not being able to visualise the full layout of a building. *A psychiatrist would have a field day with me.*

"Paul?"

Lauren was stood near the front door, in front of a large oak-framed window which she was looking out of. As he walked over, he marvelled again at how solid she looked.

*How is she doing that?* he wondered. *If we're back on Earth, surely she should be transparent.*

Sunlight poured through the window. Paul looked through and smiled as he took in the beautiful gardens outside. A gravel path led to a large grassed area, with croquet hoops dotted around. Trees were in the distance, marking the way to another portion of the grounds that he couldn't see.

"This is like something out of Pride and Prejudice," he muttered.

"I used to love that book," Lauren said.

"I remember," Paul replied, looking away from the grounds. "You kept trying to make me read the damn thing."

"Have you?"

"What do you think?"

They exchanged a smile. Paul then glanced round and saw that Joseph had walked off into the living room and begun carefully studying the wine rack.

*You can't take the wine connoisseur out of a half-angel, I guess.*

The two full-angels, meanwhile, were stood facing each other with their eyes closed and the flats of their hands pressed together. Paul walked towards them, but at the last minute, hesitated about interrupting them.

*I want to understand what's going on,* he thought. *If we've been knocked off-course, I want to know who's done it – and why.*

Lucifer sighed. "You are the sort of person, Paul Finn, who would press a button marked 'Do not touch,' just to make sure you weren't meant to touch it."

Paul was sure – absolutely, cast-iron sure – that he hadn't made a sound.

"Yeah, I would," he admitted. "After all, what's the worst that could happen?"

Both angels released their hands from their meditative poses. As they turned to Paul, he was conscious of how much taller they were than him. He was about five foot seven and Beelzebub, the shorter of the two angels by a head, was at least a foot taller.

"How ..." He paused as he tried to frame the question right. "Lucifer, up until a moment ago, you were trapped inside my body. Beelzebub, you were as insubstantial as any other spirit I've met. Now, you're both ... well, you're angels again, aren't you?"

"Correct," Lucifer replied.

Paul scrutinized the angel, trying to work out if he was being wound up, but it didn't seem likely, given Lucifer's expression.

"If you don't mind my saying," he added, "you don't seem that perturbed about being back on Earth instead of going after Poena in the astral plane."

Lucifer raised his eyebrows and Paul suddenly felt a moment of self-doubt.

"This *is* Earth, isn't it?"

"Is it?"

It had been Beelzebub that spoke that time. Paul opened his mouth to give a retort, but hesitated and looked at her closely for a moment.

"Intriguing," she murmured, almost unaware that she was speaking aloud. "Lucifer, he reminds me so much of you. Passionate and angry, but also thoughtful and with an intensity that many humans lack."

"I am in the room, you know," Paul snapped, suddenly angry. He didn't understand what was going on. He felt embarrassed about being several steps behind the conversation, and he was frustrated at being treated like a child in front of them. "If you're going to talk about me, at least have the courtesy to look at me while you're doing it."

Beelzebub blinked in apparent surprise. She regarded him in silence for a moment, but Paul refused to back down.

*No, I won't – not when I'm right.*

The female angel inclined her head, and, to her credit, she didn't glance over at Lucifer for support.

"You are right," she conceded. "I apologise."

Paul was aware out of the corner of his eye that Joseph had wandered casually – perhaps a little too casually – back into the room.

*And I bet if I had eyes in the back of my head, I'd see Lauren pretending not to listen into our little tête-a-tête.*

"This place …" he began, deciding to just move on rather than dwell on what had already happened. "It's so real … but are you saying we're not on Earth?"

This time Beelzebub did look at Lucifer, deferring the answer to him. She seemed uncertain as to how to respond.

"No," he replied. "It is not Earth. It is…"

He broke off his sentence, looking uncomfortable – and Beelzebub looked the same. Paul glanced at Joseph, and he too looked confused. *Perhaps some memories from Satan are surfacing*, Paul thought.

"Lucifer, is this place…" Joseph's voice tailed off as his eyes tracked the room again. His mouth opened and closed a few times; he seemed to be struggling to find words.

Lucifer sensed the half-angel's emotions. He smiled sadly and put a hand on Joseph's shoulder.

"Yes, my friend," he replied. "This place is the resting place of the Seven Sisters. We imprisoned them here millennia ago, after they lost the war."

# Customs House, Ramsgate – Present Day

In the moment that his friends had vanished, Kirby had experienced confusion, anger, jealousy and embarrassment, all rolled together – and Somerville had caught him in that moment of weakness.

Now, he was just ashamed of himself. He felt ashamed of his own stupid, impulsive actions. He had abandoned his friend and left with the spirit of a man who was filled with nothing more than hatred and a desire for revenge.

More than anything, however, he knew how his sister would react if she were here now and saw what he had done. Rachael was someone he trusted and cared for beyond measure; her death hadn't changed that.

*She'd be furious that I chose my own jealousy over my friends*, he thought.

"Mr Kirby?"

The detective bristled at the "Mr" prefix. To everyone that knew him, he was Kirby. Not DS Kirby, not "Sarge", not "Mr Kirby" – just plain old Kirby, and anyone who said different clearly didn't know him very well. Somerville's use of the prefix told Kirby everything he needed to know about this man. He didn't like him and doubted he could ever begin to trust him, but still he didn't leave. He remained, desperate to feel like he was helping in some way – and right now, given the choice between sitting by a hospital bed or standing here and actively doing something, whatever that might be, then he knew what he would choose every time.

*I don't necessarily have to like the choice I've made, though.*

"Yes?" he replied curtly.

Somerville smiled. "You don't like me very much, do you?"

Kirby sighed. *Am I that obvious?* He then realised that he didn't care all that much; he *didn't* like Somerville, this … slippery, evasive serpent of a man.

They were in the cabinet room of Customs House, with Somerville at his usual place at the head of the table. Kirby observed that the director seemed to have adapted well to his new existence as a spirit, and it didn't seem to have even occurred to him to not continue in his role as leader of the Seekers of Truth.

Two Seekers were sat at the table, on either side of him, working on laptops, doing something that Kirby wasn't privy to, despite his interest.

He *was* curious, he couldn't deny it, but knew that there was no point in questioning these other Seekers directly. It was clear they only took orders from Somerville, regardless of whether or not he was in a physical form.

Kirby had been staring blankly out of the window for the past fifteen minutes, watching the angels massing in the sky and knowing that the battle was imminent. The detective didn't feel particularly inclined to answer Somerville's question right away, so he leaned across the window pane and asked his own question.

"What are you working on?" he asked. "You can't kill an angel through the internet, you know." He paused, then added an afterthought. "Although, I wouldn't be surprised if there was a website about it somewhere."

"There are several," Somerville replied. "I've looked. They're not accurate."

Kirby shrugged. "Well, I'm sure Lucifer and the others will be relieved to know that."

Somerville gave a smile that was completely devoid of humour. He changed the subject. "I've been in contact with all of the Seekers of Truth."

Kirby frowned. "Why?" he asked. "There's only about twelve of you, aren't there?"

"That wasn't true even when your sister worked for us."

"My sis … Rachael was one of your better Seekers," Kirby replied after he was sure his voice wouldn't shake. "You lost a loyal member when she died."

To his surprise, Somerville looked down at the floor, apparently needing to compose himself as he thought about someone he had been very fond of.

*Is that genuine*, Kirby found himself wondering, *or just another act?*

Somerville's reputation as a hard-nosed bastard preceded him. Even Rachael, who had been loyal to the Seekers during her tenure, had admitted that her superior was often difficult to get on with, and that had been one of her politer responses.

"Yes," Somerville replied in a quiet voice. "Yes, I did. She was one of the best Seekers we've ever had. It was such a shame we parted on bad terms."

Kirby frowned. "I didn't know that," he confessed.

He wanted to change the subject. He didn't feel inclined to talk about his beloved sister with this man, especially if his famed temper had been involved.

"So how many people belong to the Seekers of Truth?"

Somerville barely had to think. "We have twelve hundred active members, with a network of four hundred or so ex or retired members that give us other support should we need them."

Kirby chose not to speculate what "other support" meant.

"So why are you contacting all your members?" he asked. "To see if they've seen the angels in the sky?"

Somerville smiled. "Oh no," he replied. "I don't need to ask them that. I know they've all seen it. They wouldn't have been able to join the Seekers of Truth if they weren't able to see what's really in front of their faces."

Kirby sighed. It felt like pulling teeth, with him having to push for answers every step of the way.

"So I'll ask again, Mr Somerville," he snapped, unable to keep the irritated tone out of his voice. "Why —"

He paused as he saw a flicker in the corner of the room. He blinked, but the thing, whatever it was, had gone.

*Must have been the reflection off a car.*

Then the flicker happened again, and then again. He had heard Paul's description of an angel arriving on Earth, and this didn't seem like that. There was no "door" in mid-air. Instead, it was just a mass of energy in the air.

"It's started."

Kirby's stomach churned with nerves as he realised that the Seeker meant.

"The angels are coming here?" he asked. "Their argument's with the spirit world, not us."

Somerville looked at him with a flash of anger and annoyance; Kirby could see how he had gained such a fearsome reputation.

"It's not an angel," he snapped. "They're invading the astral plane, not here. Poena said that she would be back; I just didn't expect it to be that this soon."

"You think spirits are invading Earth? Then you're crazier than –"

A new – yet achingly familiar – voice broke into their conversation. "Hello, Kirby."

———•●•———

Poena reappeared in the astral plane, and it took her a moment to readjust.

*Being human is a … strange concept*, she thought. *I can see why it holds so much fascination for the spirits that surround me … but why would anyone want to leave this realm? Humans like those pathetic Seekers spend so much time trying to get* in, *why would they ever want to go back?*

She felt the anger return as she saw the angels surrounding her realm – hers, in every way that mattered. She had controlled it for an age, even with the Sisters guiding them – she was recognised as the true leader here, and the spirits would do as she instructed.

The spirits were still swarming round the sealed breaches, waiting for her, and she called out to them now. She felt their joy as they realised she had returned. They had been looking forward to feeding.

"Be patient," she said. She spoke quietly, but her voice still carried across the void to all of them. "I will give you what you wish for, but right now we must fight a bigger threat."

They gathered and swirled around her. She rejoiced as she felt their loyalty and their love. They trusted her, and she would repay that trust.

*I will lead my people to war,* she thought, *and this time, the Seven Sisters aren't around to drag our heels. We will destroy all those in our path.*

❖

Alcyone paused in her search for Paul. Something greater had caught her attention.

*Poena,* she thought. *No!*

Before she could react, something else struck her. *There are … people in my realm. Why? Why are you here?*

At the same time as this maelstrom of thoughts coursed through her mind, she sensed a residual image of something on Earth – of a spirit moving across the physical plane.

*I need to begin somewhere,* she realised. *I shall start there.*

# Astral Plane – Present Day

Joseph's memories about the Seven Sisters had returned and he was appalled at what he was now able to recall. He looked at Lucifer, who evidently already knew what Joseph was only just now remembering. To his credit, he didn't shy away from Lucifer's gaze.

"Why did you trust her?" Joseph whispered. "Why didn't you listen to me?"

Lucifer shook his head. "I was young and petulant, Satan," he replied softly. "You and Beelzebub will remember what I was like. I wanted to end the war, and I believed that we deserved to win."

Joseph swallowed. "We should leave. Now," he said. "We mustn't wake the Sisters. They won't make any of us welcome – especially not you, Lucifer."

He strode to the front door and rested his hand on the handle, urgency overwhelming any rational thoughts for a moment.

Lucifer held his hands up placatingly. "Satan, the Sisters are in hibernation. Nothing *can* wake them up."

Joseph shook his head. He was clearly disturbed by what he had remembered, and wanted to leave the place that was tied up strongly with those memories and emotions.

Paul had watched his friend's anxiety affect his usually calm behaviour with concern. "Joseph," he said slowly as he processed what his friend was saying, "are you saying that this place belongs to the Seven Sisters?"

Joseph breathed out. He didn't reply to Paul's question, as he was too caught up in the emotions of his returning memories. "We … consented to that, in the end?"

"I thought we were doing the right thing," Lucifer said, hot embarrassment flushing his cheeks. "Even after I saw the error of my ways, the Almighty had made up his mind. He was determined to show his own superiority over everyone – even them. He would never have listened to us."

"But Poena betrayed you, Lucifer," Beelzebub cut in. "She betrayed all of us."

Lucifer looked at this friend. He seemed unable to speak for a moment as he thought about what Beelzebub had said; having not seen her in such a long time, he hadn't thought they would disagree so quickly.

"What do you mean?" he asked.

"Lucifer, you were manipulated by Poena." Beelzebub was staring intently at him now, determined to get her point across while she had everyone's attention – human and angel alike. "We did have a choice, you and I," she went on. "All of us had a choice. Poena came up with the idea, and we talked you round in the end … but did we try hard enough to convince the Almighty that the plan was flawed?"

She looked at Joseph. "We all know how important the Sisters are to us, and we accepted the Almighty's decision to go ahead with the plan. We knew the Almighty wanted the control that a power vacuum would afford him. With the

Sisters gone, the Almighty was the most powerful being in existence."

Paul swallowed. "What happened?" he asked. "What did you do to the Sisters?"

Joseph's wings sagged in sorrow. "These spirits are angry and resentful," he said, "and we've got no-one to blame except ourselves. We humiliated them ... and the Sevens Sisters as well."

"What happened?" Lauren asked. "What did you all do?"

Joseph shook his head, unable to speak, so Lauren turned to Beelzebub.

"You've shared my mind all my life," she said, anger inflecting her voice. "We've lived on Earth and in the astral plane together. What aren't you telling me?"

Beelzebub didn't flinch from Lauren's gaze. Her wings rose and ruffled as she felt a moment of annoyance, and she took a step forward. Lucifer gripped her wrist, but she shook it off.

"You dare talk to me like that?" she snapped. "I am an *angel*, Lauren!"

The air almost crackled between the two of them as they stood across the hallway from each other. Lucifer and Joseph looked between them, hesitating to get involved. Paul, however, didn't have the patience.

"Enough!" he snapped. "This is not the time!"

Lucifer nodded his agreement, and stepped in between the two women. Paul caught Lucifer's eye. "What happened?" he asked. "Why are we here? Just *tell* me!"

Lucifer didn't waver. His body language changed subtly; he seemed to have accepted that the truth couldn't be hidden any more. He looked at Beelzebub and Joseph in turn, then sighed. He lowered his wings submissively.

"Very well," he said. "Very well. You need to know."

Paul saw Lucifer's hands ball into fists for a moment, then release as he nodded again. Giving them a steady gaze, he raised an eyebrow.

"Are you ready?"

"We're going inside your memories again, aren't we?"

"Yes."

Paul swallowed hard, but refused to show his fear. "Let's do it."

# Customs House, Ramsgate - Present Day

Rachael Kirby was back in a room she thought she would never return to. She felt very uncomfortable being here, but couldn't say why.

*I wonder if it has anything to do with my death*, she wondered. *Right now, I wish I could remember everything.*

She sat at the other end of the table to Somerville, in the seat she had occupied as deputy director. She watched the two men carefully, giving them time to sort through their emotions. Kirby was grinning stupidly as he looked at her through red, puffy eyes. The mix of emotions was a strange one, but a mix she could understand. If her "body" could have produced tears, she knew it would have done so.

It felt good to see her brother again. Although they had spoken to each other through the barrier, it wasn't the same as being physically together, like they were now; despite that, a thought was niggling at her, and it wouldn't easily go away.

*What are you doing here anyway?* she asked herself. *You never really liked what I was doing. You can't have joined the Seekers, surely ... and why does the thought of you working closely with Evan bother me so much?*

She found it difficult to look down the table at the leader. Her memories of her last few days on Earth were hazy – that was normal enough, since the transition from physical to spiritual existence was often quite traumatic – so she couldn't be sure, but she had a vague memory that the two of them had an argument of some kind before she had died.

*Do you still remember the argument?* she wondered. *Do you still have a grudge, even after all this time? It wouldn't surprise me – I know you. You can be a bastard at the best of times.*

Somerville was surprisingly quiet. He hadn't given any reaction when he had seen her coalesce in the corner of the room. His face had remained impassive since she had arrived. Whilst his emotions were usually closely guarded, Rachael had expected more of a response; after all, they hadn't seen each other for four years, and she had been a trusted member of the Seekers for years before her death.

*If someone doesn't start this conversation off,* she thought, *we'll be sat in silence for the rest of the day. Looks like it had better be me.*

"Well," she said, "it's good to be back … although there's something to be said for the conversation."

Her brother chuckled. "You're looking a bit …" He hesitated as he searched for the right word; "… see-through, Rach."

Rachael rolled her eyes. "Yeah, well, I'm dead," she replied with a shrug of her shoulders. "What do you expect?"

The siblings jumped as Somerville slammed a fist on the table. His face was contorted with sudden anger as he pushed his chair away from the table and stood up; Rachael watched his ability to make physical contact with every object around him with envy.

*He's still a powerful personality*, she thought ruefully. *He probably doesn't know he's doing it.*

"You are sitting there, making jokes!" he snapped, pointing a finger first at Rachael and then at Kirby. "We are here on the cusp of a major shift in the way our realms exist, and you are talking about … fripperies!"

Kirby deliberately didn't react, or even move, as the older man shouted. His police training had kicked in and he remembered something his old sergeant had once said to him: *Let them talk, son. They'll use enough rope eventually to hang themselves.*

That was the training; however, and he often got into trouble for not taking it entirely seriously; he had a mischievous streak that he couldn't entirely constrain.

Without taking his eyes off Somerville, he addressed his sister. "Rach, was your boss always such a prick?"

Somerville's eyes seemed to bulge out of their sockets. He wasn't used to being spoken to like that, and Kirby wouldn't have dreamt of doing so with most people, but Somerville was annoying him in a very deep-seated way.

Rachael had drawn in a breath at her brother's question. Despite her vague discomfort for reasons she couldn't explain, Somerville had been her superior and her friend for a long time and, in spite of his sometimes atrocious temper, she had respected him.

"Kirby…" she began under her breath. Her brother waved a dismissive hand in her direction, but she wouldn't let him get away with it that easily. She stretched forward and managed to concentrate enough on the solidity of her hand long enough to grab his wrist. He looked round at her and went pale. Rachael couldn't understand why until she followed his eye line and looked down. She was stood in the middle of the table, and her waist and legs were out of sight beneath it.

"Rachael, you … you're …"

Rachael shook her head, suddenly feeling emotional. "I'm dead, Kirby. What do you expect?"

"Enough."

That one word from Somerville, delivered in a calm and measured tone, stopped their interaction. Kirby realised he had lost the initiative. He had been so happy to see his sister that he had forgotten the other issues that were far more urgent.

*And I hate it that Somerville's been the one to remind me of that.*

His sister squeezed his arm in apparent understanding, and she floated out from the middle of the table to stand next to her brother.

"Why have you come back?" Somerville asked her. His arms were crossed, and he kept glancing back at his computer. "Have you returned to fight Poena by my side?"

Rachael looked at him carefully for a moment. She'd come back to gain strength from the one person she trusted above all others: her brother. For some reason, she didn't want to talk about it in front of Somerville.

"I'm here to support someone who's planning to confront Poena," she replied. "I know what you're planning, Evan. I didn't work with you for so long without knowing what goes through that cunning brain of yours. I won't have any part of it."

"'No part in it'?" the leader repeated. "Poena abducted me, killed my physical body, and is now hell-bent on raising an army against the angels and humanity, and you refuse to join my army in fighting them?"

Kirby stood up abruptly, his chair clattering to the floor.

"You're raising an army?" he exclaimed. "We don't need a third side in the war!"

Somerville's eyes moved back to his laptop, and he suddenly smiled. The Kirby siblings were caught off-guard by the sudden change in his demeanour.

"It seems that I might well be able to do without you in any case, Rachael," he said. "How many Seekers did we have when you were alive?"

"Twelve hundred and fourteen," she replied automatically. The information was imprinted on her brain, so she didn't even need to hesitate.

"How many do you think would fit along the marina?"

"You've not brought them here?" Rachael asked in shock. "Surely you wouldn't be that stupid? Twelve hundred people walking down that harbour front … Evan, you always wanted the Seekers to be a secret society!"

Somerville finally tore his eyes away from the screen.

"I think you'll be rather proud of me, Miss Kirby," he said.

She frowned. "Why?"

"Look out the window."

Kirby followed his sister over to the window. She was worried about what she was about to see as she reached it first. Her brother stopped in his tracks as she gasped and placed a transparent, shimmering hand on the glass.

*I don't know if I actually want to see,* Kirby told himself, then corrected his thought. *You're a detective sergeant in the police force. For god's sake, just look, Kirby – if Rachael can do it, then so the bloody hell can you.*

Knowing that he wouldn't ever hear the end of it if his sister had found the courage to look and he'd remained loitering in the background, he stepped up to the glass … and gasped as his eyes took in the sight outside.

"The Seekers are all here," Somerville said from behind the siblings. Kirby didn't need to look at him to know that he was looking smug. He certainly sounded it.

"But they're all …"

"We could all project," Rachael cut in. Her eyes hadn't left the vista before her, and neither had her brother's. "We can all leave our bodies, even without going to the astral plane."

Kirby watched the human spirits pour down the street, mingling in and out of each other and either floating or walking down the marina, right towards Customs House. None of them entered, but they gathered and massed around the building, every one as transparent as his sister.

"We are going to lead the charge from Earth," Somerville went on. "The spirits have humiliated us, and Poena has hurt the Seekers by killing me. It's time we punished her in return."

Kirby heard the hate and rage in the man's voice, and he turned round in alarm. He saw Somerville, still at the head of the table, with his eyes blazing and his fists clenched at either side of him.

"You're going to join with the angels?" Kirby asked in astonishment.

Somerville nodded. "I will allow you both one last chance to come with me."

"You're insane!" Kirby laughed – he couldn't help it, he actually laughed in the face of this man whose fists were clenched so hard in anger that his knuckles were white. "I can't believe I was about to listen to you! I must have been crazy to even consider it!"

Somerville sneered at him. "I should have realised that you were too much of a coward," he said dismissively. He turned to his former deputy. "What about you, Rachael? You're a spirit already, so whose side will you choose? Your new friends … or your old friends on Earth?"

Kirby scowled and opened his mouth to snap a retort, but Rachael silenced him.

"I can fight my own battles, brother," she said quietly. "I'm a big girl now."

Somerville grinned; it was a wolfish, abrupt smile that didn't entirely touch his eyes, but enhanced the menace he was exuding.

"I always knew you'd return to me, Rachael," he said. "Despite how it ended, I –"

"I don't remember how it ended," she snapped with such a blend of anger and sadness that even Kirby took a step back in surprise.

Somerville blinked in surprise. "What?" he asked.

"I don't remember how I died!" she repeated, frustration laced through her voice. "You may remember, my brother may have heard about it afterwards, but I remember nothing about it! No-one does, Evan, no spirit can remember the nature of their death! It helps them move on!"

"Move on?" Somerville repeated her words, but clearly didn't understand them. "Move on? But … dying is just part of the journey. We continue to learn."

Rachael was silent for a moment, her eyes suddenly full of sadness. "I don't know if you'll ever understand, Evan," she said quietly, and with a touch of sympathy in her voice that

Kirby was surprised to hear. "Most people will understand after they die, but you … you've always been a lot more closed-minded than you think you are. Whether or not you can change, I just don't know. You stopped caring about the physical realm. There's so much more to think about after you die."

Somerville seemed thrown by his one-time protégé's words. His fists were clenching and unclenching and his brain seemed to be ticking fast as he processed what Rachael had said to him.

"Where's Christina?" she asked.

Kirby's insides churned. *I didn't ask about Christina,* he realised. *I didn't even think about her. I was being too selfish and jealous to remember her.*

He had to force his own mixed emotions to one side as Rachael went on. "I remember her. She and I worked together – and she was good."

Somerville drew himself up to his full height. "I wouldn't know where she is. I've not seen her since she left –"

"Don't lie to me," Rachael replied, and her voice was as hard as steel. Kirby could get angry on occasions, but he had nothing on the icy tone that had suddenly appeared in his sister's voice.

"Don't you dare lie to me," Rachael said again. "I know you, Evan! Don't forget that I know how you think and how you act! The walls between the worlds are falling down, and you would have wanted to find out how to turn that to your advantage!"

"I have had a spirit kill me today, and yet here I stand," Somerville said. "My physical body may be dead, but the important part of me is still alive! I was able to beat her by staying alive. I will not be beaten by the likes of you. "

"You've shown no interest in Christina at all," Rachael said with a frustrated sigh.

Somerville frowned. He'd had enough of having to justify himself to anyone, even Rachael. "So what?" he snapped. "What possible influence will she have on proceedings now? She's dead."

"She's also outside your window."

# Astral Plane - Present

"So the spirits ... and Poena ... were winning?"

Lucifer nodded. He had shown the humans his memories of the first, ancient war between angels and spirits, and it had left Paul breathless as he tried to absorb all the information.

"Yes," he replied. He glanced at his fellow angels before carrying on. "There were only a small number of spirits, compared with many more angels, and we thought it would be a foregone conclusion that we could win."

Paul raised an eyebrow; he was astounded at the arrogance that Lucifer had admitted to on behalf of the angelic race. Lucifer looked vaguely awkward at the admission, but continued anyway. "Poena was their leader," he said, "and she was – is – an incredibly intelligent spirit. She united the spirits in a way that we didn't expect. They became organised ... and she was able to convince the Seven Sisters to ally themselves with her."

"She's a hard bitch as well, by the sounds of it," Lauren added.

Beelzebub nodded. "If she were human, I believe that would be accurate," she said. "Poena was fanatical about not only winning, but also about seeking revenge on her ... slave masters, as she saw them."

"Angels," Lucifer added – although Paul had already realised that. Paul glanced at Joseph, who seemed overwhelmed by all the memories he was recovering.

"You okay, mate?" he asked.

"Yeah," he said thoughtfully. He was staring into the distance, but he seemed grateful that his friend was looking out for him. "Yeah, it's just … I've got a lot to think about."

Lauren smiled at her brother, glad he was okay, but something was clearly pressing on her mind. Beelzebub noticed, and nodded encouragingly towards her.

"Ask your question," she prompted.

Lauren frowned. "Who exactly are the Seven Sisters?" she asked. "I mean, I've heard about them in mythology, but I'm amazed that they were actually real."

"Some mythologies have a basis in fact," Lucifer said, "and this is one of them. They are the oldest spirits in the universe, and each Sister is as powerful as a legion of angels. How Poena was able to convince them to join the war, I do not know. Suffice to say, they did – and they changed its course."

"We started to lose."

Joseph had said that. He stood with his back to the front door, looking tense. While his head didn't move, his eyes glanced to Lucifer.

"And when they drew both sides to a standstill, you and Poena were furious at that, weren't you? Both of you wanted to win."

Lucifer made eye contact with his old friend, unwilling to look away from the painful memories that showed in Joseph's eyes – *Not any more*, he thought. *I must confront my past – as I hope Poena confronts hers one day.*

"Yes, I wanted us to win," he said. "We were at war — each side was determined to be victorious. So when Poena approached me with a deal, I agreed to it because I thought it would give us the upper hand again."

Paul was curious. "I think you need to tell us the rest of the story."

# Customs House, Ramsgate – Present Day

Kirby had turned back to the window to see if his sister was correct. It only took him a few seconds to locate Christina's spirit. She seemed to realise that someone was looking at her, and had turned her head to look through the glass.

He tried to speak, but his throat had dried up. He glanced at his sister, but she was still glowering at Somerville. For his part, the leader hadn't moved, and not even a flicker of emotion had crossed his face.

"The question is," Rachael went on, "whether Christina is here because she was summoned or because she's dead and has nowhere else to go."

Somerville shrugged. "The important thing is that she's here … and ready to fight."

*But fight who?* Kirby's mind wondered treacherously.

"In any case," Somerville went on, sounding dismissive of the siblings' concerns, "even if Christina is dead, it's no-one's fault but Poena's. I played no part in it."

"Is that what you're telling yourself?" Kirby snapped. "To make yourself feel better? If I recall, she came with you this morning after you'd practically guilted her into it."

He scowled at the director. "I wonder if you've killed before," he went on, "because you're not showing the concern I would expect an innocent man to show."

In the pit of his stomach, Kirby felt a terrible emotion: shame. For a moment, he'd considered joining forces with this arrogant man, all in the name of petty jealousy. He had felt abandoned by his friends, but now realised that wasn't the case at all. In fact, Paul had never once abandoned him. For every time he had gone somewhere else, he had remained by his friend's side ten times more and proven his loyalty.

*How could I have been so blind?* he asked himself. *I should be by Paul's side right now, instead of here.*

But then, if he had been at the hospital, he wouldn't have discovered Somerville's plans – and might not have encountered his sister.

*Some people would call that a sign.*

He laughed at himself. He was a pragmatist, and preferred seeing what was really there instead. Right now, however, the two were indistinguishable.

"We need to do something about this," he said quietly to his sister. He was facing away from Somerville, but still wanted to keep his words quiet. He didn't trust the director at all. "We have all these Seekers here. They're a captive audience."

"What are you suggesting?" Rachael asked.

Kirby shrugged. "I don't know. But the Seekers have become corrupted by him," he nodded towards Somerville, "and he's going to commit this world to war by sending twelve hundred spirits, still connected to their bodies, up to the astral plane to fight on the side of the angels. We cannot let that happen."

"You really think that my Seekers will listen to anyone other than me?"

Kirby and Rachael looked at Somerville, and Kirby's heart stopped; a gun was pointed directly at his head.

"You're a spirit …" he said in a croaky voice. "How are you holding that?"

Somerville's spirit body shrugged. "In the same way that I moved the chair earlier: by sheer effort of will. I have the force of energy to do it, so I can."

---

Terror ran through Rachael's transparent form. While the gun couldn't harm her, the same couldn't be said for her brother.

Somerville went on, talking calmly as if they were discussing nothing more interesting than the weather. "I have no compunction against killing another, Kirby," he said. "I killed one when she turned against me. I'll kill the other sibling if it means getting you out the way."

Somerville's eyes focused on Rachael, who look shocked at what he had just admitted. "You've clearly thought about it, Rachael," he said, "but I'm amazed that you never remembered that it was me who killed you."

"I didn't ever think –" she croaked. "Of all the ways it could have happened, why did it have to be you?"

"Because you betrayed me," he retorted, "and you're about to betray me again."

He looked back to Kirby. "Like brother, like sister," he said.

Kirby pulled himself up straight. His brain was fizzing with rage, and if he hadn't been facing down the barrel of a gun, then he knew he would have rushed the Seeker, and the consequences be damned.

Instead, he wrestled to keep his anger in check. He needed to control it and think clearly.

"So what do we do now?" he asked, folding his arms across his chest. "We all stand around here while the angels and spirits slug it out above our head? Perhaps we'll let the spirits just kill us. I don't think the Seekers could truly defend us, anyway."

An angry growl emerged from Somerville's throat.

"You've just stepped over the line," he said angrily. "Looks like the Kirby name is going to die with you."

Rachael panicked, but knew that her transparent form meant she wouldn't be able to do anything to stop a bullet fired from that gun.

*I can't let my brother die!* she thought. All other thoughts out of her head, and panic set in. Her mind called out for help, but she doubted anyone would hear her.

Somerville fired.

# Seekers of Truth HQ – Four Years Previous

Rachael Kirby pulled her collar up to try and at least protect a small part of her neck against the rain. She realised, however, that it wasn't working, and gave up.

*Every other part of me is saturated,* she thought. *Keeping the back of my neck dry is the least of my problems right now.*

She glanced over her shoulder for what must have been the tenth time in the last couple of minutes. Again, she saw nothing there, but still wasn't satisfied.

*There's too many shadows. I don't trust anything. At least I'm almost there.*

It was a wet, moonless night, but Rachael could have found her way to the meeting place blindfolded and turned around seventeen times. She knew this area of her home town like the back of her hand, and Customs House was a well-known landmark. The new town council was due to move in any day now, although residents had already taken up the top floor – the Seekers of Truth.

Rachael gave the password to the doorkeeper and stepped inside to the changing room. She didn't have any clothes to change into, but five minutes with a towel and a radiator would make her feel a lot better.

She didn't look round as the door opened and closed; she was too busy drying off her hair.

"Hello, Rachael, I'm glad you're here early."

Rachael spun round, surprised that someone had managed to come in without her hearing them.

"Evan, you can't be in here!" she exclaimed.

"Because this is the meeting place for a secret society?"

"No, because this is a female changing room. Yours is across the hall."

Evan Somerville laughed and shrugged his shoulders at the same time, making it look as if his whole body was laughing at the joke.

"I don't think they'll throw me out. Do you?" he asked.

She smiled and threw the towel into the laundry basket.

"Probably not," she conceded. Knowing she'd never win the argument, she changed the subject. "Why have you called us here tonight? We're not meant to be meeting until next Tuesday."

Evan shrugged again; this time, a sly grin slid across his face.

"Why do you think?"

By now, Rachael was combing her hair out. The comb paused as she realised what the director was insinuating.

"Evan –"

A flick of his hand stopped her protests in their tracks. He sighed, looking more disappointed than anything. Evan was a powerful man, the most powerful of all the Seekers – although Rachael was a close second. Her power and ability to reach further and further into the unknown was fast becoming legendary, and she always wondered how Evan felt about it.

*Looks like I won't be finding out now*, she thought in confusion.

Her leader, despite being dismissive of her protests, looked extremely calm.

"Did you honestly think I wouldn't find out?" Evan asked. "I can reach further in the astral plane than you've ever dreamed, and you and your … cabal … honestly didn't think I'd find out?"

*Shit!* Rachael thought. *This is worse than I thought.*

"Evan," she said softly, speaking carefully so that he wouldn't have cause to interrupt again, "don't call it a cabal. It's nothing of the sort. We're just … we're worried about you. Things have changed."

Somerville angrily shook his head. "No they haven't!" he snapped. "We're the Seekers of Truth! We never change!"

"But *you* do, Evan, and you have. You're so desperate for answers in the other realm that you won't consider the possibility that you could be wrong – that we need to remain in this realm, and not risk the dangers of what's beyond the veil."

She had rushed her words, afraid that if she hadn't, she wouldn't be able to say them at all. Now, with Somerville glaring at her from the other end of the room, she wished that she had her supporters from the Cabinet alongside her.

*Safety in numbers*, she thought. *Well, too late now.*

Eyes blazing with anger, Somerville took a step further towards Rachael. He looked furious, and Rachael knew that people often came off the worst when his anger reached this point.

"Who would you have replaced me with?" he asked. "I assume that's what this is all about; replacing me with someone new? Else, why would you be gathering a cabal together? We could have just discussed it privately otherwise."

Rachael drew herself up to her full height and refused to be cowed by him.

"You would never have just discussed it privately," she said, more angrily than she had planned to. "I know you, Evan. I've worked with you long enough, don't forget. And since you ask, I propose to replace you with me. I will be more cautious in our approach, and that's what we need right now."

Somerville didn't move for a moment. He was rooted to the spot, staring intently at the young protégé who had risen to become his deputy. She knew he was incredibly proud of her, and the fact he was silent and not showing her his legendary rage raised her confidence the tiniest amount. Although she and the rest of the Seeker's Cabinet had been planning to remove him as director, she didn't bear him any ill-will.

*I still respect you more than anyone*, she thought.

The Leader cocked his head to one side, almost as if he were listening to someone that Rachael couldn't hear, or as if he had heard what she was thinking.

"How long have we known each other?" he asked.

Rachael hesitated. Her superior's voice was calm and measured, as if his visible anger of a moment ago had never happened, but she knew she couldn't trust that possibility. Rumours of Seekers going missing couldn't always be attributable to the astral plane. Sometimes, there were suspicions of more earthly origins, and the finger had been pointed directly at Somerville – although never to his face.

"Six years," she replied. There was more risk in not answering. At least this way, she could hold out hope that someone else would walk into the changing rooms. "You recruited me, Evan." She smiled. "Remember that day?"

Somerville smiled back, a fond look on his eye. "How could I forget? As soon as I saw you channelling in that dingy room, I knew I'd got someone I could trust."

Rachael's smile wavered for a moment. She knew he hadn't used the word "trust" lightly. In the blink of an eye, the Leader's face changed from nostalgia back to the fury of a moment ago.

"I think you understand me," he went on. "You understand that I don't tolerate disloyalty? That I trusted you above all the others?"

Rachael nodded and swallowed, but didn't trust herself to speak. The look in her mentor's eyes terrified her, but she couldn't look away.

Somerville sighed, the anger giving way to a weary resignation. "I didn't want to have to do this, Rachael, but I know you're the ringleader of the conspiracy, and without you, it'll completely fall apart."

Rachael began to back away, but knew there was nowhere to go. The only entrance was behind Somerville, and she doubted he would step aside if she asked.

"Evan, stop it," she said. "Let's go somewhere and talk."

There was a sudden flash of light and Rachael could feel a pull, as if an enormous pressure front had somehow built inside the changing room. If Rachael had been anyone else, she might have thought that was impossible; however, she was a senior Seeker of Truth, and so knew differently.

She looked up and saw the reason for the sudden burst of light and the change in air pressure. A black whirlpool had opened in the ceiling, swirling round in a violent circle of energy. It sucked in all the light around it, and it almost hurt to look into its depths. The noise was deafening and the crackle of energy blended in with distant screams and cries of torment. She was about to die, and that whirlpool was preparing to take her to … she didn't know where, but it made her sick just thinking about it.

*I didn't realise he had the power to open a channel to another realm!* she thought urgently. *He can't travel through yet without killing himself – but I suppose that doesn't matter for anyone else, especially me.*

"No!" she said sharply. "Don't do this, Evan!"

She looked back at Somerville. His eyes were cold and hard. Whether he knew the vortex was there or not, she wasn't sure, but it was obvious what he was about to do.

"Evan!" she bellowed. "Evan, we can talk about this!"

"You've betrayed me, Rachael," Somerville said. He was speaking at normal volume, but Rachael could hear him above the roar of the maelstrom. "And I don't tolerate betrayal. Your death will serve as a lesson to all those left behind. No-one is safe from me."

The crack of the bullet leaving the gun was piercing and deadly, and it hit its mark the first time, straight through her head. Rachael's legs buckled, and she slumped against the bank of lockers, with no time to even draw another breath. She was dead before she hit the floor.

He had heard the maelstrom forming, which was how he had known he would succeed. That vortex of energy didn't appear for everybody, but Seekers were especially attuned, and always detected it when it arrived.

He heard a brief cry of "Help me!" before the whirlpool disappeared and the plain white ceiling, with its artexed patterns in their familiar shapes reappeared as if nothing had happened.

Somerville sagged against the door frame for a moment, using it to support him as he regained his strength. He ran a shaky hand through his hair and glanced up again for a second before looking away as a wave of nausea flooded over him.

*I had to do it*, he told himself. *I had to.*

He cleared his throat and pushed himself off the door frame. Straightening his tie, he checked himself in the nearest mirror, making sure that nothing was out of place and that the mask of geniality was back on his face, then turned and opened the door.

# Michael's Quarters, Heaven – The Distant Past

Lucifer, Satan and Beelzebub filed into Michael's quarters one after the other. Michael stood by the arched windows, watching each of them carefully as they entered. His face didn't give away even a modicum of emotion. All three of the younger angels looked back at him curiously, but Lucifer had a combined look of curiosity, nerves and determination written across his features.

Beelzebub and Satan remained standing, but Lucifer sat in one of the recliner chairs near to the window. Michael's eyebrows rose. *He is either confident or terrified.*

"You have been locked in conference with my father for two days," Lucifer said without any greeting. "Do you have a plan of action now?"

Michael folded his arms across his chest and rested his shoulder against the wall. His eyes were firmly focused on Lucifer, but the younger angel didn't flinch.

"We will continue to fight," Michael said.

Beelzebub and Satan reacted in surprise.

*They were clearly expecting me to rant and rave*, Michael thought. Inwardly, he smiled. *I am glad that I can still shock them occasionally.*

"What else?" Lucifer said shortly.

"And we will win."

Lucifer scowled, stood and angrily stomped to the window. He didn't reply, but Michael picked up on the angel's disapproval from across the room.

"Lucifer?" he said. "Talk to me."

Lucifer shook his head. "I do not understand," he replied quietly, his softly-spoken words belying his angry body language. "I do not understand how it is that the Seven Sisters have betrayed us by allying with the spirit realm, and yet we do not get angry about it."

Michael shifted uncomfortably on his feet. "I am not entirely sure what you are saying, my friend, but I do not like the sound of it."

"We must act decisively," Lucifer said as he turned away from the window. "Our tactics of trying to divide and conquer are not working. They cannot work while the Seven Sisters are allied against us. We decapitate the top and then the body crumbles."

Satan frowned. "Lucifer, it sounds as if you're suggesting…" He hesitated, worried about offending his friend but knowing he had to ask the question "Are you suggesting we kill the Seven Sisters?"

Lucifer didn't respond. His eyes slid across to Satan, and they exchanged a look full of meaning.

"Lucifer!" Beelzebub exclaimed. She had picked up on the silent communion between the other two angels. "You cannot be serious?"

"They've killed angels!" Lucifer raged. "Beelzebub, they've killed our friends, people we love, and now we're caught in an endless stalemate!"

"Lucifer," Satan continued, "your emotions are clouding your judgment. Think about what you're suggesting."

He looked at Michael, who had remained silent during Lucifer's proposal. "What do you think, Michael?"

Michael sighed, deep in thought. "I agree that the Seven Sisters have turned this war around," he said, "and not in the way we would like. We're losing, and we need to think of drastic measures to regain the initiative. The Almighty is willing to consider all alternatives."

Satan was appalled, and it showed on his face. "What *are* we considering?" he asked. "The slaughter of the Seven Sisters? Even if the Almighty countenanced that – and I refuse to believe He would – we couldn't do that by ourselves. Each Sister is incredibly powerful."

"You're right," Lucifer said. "Which is why we need to recruit Poena and her spirits to help us. They dislike the Seven Sisters causing a stalemate as much as we do."

Michael laughed. "Forgive me, Lucifer, but are you suggesting that we recruit our enemies into a war against the Seven Sisters?"

"Yes."

The room was silent as they all digested Lucifer's suggestion.

Michael eventually spoke up; "So ... you propose that we join our mortal enemies, defeat the Seven Sisters, and then return to our fight with those enemies?"

"How did you come up this idea, Lucifer?" Satan asked.

Lucifer flashed him a warning glare, but Satan didn't back down. Instead, he took a step forward and squared his shoulders in a challenge.

"Or should I say *who* came up with the idea?"

Beelzebub and Michael both looked confused.

"Satan…" Lucifer said warningly, but Satan ignored him.

"Lucifer, I am sure that I felt something penetrate our defences yesterday. I cannot entirely explain it, but I believe that Poena breached our external barrier … and I believe she spoke to you."

"What the –"

Before Michael could continue his sentence, Lucifer strode angrily across the room and stood right in front of his oldest friend.

"What exactly are you suggesting?" he snapped.

"Nothing," Satan replied. "I just wonder … if Poena *did* come up with this idea, then we have to be suspicious of it."

Beelzebub swallowed, reluctant to ask the question that had formed in her head, but needing to all the same. "Lucifer, are you in league with Poena?"

There was an icy silence before Lucifer spoke again. "Never say that again in my presence." He shook his head and turned to the windows, suddenly seeming battle-fatigued. "I …" Lucifer's mighty wings heaved and then sagged in weary surrender. "This is our home. Our entire way of life is under threat. I know we committed a pre-emptive strike, but the spirits are gradually eating away at our defences. Do any one of you wish for everything we love to end, and for us to be slaves? I do not want to see them dead, but if that is the only way we can succeed, then so be it."

"But can we justify the annihilation of the Sisters to let our way of life continue?" Beelzebub wondered. "Especially when we enslaved the spirits for so long and then launched the first attack."

Her wings folded around herself in an attempt of comfort. It didn't work.

Lucifer looked at each angel in turn. Beelzebub was clearly uncomfortable and upset, Satan's reason and logic were telling him that what Lucifer was saying was wrong, and Michael's jaw was set in a determined line. Lucifer just couldn't tell whether that was a good thing or a bad thing.

Lucifer walked over to the door; "I am going to see my father now," he said. "He will make the final decision."

"Then I will come with you."

Lucifer looked at Satan, surprised by the speed of his friend's reply. "You're worried that he might agree with me?" he said, more sharply than he had planned to.

Satan's voice was thick with emotion as he replied; "I need to know that the Almighty can hear all options – not just yours."

Lucifer couldn't argue the point, and nodded. "Very well."

He turned to Michael and Beelzebub. "I'm doing what I think is right," he said.

"Then you are not the angel I thought you were."

Beelzebub's words cut through Lucifer like a knife. It was almost a physical pain, hearing Beelzebub's raw, open anger directed at him. He knew, with a terrible certainty, that there was nothing he could say to change it. Without another word, he turned and left, Satan following closely behind.

"I suppose you agree with him," Beelzebub snapped at Michael, who had walked over to the window.

He turned back to face her and sighed, his wings stretching out for a moment as he thought about her question. "I agree that we're losing," he said. "I agree that we need to do something. We are at war, Beelzebub."

"Even in war, there are rules!"

Michael gave her an appraising look for a moment. She wondered what he was thinking, and was uncomfortable with the resulting silence – she was glad when he spoke again.

"You've never fought on the front line," he said, and he shrugged his broad shoulders. "I can accept that, Beelzebub. Not everyone in Heaven is a soldier. You have provided us – me – with exceptional intelligence and insight into the spirits. A lot of our early successes were due to the analysis you provided."

Beelzebub sighed and shook her head. "But they're still winning, Michael. I didn't foresee the Seven Sisters becoming involved in the conflict."

"None of us did." Michael seemed to be choosing his words carefully. "You're not a soldier. I am. I look at this realm…" He spread his arms out wide, as if encompassing everything in – and beyond – the realm, "…and I want keep it safe. I am responsible for protecting us, and I would die to ensure it. This is war, Beelzebub. It sometimes involves death."

"But it's the Seven Sisters …"

Michael shook his head, unable to answer the unspoken question, and turned back to the windows.

"They may leave us no choice," he said.

He stared into the dark nothingness of space and time, and wished for a moment that he could see how it would all end.

"What will happen to us if Lucifer succeeds?" he muttered.

Beelzebub shook her head. "We'll all be damned."

# Heaven – Present Day

Michael looked out over the army of angels formed behind him, fifty deep. The battalion had formed, they were armed, and they were ready.

Halamiel was next to him, her wings gently beating against the astral eddies as she waited patiently for his orders.

*It's time*, he thought.

He flexed his fingers and exhaled. For the first time in a very long time, he was going to war, and he knew it was the right thing to do.

"Begin."

# Astral Plane – Present Day

oena saw the angels shift position. The attack front had been formed, and now they were surging forwards.

It was time to fight for her very existence, and the existence of the beings around her.

The spirits had gathered to her side. She could feel their energy, their vitality – and their eagerness.

*We don't need the Seven Sisters to lead us into battle this time*, she told herself. *There are many more spirits now, all of whom are ready to fight for their security.*

She cried out, and her army surged forwards to meet their implacable enemy.

# Customs House, Ramsgate – Present Day

"Stop."

The bullet ceased its forward motion and fell to the floor. The soft, red carpet absorbed the impact and noise without a sound. At the same time, Somerville's spirit disappeared from the room.

Kirby released a breath he didn't realise he had been holding.

"How the hell did you do that?"

Rachael shook her head, her eyes almost as wide as dinner plates. "I didn't do anything!" she insisted. "I wanted to, but –"

"Did I do something wrong?"

Both siblings turned to the source of the question. The voice was female, beautifully harmonic and full of melody. It was pitch perfect, the sort of voice that would cause a person to beg just to hear again, even for a single second; it had the ability to touch someone's heart and make them feel joyous.

Where the voice came from, however, there was nothing. Not just an absence of an entity, but literally nothing.

Cutting through the wooden table was a void. It was black as night and drawing in all the colours of the air surrounding it. Kirby drew in a breath, cold cutting into his heart for a moment as his eyes focused on the black oval.

"What is that?" he whispered. His voice wavered for a moment as he continued to remember the sheer beauty of the voice that had emanated from that spot. His eyes couldn't draw themselves away from the empty void.

"I … I don't know," his sister replied. Kirby was able to pull his gaze away and glance at Rachael. She was as engrossed as he was.

*Strange*, he thought, *now that I'm not looking, I can think clearly again. What is that thing – and how does it have a hold over us, like the voice?*

Rachael shook her head. "It feels … it feels like I should know what it is."

"Indeed you should, Rachael Kirby," the voice said again, and made Kirby almost melt, until he remembered what he had just thought. He felt his head start to turn back towards the void, but he closed his eyes tight and refused to move. *I will not be beaten!*

"Why is … Kirby fighting his natural instinct to look at me?"

"Are you … an angel?" Kirby asked.

*How do you know my name?* he wondered. *Can you read my mind?*

He realised then that the voice had fallen silent, and he felt the chill pervading the room again, stronger this time, and he wondered if it might have been due to his statement.

*What did I say?*

"An angel?" the beautiful voice asked, and this time, it was tinged with a layer of anger at the mere suggestion. "Do I look like an angel to you?"

His eyes almost reopened out of habit, but he resisted the urge.

"You don't look like anything," he pointed out. "I can't see anything except … nothingness."

"And it's bloody hard to look away," Rachael muttered through gritted teeth.

Suddenly, the voice was back to its apparently-default tone – one of perfect harmony and melody. "Oh, have I … I haven't materialized correctly? I've channelled into the void instead of your realm."

"You're … a spirit?" Kirby asked, his police training coming to the fore of his mind again: when you don't understand what a suspect is talking about, then ask follow-up questions until you do.

There was a silence for a moment, then he heard Rachael exclaim in surprise and say, "I think she's more than that, Kirby. It's okay; you can open your eyes now. It's safe."

Kirby trusted his sister, but he still eased just one eye open cautiously. He saw that Rachael had managed to tear her gaze away from the void, as the voice had called it, and was looking at him instead with a strange look on her face.

He looked round – and his eyes almost bulged out of his head. The voice's owner had waist-long hair that was so blonde it was almost white, and her features and frame were so delicate that Kirby was reminded of a porcelain doll that Rachael had kept in her room as a child. She was shorter than him – barely five foot – and, while her feet were on the floor, there was something about her, as if she had barely-suppressed energy surrounding her, and she was only just balancing on the tread of the carpet.

She had a look of curiosity on her face and, when she spoke, her voice sang to Kirby's heart, but he tried to restrain the emotional response.

"Who do you think I am?" she asked, looking genuinely curious.

Kirby hesitated for a moment, then mentally shrugged. She was asking him a direct question and, in any case, he wanted to see if his suspicions were right.

"You can't be an ordinary human spirit," he said as he worked through his thought processes. "If you were, you'd be transparent like my sister. No offence, sis."

Rachael looked down at her faux body. "None taken," she replied wearily.

He grinned at her and carried on. "If I take your word at face value, then you're certainly not an angel. Are you Poena?" He paused to think, then shook his head. "No, because then you wouldn't be here. You'd be fighting in Heaven."

She raised a delicate eyebrow, clearly fascinated with his thought processes. "You have told me who I am not," she said. "Now … tell me who I am."

"You're one of the Seven Sisters."

The doll-like girl closed her eyes in relief. "That's who I thought I was too," she replied. "But it's been so long … I'd thought I was confused, or that I'd somehow forgotten."

Rachael was immediately curious about this woman, who was clearly so much more than the dainty physical form in front of her.

"What have you done with Somerville?" she asked.

The Sister looked confused, and Rachael realised that she didn't know who she was talking about. "The spirit who was in the room with us a moment ago?"

"You refer to the angry spirit?" the Sister asked. "He planned to kill you, and that was not acceptable. I sent him to be with his spirits outside this room."

Rachael exchanged a glance with her brother, and they both walked over to the window, where the spirits were still mingling below. Something was different now, however; Somerville was in the centre of the marina, silently gathering the Seekers around him.

A silent communion seemed to be happening among them. Almost as one, they all looked up at the sky just as the darkened shapes of the angels moved forward to attack the unseen spirits. Somerville rose from the ground and headed towards the battle, and the rest of the Seekers' spirits followed.

"They'll be slaughtered," Kirby whispered. "They're going to die."

"Then Somerville will die with them," Rachael replied as she watched them go.

"Good," her brother said empathically. "The battle will hopefully be the last thing he ever sees."

"You talk of battle," the Sister said from behind them, and the siblings turned to face her. "Have the angels and spirits resurrected their ancient war?"

"Yes," Rachael replied, suddenly intrigued even more in this ancient being. "Can you stop it?"

The Sister thought for a moment, then nodded.

"It is possible," she conceded. "I can wake my fellow Sisters, and we can bring it to a halt."

"Then let us help you!" Kirby said urgently. "This war is a bad thing for *all* the realms. It needs to be stopped!"

"We will need something first," the Sister said, her lips setting in a hard, angry line that seemed in conflict with such a beautiful face. "A long time ago, our desire for peace was overridden by a selfish, naïve angel."

Rachael frowned. "You wish him to be … prosecuted for that?"

"No," the Sister said, "I wish him to die for that."

# Astral Plane – Present Day

Paul slumped back against the wall. It was surprisingly cool through the wallpaper – *Why would the Seven Sisters even need wallpaper?* – and ran a hand through his hair.

"You tried to kill these … these Seven Sisters?" he asked Lucifer. He felt empty and exhausted for a moment, his emotions having been dampened by what he had heard. "You … thought their deaths would stop the war?"

Lucifer, looking chagrined, nodded. "I believed Poena when she told me that their deaths would change the dynamic between our realms," he replied in a quiet voice that was unlike him. "They were … are … powerful beyond measure, and I believed Poena when she said that they were holding us back."

He glanced at Beelzebub and Joseph, who remained silent but didn't flinch away from his gaze.

"When Poena convinced them to fight," he said as he looked back at Paul, "we all knew we were doomed."

"Can you really blame a race of slaves from rising up against their masters?" Paul said angrily. He was aware of Lauren and Joseph on either side of him, but having his friends there didn't stop his anger rising. "Slaves who want their freedom will do anything to free themselves."

"We didn't want to *become* the race of slaves," Lucifer replied, trying to keep his voice even. "We were willing to do anything as well … and I thought that Poena's plan was as good as any."

Paul pushed away from the wall, using the forward motion to propel himself towards to the angel.

"You lived inside my head!" he bellowed, unable to contain the sudden rage that erupted from within him. "You've shared my mind, and I trusted you, Lucifer! I trusted you, and it turns out you were listening to Poena advocate murder against these Sisters! You bastard!"

He shoved Lucifer with his hands. In retrospect, he wasn't sure how he had done it, but he actually reached up to the seven-foot angel and shoved him backwards. Lucifer was caught off guard and his wings spread out wide to help him balance. A gust of wind pushed past Paul's face as the angel's wings beat and lifted him off the ground. Lucifer looked shocked at the assault, as did everyone else.

Beelzebub stepped in front of Paul and her eyes blazed with anger.

"Lucifer is a leader of angels," he snarled, a fury whipping every word. "Whatever you have done for him, you do not have the right to assault him!"

Lauren pointed a finger at the female angel that had shared her own head for so long. "Back off!" she snapped. "Paul's my friend – and you're my angel! He's entitled to be angry."

"Enough!" Joseph said, loudly enough to be heard by human, spirit and angel alike. Looking round, he realised that everyone was now staring directly at him.

"It's started," he said.

Paul frowned. "What has?"

"The war. The barrier has been breached. Spirits and angels are fighting."

Paul couldn't suppress the shudder that travelled down his spine. The angel almost sounded afraid.

"Then you'd better finish the story," he said, "and quickly."

# Heaven – The Distant Past

It was all over. The battles had all been fought and the war had been won, but at a terrible price.

Michael looked out over the cosmos as the final parts to the barrier were erected. He should have felt proud, he knew. Instead, he felt a terrible sadness at the price that everyone had paid.

He had been alone, but realised that someone had now joined him, floating out on the magnificent vista of the universe away from the Heavenly Citadel. He was floating on a stream of galactic wind – and now Lucifer was by his side.

In the final few months of the war, Lucifer had changed. His face was harder and more lined with stress, and he seemed a lot more tense.

*He has aged*, Michael thought, a difficult task for a race that was immortal.

Michael didn't ask how his protégé was feeling; he didn't need to. They sat in semi-companionable silence for a while until Lucifer spoke.

"How is my father?"

Michael was surprised. "Why don't you ask him yourself?" he prompted. "If anyone can have unfettered access to the Almighty, it's his son."

Lucifer shrugged. "My father and I have not spoken since the … debacle of the final battle."

*I'm not surprised*, Michael thought, but didn't say anything. *I am appalled at how badly it went, but the Almighty must accept some of the blame for agreeing to Lucifer's plan the first place.*

"Angels died under my command, Michael."

It was a statement of fact, rather than a question. Michael nodded. He wasn't going to pull his punches. Lucifer had made a horrendous mistake.

"Yes," he replied. "Yes, they did."

"How was I so naïve?" he wondered aloud, and, for the first time in a long while, Michael didn't know what to say in return.

❖

Lucifer, stricken with fear and grief, flew through the warzone, looking desperately for his friends. He almost flew into the body – just the body, as the mind was gone – of a brother angel, and he jerked back in shock. Tears streamed down his face as he flew round it and continued searching, fighting the urge to look back over his shoulder to face his mistake.

"What have I done?" he asked. "In the name of all that is holy, what happened?"

"*You* happened, 'fer."

Lucifer spun round, his wings beating hard with relief as his heard his old friend's voice, but his face fell as he saw the fresh wound on Satan's side.

"What … what happened?" he croaked.

"I met Poena," Satan replied. He was trying to hide the pain, but he couldn't mask the wince that moved across his face. "She wasn't very happy to see me."

He tried to smile, but it turned into another wince instead. Lucifer reached out a hand to help him, but Satan waved him off.

"I think you've done more than enough damage," he said sharply.

Lucifer swallowed and accepted the stinging comment. He expected that there would be a lot more to come.

"What happened?" he whispered – although he knew that Satan would hear him, even in the depths of space.

"Poena was treating you like the naïve fool you clearly are," Satan snapped. "Did you really think that she would allow the spirits to unite with the angels in order to kill the Seven Sisters?"

Lucifer opened his mouth to reply, but found that he couldn't. Instead, jumbled, mixed-up images crossed his brain; images of himself, leading the entire angelic army into battle against the Seven Sisters and expecting the spirit army to support them. Instead, they walked straight into an ambush.

When the spirit army had arrived, they had attacked the angels, and not the Seven Sisters. Suddenly, battalions of angels were caught between two avenging armies, and the Seven Sisters had been forced to fight to defend their lives and kill both angels and spirits, which they had vowed never to do.

"Are the Seven Sisters…?"

Satan nodded. "I assume they must have realised that neither side was going to stop, and that if we were capable of trying to kill them once, we could try it again."

"Will they ever come back?"

Satan scowled at his friend. "Why ask me?" he asked angrily. "The Sisters are far wiser than any of us. How can any of us know what they're thinking? All I know is that they've gone into hibernation. I don't know if we'll ever see them again."

Lucifer was silent. The angels had managed to find a second wind against the spirits and had gone on to secure a less-than-triumphant victory. Imprisonment of the spirits in their own realm was the best angels could hope for now.

"It's all gone wrong," he whispered, "and it's all my fault."

# The Front Line – Present Day

Michael felt alive.

This was when he came into his element, fighting for survival – not only for himself, but for the existence of his race.

*They will not* win! he told himself *We are superior! We are angels!*

Angels and spirits swarmed around him, fighting their own battles against each other. His heart swelled with pride as he watched his angels swoop in and out of the astral plane, attacking the spirits. While the spirits were fighting back, Michael knew that his battalion would eventually win. He was a patient angel, and would remain here as long as it took to beat the spirits into submission again. He himself was searching for Poena; she was his personal goal, and he was determined to confront her personally.

*Lucifer regretted what he did to the Seven Sisters, and I understand that,* he thought. *It was a mistake, but only because we were focused on the wrong target. He saw the light in the end. She tried to break us apart, and now she needs to suffer.*

*She will die, and I will be the one to kill her.*

—•◆•—

Poena's rage was white hot and focused. While she had seen for herself the angels in the sky, she had wondered if they would actually go through with the attack.

*Michael has gone insane!* she thought angrily as she parried an attack by an angel and sped off in a different direction in the blackness of space. Angels were powerful beings by themselves, and a spirit wouldn't be able to win one-on-one against an angel.

*That's what Michael is planning,* she thought. *That we'll be divided and conquered, that we've forgotten how to fight.*

Poena knew that he was wrong. She had learnt from the last war, and from the Seven Sisters. The spirits now fought in packs of six, each pack separating angels off from the main army and wearing them down – and there were many spirits.

Her anger was boiling, but it still let through a small feeling of … something. She stopped looking for the rest of her pack, narrowly avoided an angel and the three remaining spirits of another pack fighting to the death, and looked for the feeling's source. It didn't take her long to find it.

"We've been betrayed," she whispered.

◄●●►

Somerville was free. He had managed to break his way back into the astral plane by breaching one of the scars that had formed after his earlier attempt. Now, he and his fellow Seekers were in the depths of the astral plane, unencumbered by the restrictions of their mortal bodies.

He paused for a second as he looked out onto the scene before him – angel against spirit.

*And the spirits must lose,* he thought angrily. *If this Poena is any indication, then they have become too arrogant and will not stop with the angels, but move onto humanity as well.*

# Heaven – The Distant Past

Lucifer wished that Beelzebub would stop talking, but she didn't, and he knew why. He needed – no, he deserved – to know.

"One thousand, three hundred and forty-two angels died in total," she said, looking into the middle distance as if reading from some internal list. "We haven't been able to locate their souls."

"In truth," Satan chimed in, "I doubt we ever will."

Lucifer swallowed. His eyes were closed; he couldn't bear the look in their eyes as they spoke. He wasn't sure if he could speak, but he knew his friends wouldn't say anything more until he had.

"What is happening?" he asked. Angels rarely felt apprehensive or unsure, but Lucifer felt both now, and it didn't sit well with him.

"The barrier between our realms has been completed," Beelzebub said. "The astral plane is now sealed off from us and the physical plane. The spirits are prisoners."

Lucifer finally opened his eyes and looked imploringly at Beelzebub. "Have the Seven Sisters responded to us?"

Satan shook his head. "No," he replied. "We do not know where they are."

"I need to talk to them!" Lucifer explained. "I need to explain about Poena, and how she influenced me!"

The three of them were in the Celestial Observatory. Satan was sat on one of the stone benches; he was so still that he looked as if he were meditating.

Lucifer shook his head as he realised what he had said.

"I was angry," he said out loud, but the words sound hollow. "I didn't mean…"

He then asked a question that he knew he wouldn't get an answer to. "What will happen to our ancestors? Will we ever see them again?"

# Astral Plane – Present Day

"Your *ancestors?*" Paul demanded. "What the hell…?"

He glanced at Joseph. With the tension between them all as high as it was, the angel/human hybrid was the only one he felt would give him an honest answer without any anger behind it.

"Mate, what the hell is going on?"

Joseph gave a weak smile. He had been able to accept the memories that had resurfaced, but Paul could tell they still disturbed him.

*I'm not surprised,* he thought. *They've affected me, and I'm seeing it second-hand.*

"The Seven Sisters are revered by all angels," Joseph said in reply to his friend's question, "including the Almighty."

Lauren laughed. "There's something out there that the Almighty reveres? Bloody hell, I'd better be careful if I ever bump into one."

"If you ever bumped into one," said Beelzebub, "you might not live to tell the tale."

Lauren frowned and opened her mouth to snap a comment back, but stopped herself. She realised that the angel had been trying to make an effort to reconnect with her host, rather than provoke another row.

Paul looked at Lucifer; he was hovering a couple of feet in the air, his wings gently beating to a steady rhythm. His face looked as if it was set in stone, and Paul wasn't sure if that was a good thing or not.

"Why do you revere them?" he asked the angel.

*I won't apologise for what I said or did*, Paul thought. *I was angry, and I felt like you'd deliberately kept something from me while you'd lived inside my head.*

Lucifer made eye contact with him and Paul began to wonder if the angel could still hear his thoughts, even from a distance. *Can you?*

They maintained eye contact for a moment longer. Lucifer broke the gaze first, and Paul was convinced he saw the ghostly flicker of a smile. The angel floated back to the ground and tucked his wings back behind his back.

"The Seven Sisters ..." He seemed to be thinking how best to phrase his reply. "They gave birth to the first generation of angels ... including the Almighty."

Paul shifted awkwardly on his feet, and glanced at Lauren. She didn't seem to know what to say, and neither did he. Joseph had crossed his arms over his chest and was looking at a piece of artwork on the wall. He had clearly known that already, and wanted to give his friends time to absorb it.

"They ..." Paul cleared his throat. "One of them is the Almighty's mother?"

Beelzebub nodded. "And another is the mother of Michael."

"Sorry," Lauren said, askance, "but have I understood that right? The Almighty was willing to kill them in order to stop the war. He was willing to kill his own mother?"

Lucifer didn't shy from her gaze as he replied. "I was young and stupid," he said, "and I thought Poena had the answers we needed to push the war in our favour."

Paul frowned. "Why would they fight their own children?"

Joseph turned away from the piece of art. "Another Sister is the mother of Poena, and she was better at manipulating the Sisters than we were."

Paul's mouth opened and closed for a moment, and Joseph carried on in order to fill the silence. "Angels and spirits are cousins, Paul," he said.

"That's why I changed my mind," Lucifer said slowly. "They gave us life. How could we take away theirs? The Almighty became even more determined than I ever was, but thankfully, the choice was taken out of our hands."

"The Sisters wanted to live?" Paul asked.

Lucifer nodded. "They put themselves into hibernation, away from the war and the Almighty, to prevent the angelic army doing something we would later regret. That was too hopeful."

He tried to smile at the weak joke, but it didn't last. Paul was eyeing Lucifer carefully, and the angel seemed uncomfortable under the human's penetrating gaze.

*You can hear my thoughts. I know you can.*

Lucifer inclined his head ever so slightly.

*I can't help wondering one thing …* Paul thought. *How did the Seven Sisters get into hibernation before your forces or Poena's forces killed them?*

Lucifer looked relieved, as if glad that someone had asked that question.

*Redemption*, was the first word that flashed up in Paul's mind. *They were never aware that the message came from me, but I got them out safely, so they could hide.*

Paul kept his face neutral, but was relieved nonetheless. *It worked. You saved them. Now we can get them to help us stop this war for good.*

*It might not be as simple as that.*

# Astral Plane – Present Day

*Be careful what you wish for. It might come true.*

Kirby's mother had used that expression when he had been little, and it had stuck with him throughout his life, even more since he had joined the police force. Meeting people from across the spectrum of life, either as victims or as criminals, had given him a deeper respect for the saying. People either didn't know what they wanted, or wanted something so badly that they would go to any lengths to get it.

*I just wanted to see what Paul saw,* he thought. *I caught a glimpse of it this morning, and that wasn't enough. I still thought there was more I wanted to see, because Paul had seen it. I wish I'd … I'm glad I've experienced it, but I want my normal life back now please.*

Below them, a war raged.

*I thought I'd got a good imagination,* Kirby thought, *but this is nothing like I assumed it would be.*

Angels and spirits were fighting hard, each side refusing to give a single inch of space. The angels were tall and magnificent, their powerful wings beating to propel themselves forward. The spirits were harder to distinguish to a human eye. Kirby caught a glimpse of an ethereal being, looking like a human, ghostly shape, and other times it looked as if an angel was fighting itself.

"Is this harming Earth?" he asked, concerned for the planet's inhabitants. He remembered the sight of the angels massing in the sky, blocking out the sun and being intimidating just by their presence. Now, they looked terrifying.

Alcyone had managed to remember how to move back into the astral plane, and how to bring passengers with her. She looked at the human, impressed. "You worry about your world?" she asked him. "That concern does you credit."

Her eyes returned to the view beneath them, her face now an unreadable mix of emotions, and fell silent. Rachael cleared her throat.

"I can't help but notice," she said nervously, "that you didn't actually answer my brother's question."

Alcyone looked round and faced Rachael. "You are right, my child," she said in an airy voice. "I have not answered it, because I do not have an answer to give. Some things are beyond even my ability to see."

"What happens now?" Kirby asked. "Can you just ... click your fingers and stop this?"

"If only it were that simple," she replied. "Before I do anything else, I need to see Lucifer. For my Sisters to be willing to help, I will need to convince them, and Lucifer's death is the best way of doing so."

Kirby had tried to argue with her as they had travelled here, but she had ignored him. He knew that wouldn't change now, so despite his dislike of Alcyone's plan, he kept his own counsel. He didn't plan to upset the Sister too much. She was, after all, the one enabling him to breathe while floating in the cold vacuum of space.

*I'd rather like that to continue, thank you very much.*

"And now we must move on," Alcyone said suddenly.

Rachael was curious. "Where are we going?" she asked.

"Somewhere you have never been," Alcyone said, and a vague smile spread across her porcelain features. "You can both help me find Lucifer. We must go to Heaven."

Rachael reacted immediately. She looked alarmed at the thought. "I'll be killed if I go there!" she exclaimed. "Angels will strike me down on sight because of who I am. If you don't believe me, then look down!"

"They'd answer to me first," Kirby retorted.

She smiled at her brother, genuinely appreciative of his support. "You're a good man, Kirby," she said, "but I'm afraid you'd suffer the same fate as me. Humans never travel to Heaven."

"Well, except for Paul, Joseph and Lauren."

Alcyone's head snapped round and her face darkened. "Three humans went to Heaven?" she asked.

Kirby nodded, caught off-guard by the sudden change in her emotions. "Y-yes," he stuttered.

The Sister shook her head. "I have been asleep for too long," she whispered. "Things have changed so much."

Kirby nodded, but he wasn't sure if she took it in. Alcyone was looking off into the distance, now oblivious to the chaos and savagery below.

"Satan and Beelzebub were hosted by Joseph and Lauren," he said. "They … they woke up about two years ago."

"So many of my children," Alcyone said vaguely, mostly to herself. "So many lost … I cannot save them all."

Her face hardened. "But I can do something. Lucifer can die, and then my Sisters will help me stop this war."

Kirby had so many questions, but there wasn't time for them all.

*How can I stop this?* he asked himself. *What can I do?*

# Astral Plane - Present Day

The Seekers were now in the heart of the battle; they had charged forward and joined the angels in their fight. For a moment, the angels looked at them with amusement – until they considered how many spirits there still were. Their attitude quickly changed, and they grudgingly accepted the human souls onto their side.

Michael looked on with amazement – and a certain amount of respect – as this band of twelve hundred humans launched themselves at the astral plane spirits with an anger and rage that he would have expected from his own army, but not from others.

*How did they all manage to breach the barrier so easily without me knowing?*

His eyes quickly found the leader of the group: his anger burnt the brightest of them all, so much so that Michael could almost taste it.

He steered himself down towards that human spirit and blocked his way.

"What are you doing here?!" Michael demanded. "Why have you brought your humans here?"

Somerville's features had been contorted in anger, but when confronted by this tall, powerful angel, they swapped to one of surprise and awe.

"We've come to help!" he yelled over the noise of the battle all around them, not realising that Michael could have heard a whisper from the furthest galaxy if he were concentrating properly. "Poena humiliated us – and me. We are the Seekers of Truth, and we will not allow Poena to bring her chaos to Earth!"

———•●•———

Poena heard her name being spoken. Even from across a vastness where she was battling Halamiel with two packs of other spirits, she could still hear it. The battlefield was vast and loud, but her eyes quickly focused on the source of her name.

"I was right!" she bellowed. If she had been human, she would have known the phrase "bloodlust" and recognised that as what she was feeling right now. Her ancient cousins, after having enslaved the spirits for so long, *were* conspiring with humanity after all. Her rage took over her rational thoughts; she broke off her attack and sped towards the conspirators' meeting place.

Her rage blinded her to a lot of her surroundings. While she was aware of the dangers with the warring angels and spirits, she had tuned out everything else – and so was caught by surprise when she was suddenly sent barrelling sideways and completely off course.

She managed to steady herself after a moment, but her nebulous, shifting form was caught in a tight stranglehold. No matter how much she moved and twisted and tried to pull away, she was held tightly in place.

*I've been caught by an angel!* she thought, angry at herself more than the situation. *How can I have been so stupid!*

Her vision finally settled on her captor, and she was shocked by what she saw.

"You're a human spirit!" she growled, trying to hide her surprise.

"I'm more than that!" the human yelled. "I'm your worst nightmare, because you stole my body!"

Poena looked again, and realised who the spirit was.

"Your name is … Christina?" she said, a quaver of uncertainty edging her voice. The sounds of the battlefield were suddenly so far away. "I used your body on Earth."

"And you left me for dead," Christina said, her mind taken over with furious anger. "Now that I'm free of my body, what's to stop me killing you right now?"

"You're human," Poena snapped back disdainfully. "You could never kill me."

"But I'm sure I could hurt you," Christina said ominously. She had maintained her human form, despite now being a spirit, and the smile that spread across her ghostly face worried Poena.

"What do you want?" she demanded.

It was Christina's turn to sound surprised. "You know I want something?"

"I shared your head," Poena said coolly. "I can read you."

She shuddered at the thought of being able to read a human, but suppressed it as much as possible. She needed to confront the conspirators, and she couldn't do that while she was trapped here with this spirit.

"I need to find my friends," Christina said. "I need to find my boyfriend, Paul."

"The human who travelled to Heaven?"

"Yes!" Christina said excitedly. "You know him?"

"Only from your memories," Poena snarled. "He's human. He's not important."

Christina paused for a moment, her metaphysical grip still maintaining its tightness on Poena's form, and a strange look crossed her ghostly face.

"You're lying."

Poena was lost for words. She couldn't remember the last time that happened, but it happened now.

"You thought the process was one way?" Christina demanded. "When you took over my body, you had access to my memories. Why did you not think that I would be able to do the same? Because you're arrogant and overconfident, that's why – and, because you're the daughter of one of the Seven Sisters, you think you know everything! Well, I can tell you that you don't! Paul's important to me. I love him."

She considered Poena for a moment. "I know why he's important to you too, in a way. He's got Lucifer sleeping inside his head, and you think Lucifer's … weak?" Christina inclined her head to one side, as if she were sorting through some alien memories. "You're furious with him for not seeing through your plan."

Christina shook her head. "You're carrying round so much anger," she said coolly. "You'll never be happy. I can't keep this anger inside of me. I love Paul, no matter what. Now, tell me where my boyfriend is!"

Poena was appalled, primarily at herself for letting her guard down sufficiently to allow this mere human access to her thoughts, and now at this situation. She considered her options.

Being a child of the Sisters gave her certain powers, and she made use of them now to stretch out her mind and sense the being that was so important to Christina. If she had been human, her legs would have buckled as she discovered his location – and then realised the opportunities.

*I wanted the Seven Sisters … including my mother … out of this,* she thought. *I want to prove I can win this war without them – and if Paul is trying to wake them up, then perhaps Christina will be a distraction.*

She stopped herself. *If Paul is there, then Lucifer will be there as well! If I could … I could kill him. I would be a hero, and it would prove a viable symbol to the angels that we are stronger than them.*

"I will transport you there myself if you wish," she said.

Christina eyed her, as if trying to work out how genuine she was, but obviously she hadn't seen all of Poena's thoughts – *Or, at least, can't still see them now*, she thought with satisfaction.

Slowly, she nodded. "Okay," she said. "Okay, you can take me there. It'll be quicker with someone who knows the way. But I warn you: any funny business and I *will* hurt you."

Poena concealed her amusement well, she thought. *As if I am truly interested in* you. *All I care about is winning, and if that means killing Lucifer to do so, then so be it.*

Casting one final glance across the battlefield, and feeling confident that the spirits would cope well without her for a short while, she focused her energies on their new location – and the two spirits vanished.

⬤•⬤

Michael stopped talking and looked around. He frowned as he felt a disturbance near him. Something had shifted away from the battlefield.

*What was it?* he wondered. *Who was there?*

He caught sight of the raging battle again and knew that he didn't time to worry about something like that – or, indeed, about the human spirit floating in front of him with his righteous anger burning bright like a beacon.

"Do whatever you feel is right," he said shortly. "I have far more important things to worry about. Just remember whose side you are fighting on."

Somerville's eyes blazed brightly against the star-lit sky, and he grinned broadly.

"I'll not forget!" he bellowed as his spirit barrelled away from the senior angel.

*My own*, he thought in the privacy of his own head, and he led his Seekers of Truth to war.

# Astral Plane – Present Day

"Lucifer … one of these Sisters is your grand-mother?"

Paul was still struggling to come to terms with everything that Lucifer had told him. The angel nodded, and Paul's head almost shut down with an overload of information.

*This isn't happening,* he thought. *I'm dreaming and I'll wake up in a minute.*

"So…" said Lauren, her eyebrows quirking upwards. "How's everyone's day been so far? Anything else anyone wants to talk about?"

Her brother and Paul grinned at her comment, but the two full-blooded angels scowled at her.

"I have just told you about a shameful portion of our history," Lucifer said, "and you are making jokes."

Lauren shook her head. "It's a way of relieving stress and tension," she said. "I'd say there's quite a lot to be stressed and tense about, wouldn't you?"

"Agreed," Beelzebub said simply. She didn't look directly at the human, but Lauren noticed that her body language had become less formal.

*I'm glad,* she thought. *I didn't really fancy an angel, even a dis-embodied one, being angry at me for long.*

Paul turned to Joseph. "My friend, I think we're beyond the point of you and I being able to solve this by negotiation."

"Yes," Joseph replied with a nod of his head. "Now, all we can hope for is stopping any further bloodshed."

Lauren frowned. 'Do angels bleed?"

She blinked in surprise when angelic and human eyes focused on her. "What?" she said defensively. "I'm curious."

"There is only one way this war will end," Lucifer replied. He hadn't taken his eyes off the window and the views of the garden beyond it. "I can see no other way for the two sides to be reconciled."

Paul was confused by what Lucifer was saying, as well as why he was saying it in such a philosophical and sorrowful tone.

"What are you saying?" he asked the angel. "What do you think needs to be done?"

Lucifer finally turned away from the window and looked into Paul's eyes. He projected his thoughts directly into Paul's head. He didn't want everyone debating it.

*Poena or I will need to die. We need to regain the trust of the Seven Sisters, who are the only ones who can end this war and bring the two sides together. They will only agree to do so without a ... figurehead from the first war around.*

"Paul?" Joseph's voice came from behind him.

"Yeah?"

Paul spun round on his heel, his emotions in conflict. He knew he had heard Lucifer right, and it scared him; despite their earlier disagreement, Paul was very fond of the angel — and certainly didn't see the need in him dying.

*There's got to be another way*, he thought.

*There isn't.*

*There's* always *another way.*

*Can you think of it?*

*… No.*

Paul realised that Joseph had spoken to him, but had been so focused on Lucifer that he had tuned everything else out. The half-angel was stood by the staircase, looking up to the first floor landing, and he followed his friend's gaze. His jaw slackened as he realised that there was a figure stood there, smiling at him.

"Chris…"

"Hello, Paul," she replied. "I'm glad I've found you."

Needing to know, Paul blurted out, "Christina, are you … dead?"

She nodded. "Yes, Paul." Her eyes welled up with tears as she went on; "Poena took control of my body … and when she left, I couldn't return. I found out I was dead by seeing my body slump to the pavement … what a way to go."

"I know about you being a Seeker of Truth."

She smiled at him. "So we're even now?" she said, keeping her tone light. "No more secrets?"

Paul smiled back. "No more secrets, I swear."

Christina hugged her arms around herself and shook her head, her voice trembling as she spoke. "I died, Paul."

Paul breathed out, determined to keep a tight lid on his emotions. His hands involuntarily balled up into fists and he bit down on his bottom lip so hard he worried he would draw blood.

Lauren had no such compunctions. "Paul —" she began, and took a step towards him, but that was as far as she got as

Paul abruptly shook his head and took a step backwards. He felt his back hit the front door of this strange building, located in the middle of a strange area of the astral plane, and he rested against it, welcoming its coolness on the back of his head.

"Chris, I…" He didn't know what to say, and he had to admit it. Everyone seemed to understand.

Poena had been disorientated when she first arrived here, the home of her ancestors, because a physical body had formed around her.

She was slim and average-height, but carried herself in such a way made her appear taller, with pale skin and waist-length, jet-black hair – and a look which Lauren and Joseph would both describe as haughty. Joseph had recognised her immediately from descriptions Michael and Micah had given her, and her arrogant demeanour gave her away more than anything else. He took an instant dislike to the woman.

"This is how the Seven Sisters' resting place has appeared to you all?" she spat, disdain dripping from every word. "How decadent and … human."

The way she said the word 'human' told everyone that she hadn't meant it as a compliment. Beelzebub's wings uncurled and her jaw set in an angry line. Next to her, Lauren's fists almost went white with anger as they strained to be used.

"What the hell is *she* doing here?" Paul growled.

Christina looked over at Poena with a scowl. "She brought me here," she said. "I couldn't have got here without her."

"Well, she can leave now," Beelzebub growled. "She has no right to be here."

"I'm touched by your concern." Poena folded her arms across her chest and glared at Beelzebub. "You're aware that a war between our peoples is raging outside this realm? Don't tempt me to start the war in here as well."

"You'd be a fool," Joseph said with a certainty that even surprised him. "We're in the realm of the Seven Sisters. You know what would happen if we fought in here."

"Hello, Poena."

Poena slowly turned towards the voice, her face frozen in an expression of shock.

"Hello, Lucifer. How lovely to see you."

Paul glanced at the angel that had, until recently, shared his head, and was surprised to see him looking quite calm.

"I always knew that, one day, we would meet again," Lucifer said. "Your betrayal wouldn't keep us apart forever."

A slight flicker of Poena's left eyebrow was all the emotion she showed.

"The conspiracy has reached the Seven Sisters," she said angrily, looking round the large reception area before turning her attention fully back at Lucifer. "I was right to try and destroy them, all those years ago."

"And I was wrong to have ever listened to you."

Poena made a disparaging face. "You were a naïve fool," she retorted, "but it meant that my hands were clean. It's a shame my plan failed. Now I have a second chance."

"I am prepared to face up to my crimes," Lucifer retorted. "I am guilty of being a fool, and an angry one at that. I wonder if you are willing to do the same."

"Why are there so many people in my home?"

Three more individuals were suddenly up on the first floor; Beelzebub, Lucifer and Poena looked round to the voice's origin and immediately fell to one knee. It took Joseph a moment longer to recognise the middle figure, but his eyes widened as Satan's memories told him who it was, and he, too, fell to one knee.

That left Paul, Christina and Lauren standing, each of them confused as each other.

*That's a Sister.* Paul blinked. *It has to be. What the hell are Kirby and Rachael doing with her?*

He looked at Kirby, who rolled his eyes apologetically at the abrupt intrusion. Paul managed a half-smile in acknowledgement. He couldn't manage any more.

"You're human spirits," Poena snapped from her knelt position. "You dare to travel with one of the Seven Sisters?"

"They travel with me at my insistence."

Alcyone had looked confused as her eyes roamed the human interpretation of her home, the place she had slept in for an incredibly long time and where her six Sisters still slept to this day. Now, however, her gaze focused on Poena.

"We joined the war because you convinced us," she said, anger tingeing the beautiful currents of her voice. "We believed that you were losing, and you made us believe that the angels were annihilating you."

Still kneeling out of respect, Lucifer and Beelzebub shared an awkward glance. Paul, standing further back, looked to Joseph, trying to understand what was going on, but Joseph just shrugged.

"They were winning!" Poena protested. "Your children were dying!"

"And now I find out that the angel's plan was your plan. You tricked Lucifer into trying to kill us."

Her eyes glanced at Lucifer for a moment. "I do not forgive you for what you did," she said coolly, "but now I understand why you did it."

*But he knew that what he did was wrong!* Paul thought. *He wanted to correct his mistake!*

There was no indication that the Sister had even registered Paul's existence, and she carried on talking. "Now war has started again between my children … and yet I am not summoned. I wonder why this is."

Finally, she looked at the humans that were huddled together – Paul, Lauren and Christina were all close to Joseph, as if the angel's presence could have protected them. She looked at Paul. A shiver ran down his spine, but he refused to be cowed by anyone, not any more.

"You are Lucifer's host," she said simply.

Paul nodded. "Yes. Lucifer slept in my head for a time."

"I can see the resemblance."

"Are you Lucifer's grandmother?"

Alcyone looked at him coolly for a moment. Everything else seemed to fade away as they maintained eye contact.

"I am the mother … and the grandmother – of so many," she eventually replied. "I love them all equally."

"You love them as your children," Paul said, finding his confidence. "Do you understand love? Truly understand it? The love of a partner or a child; someone you can trust implicitly and beyond question, and to love them even beyond death."

He looked over towards Christina and gave her a small smile, which she returned.

Alcyone was quiet again; Paul wondered for a second if he had overstepped some unspoken boundary, but he didn't care.

His girlfriend, regardless of her standing in front of him now, had died on Earth, and Evan Somerville, while not directly responsible, hadn't even cared. He had said that he loved her, once upon a time, but showed that he was more interested in manipulating peoples' emotions than giving a part of himself to someone he loved.

He couldn't have stopped the tears from running down his cheeks even if he had wanted to – and, right now, he didn't feel inclined to even try.

"My Sisters and I gave birth to the cosmos," Alcyone said thoughtfully. "When the war came to pass, I felt the death of each and every one of those who died … and it hurt me, every single time. I did not wish any more of them to die, but Poena disagreed with me, and Lucifer naïvely followed for a time."

Paul sucked in a breath, then released it slowly. He brushed the tears away. There were more urgent matters to deal with.

"You blame Poena and Lucifer for your enforced hibernation?" he asked.

Alcyone's eyes blazed. "We were humiliated," she snapped, "and we always held Lucifer accountable for that. Now, I learn that Poena was ultimately responsible, but that does not excuse Lucifer's actions."

"Mother!" Poena exclaimed with sudden passion, standing up and looking at Alcyone. "I did what I felt best! The angels would have continued with their warfare until all the spirits were dead."

"Are you sure that you have not got that the wrong way around?"

Poena's mouth opened and closed for a moment. She looked round at Lucifer, who had remained deliberately still. He wasn't looking up at either her or Alcyone.

"Lucifer joined me willingly!" Poena went on, now sounding slightly hysterical. "He played a part in my plans!"

"Yes, and he will pay," Alcyone said. She was walking down the steps, never taking her eyes off Poena as she did so. "But I also sense that he accepts his punishment willingly, as befits someone who has learnt and changed over the years. You, Poena, have not changed, however. You are still the same being I remember from all those years ago."

"I am the leader of the astral plane!" Poena shouted. Everyone – human, angel and spirit – in the strange mansion remained silent, watching her increasing anger with curiosity and sadness. "I am the leader in every way that matters! You never allowed me the freedom to win. I should never have asked for your help!"

"I am glad you did ask," Alcyone replied. She had reached the bottom of the stairs, and was now only a few steps from Poena. "Although I regret saying yes. We should have brokered a deal, not gotten involved in a war amongst our children."

Poena sneered contemptuously. "Then you are a coward."

The next few movements happened in a blur. Paul blinked furiously and tried to replay the images in his head, but there was too much to analyse: Alcyone's sudden look of murderous rage, Poena's belated realisation that she had gone too far, and Alcyone's abrupt, savage actions.

When everything had settled down again, Poena was … gone. Just gone.

"What …?" Lauren began, but was hushed by her brother.

Alcyone looked at the kneeling angels. "Stand," she instructed them. As they obeyed, she continued talking. "I did what I had to do. I do not wish death on anyone unnecessarily, but know that it sometimes must be done. Poena would have led her realm to destruction."

She turned to Lucifer. "You must accept a similar punishment as well," she said. "Each realm must pay a price."

Lucifer meekly nodded, which seemed odd to Paul; he knew that Lucifer wasn't timid at all. Even the fiery Beelzebub next to him, stood quietly by. Paul looked around the room, caught with a sudden urgency. No-one seemed to be questioning Alcyone's logic, and he was stunned at the lack of alternatives.

"This is insane!" he exclaimed. "You actually believe this? That your own grandson must die to resolve a war?"

Alcyone looked surprised by Paul's interruption, but seemed to scale down her expectations as she realised that Paul was human, as if she expected nothing more from a being who knew nothing of her ways.

*Sod that*, he thought. *I know enough.*

"Poena was cruel," Alcyone said. "I see that now. She paid the ultimate price, but there can be no peace without the angels paying similarly."

"You're wrong."

Alcyone didn't speak, nor did she register any emotion on her face. She regarded Paul steadily and thoughtfully, and he did the same back to her.

*I wonder how many times in her long life she's been told she's wrong,* he wondered, *instead of treated with reverence and respect because of who she is.*

*Ah well,* he went on inside his head. *In for a penny …*

"You honestly think that one person is responsible for this?" he asked, and couldn't entirely keep the incredulity out of his voice. "Lucifer saw the error of his ways, and was devastated when he couldn't talk the Almighty out of his decision. Michael got over his humiliation to defend humanity during the angelic civil war. Poena festered in her own anger, but had always been proud of her fellow spirits, and was fighting for them now. Time has moved on, but *you* haven't."

He shook his head. "The two sides are beyond the point of no return. Your children are at war. Do you honestly believe that the death of one more will undo the damage of generation upon generation of history? History which, by the way, you weren't present for."

Alcyone's face remained neutral. "Let us look at this war," she said, "that you seem to know so much about."

She nodded to a spot over his shoulder; Paul followed her gaze and gasped in shock. The entire front wall of the mansion had vanished. Instead of the fields beyond, the dark astral plane was laid out before him, and he could see the battle beneath him, angel against spirit against Seeker.

He glanced behind him and the mansion was still there, looking as solid as it had been a moment ago, and everyone was still frozen in place as he looked at them.

*This is insane,* he thought, but dragged his eyes back round to the spectacle before him and tried to focus on detail.

# The Battle – Present Day

Michael had to concede a certain amount of grudging respect for these twelve hundred "Seekers of Truth", as they styled themselves. They had fought bravely and even now, with a third of their number dead and sent spiralling away into the darkness, they continued fighting.

*How is this going to end?* he wondered. Michael had never been one for introspection until the events of the Civil War, when Lucifer and his loyal followers had been imprisoned inside human bodies as their punishment.

Michael had stayed behind during the Civil War and commanded the kingdom's armies, mostly to prevent the atrocities he knew would happen if anyone else had led them, but although he had ended up fighting his brothers and sisters he secretly agreed with much of what they had believed in.

For a brief time, he had felt like a coward for staying behind, but those that he loved and cared for – those angels who were gradually coming back to Heaven as their hosts died – all told him differently. They respected him for his principles, and for what he had done with honour and courage during the war.

There was something he had never confessed, however, even to his closest comrades-in-arms – not even to Lucifer, who he loved almost like a son.

During the first angel-spirit war, back in the far mists of time, he had seen the logic in Lucifer's suggestion and hadn't argued with him that day in his quarters because he had thought it might have been the quickest way of ending the war. By the time Lucifer had begun to have second thoughts, the Almighty was committed to the plan, and so, therefore, was he.

He narrowly avoided being caught by a group of spirits, who didn't pursue him but narrowed their focus on another angel instead. Michael continued flying. He had to concede, his opinion had begun to change as he had watched the Seekers join the fight – and he had watched more death happening before his eyes. They all believed in the sanctity of their own realms, and each side wanted nothing more than to protect it against those they distrusted most: each other.

He pulled himself upright and surveyed the scene of chaos, anger and fear before him – and saw his part in this destruction.

"What have I done?" he asked.

"Michael!"

He pulled himself out of his sorrow; Evan Somerville's spirit had appeared by his side. He was grinning exultantly.

"Michael, we have them, I'm sure of it!" he bellowed. "If we keep up this momentum, we will win."

"But at what cost?"

Somerville blinked. "What do you mean?!" he retorted, hoping that the angel would be able to hear him over the noise of the battle.

Michael shook his head. "You would not understand. I have lived far longer than you could ever imagine, and *I* barely understand. But … what if we're wrong? What if we're all wrong?"

"Wrong? Wrong?!" Somerville looked astounded by the angel's comments. "How can we be wrong? The spirits must pay for what they've done!"

Michael shook his head. "I need to find Poena and Lucifer. We must talk. I must keep looking."

The angel beat his wings and flew away, leaving a confused Seeker of Truth in his wake. Somerville shook his head as he watched Michael go.

"You are wrong," he muttered. "You are incredibly wrong. We must go on fighting, because this world must change. It must change … and why should it not be *me* who changes it?"

# A Hidden Dimension –
# Present Day

"Because you'd change it to a world of hatred, anger and vengeance."

Paul answered Somerville's question without even realising he had done so. He had been so engrossed with watching the events on the vast screen that Alcyone had created. It gave him hope; if Michael were able to change, even after all that, then what was to say that someone like Alcyone wouldn't be able to as well?

The image disappeared, and he had to adjust his vision. He was back in the empty, white void that he had found himself in earlier the same day. As his eyes adapted to his surroundings, he realised Alcyone was stood in front of him.

"You and I have been here before," she said.

"You were the one who brought me?"

The Sister inclined her head. "Yes."

"Why?"

"To prepare you."

Paul hesitated. "For Lucifer's death?"

"I was still waking from my slumber when I brought you here, but even half-awake, I knew what needed to be done."

"But I've told you –" Paul stopped himself. He had honestly believed that, by speaking so bluntly to this woman, or spirit, or whatever she was, that she would be convinced by his argument.

*As if it would be so simple.*

"Lucifer's death won't change anything!" he said desperately. "It won't act as any sort of symbol."

"If I cannot convince you," said Alcyone with a strange look on her face, "then perhaps others can."

All of a sudden, Lucifer, Joseph, Lauren and Kirby were in the white void alongside them. Alcyone didn't give them any time to adjust; she stepped straight in front of Lucifer, who drew himself up to his full height.

"You know what Paul and I have discussed?" she asked him, and he nodded in reply with a sorrowful – and resigned – gaze.

"I do," he said politely.

"And what do you think about it?"

"If you believe it will heal our realms, then I will go willingly into the light."

"Lucifer!"

Paul and Joseph had exclaimed the angel's name together, and both were as appalled as the other. Alcyone looked annoyed at their emotional outburst.

"Your theatrics are becoming tiresome," she said. "The angel has been brought to this realm for his punishment. Will you carry it out in order for the healing process between the realms to begin?"

Paul was disgusted at even being asked. "No, I will not!" he snapped. "Lucifer is an angel, one of the most senior and experienced angels in heaven, and he should not have to die for a proposal he made out of fear and anger millions of years ago!"

Lucifer looked at his human host with a mixture of surprise and curiosity. He hadn't expected such a vocal response or defence from anyone.

Paul ignored him and continued speaking to the Sister, unwilling to stop forcing Alcyone to listen to him; "We have just watched Michael wonder if he has made a mistake, and we've also seen how arrogant belief from a human spirit will keep them fighting until they all die!"

He gritted his teeth. "You've also just killed Poena for her supposed crimes and for calling you a coward. Isn't *that* theatrical? How many have to die in the name of healing in order for this realm to move on? From time to time, someone has to just say 'enough is enough', be mature and move on!"

Alcyone's face darkened as he spoke. "You, a mere human, would speak to me like this?"

Something clicked inside Paul's head. "You're the Almighty's mother," he said. "The Almighty and Poena were siblings."

Lucifer looked alarmed, as if that wasn't something many people knew – or should know. Lauren threw Paul a concerned look, but Paul was too angry to stop.

Alcyone, for the first time, looked alarmed. "How can you be sure of that?"

"Because the Almighty was just as sure of himself and just as confident that his opinions mattered more than anyone else's. You can't see one simple truth. The true architect of the plan is dead, and all Lucifer has ever wanted is to return to his friends and his family and make amends for his actions."

He shook his head in weary resignation. "He willingly slept in my head while I lived, in order to let me have a full life. He gave up some of *his* life in order to let me have mine.

Well, now it's time for me to return the favour. If you must kill someone, then kill me instead."

"Paul!" Lauren exclaimed. "You can't do that!"

"Yes, I can," he replied. "Lucifer is needed in Heaven. I'd never belong there."

The Sister was looking at him carefully, and Paul could tell that she was truly considering his proposal – which gave him hope a sudden surge of hope. He didn't interrupt her as she quietly thought things through. Eventually, she shook her head.

"No," she said. "It would not work. You know nothing of our realm."

"And neither do you!" Paul snapped. "You've been asleep, Alcyone – how can you possibly know the depth of feelings behind what's going on here?"

He pointed to Lucifer. "He is the Almighty's son by an angel who was once human! If that's not the perfect symbol of what is possible when sides reconcile, then I don't know what is!"

Fury was now evident on Alcyone's face – fury at being challenged and defied. She started to radiate some sort of energy, a golden outline round her body that seemed to warp her expression. Joseph and Lucifer took a step back at the power she was beginning to emanate. Paul, however, stood his ground, resisting it with every fibre of his being.

*I'm done running*, he thought, *and I'm not being dragged around anymore. It's time for me to lead.*

"I am one of the Seven Sisters," Alcyone said darkly. "I am the final appeal, and my word is law!"

"Then the law is moronic!" Paul yelled. "And that makes you just as corrupt as Poena!"

That was the final straw for Alcyone – and her human form. She began to twist and distort against the whiteness of their surroundings, and Paul had to root himself squarely in order to make sure he didn't get pulled towards the swirling shapes and energy in front of him. Alcyone's human form had disappeared into an angry mass of black and red swirls, growing exponentially bigger as it continued to mix and blend together.

"Paul!" Joseph yelled from behind, and Paul took the hint. He took a step backwards, still entranced. Lauren and Rachael were watching in horror the twisting, horrific mass in front of them.

"How is Paul not terrified?" Rachael asked in morbid fascination.

"He probably is!" Lauren retorted.

She was fighting every instinct in her spiritual body, which were all currently yelling at her to run away as fast as possible. *But run away to where?*

Beelzebub had appeared on the other side of her, curiosity written across her face.

"Why is he just standing there?"

"Because that's what you do," Lauren said quietly. "You confront your emotions. You don't hide them behind a fake exterior. That can ... well, that can lead to war."

Beelzebub's gaze broke away from the Sister's new, rapidly-changing form and made eye contact for the first time with Lauren; a measure of understanding flickered between them.

⬤•⬤

On the battleground, Michael knew with a jolt what had happened to Poena.

*Not many people could simply kill her*, he thought.

Something caught his eye. Above him – above all of them – a swirling, circular mass of energy had broken through from another place – a side realm that Michael knew well – and was blocking out some of the remaining stars. Knowledge of what was happening made him falter.

"No," he breathed. "Lucifer. NO!"

He pulled his wings into a tight curve, barrelled upwards and disappeared through the walls of the realms.

Somerville watched him go, anger bubbling deep inside as he realised that the angels were beginning to turn against *him* as well.

"We are betrayed," he muttered.

"Yes. By you."

His spiritual form spun round – and was confronted by Rachael and Christina.

"What the –"

Rachael shook her head and continued talking. "This is the time for you to listen, Evan," she said. "Not to talk."

"Your righteous anger against the angels and the spirits would be a lot easier to cope with," Christina said, "if it wasn't so full of …" She paused, thought for the right word, then smiled, "… crap."

"How did the pair of you find me?" Somerville snapped.

Rachael smiled. "We seem to have developed the ability to sense your thoughts," she said. She glanced upwards at the swirling mass above them. "We had to escape to get away from the Sister, so we decided to come and visit you."

Christina rolled her eyes. "No need to thank us."

"Have you not seen what is happening?" Somerville asked angrily. "The spirits and the angels have turned against us! They've betrayed –"

"It's not all about you, Evan!" Rachael snapped. "This war goes far deeper than you'll ever know, and your interference is only making things worse! It's brought Earth into a conflict it has no place in, and your Seekers are dying for it!"

"It's time someone stood against you, Evan," Christina went on. "Your arrogance and deluded self-belief is causing more chaos than it's stopping."

The leader drew himself up to his full height. "I would do it all again if I had to."

Christina and Rachael exchanged a glance, full of meaning, and Christina nodded.

"That's what I was afraid you would say," she said, looking back to him. "Evan, we're taking command of the Seekers away from you. No more deaths. Not today."

Somerville burst out laughing. "You honestly believe you can lead the Seekers better than I can?" he asked in between his staccato laughter. "How can you possibly take control so easily?"

"Look behind you," Rachael instructed him.

Automatically, he did as Rachael had told him, and his eyes widened in shock as he saw a group of six spirits heading straight for him.

"What the –" he began, and glanced back at Rachael and Christina, who were blocking his escape. "Help me!" he begged. "You've got to help me!"

The two spirits just smiled at him, and by then, it was too late.

"NO!"

Neither Rachael nor Christina moved as they watched what happened next. They knew it had to be done, and it felt right that there be someone to witness it.

Above them, the Sister's form kept swirling and growing larger.

———••———

Michael appeared in the side dimension and smiled as he saw Lucifer, looking no different from the day, two years ago, when they had been briefly reunited in Heaven.

"There's no time for emotional reunions," Beelzebub said urgently, stepping in to Lucifer's side. "We have a more pressing problem."

The other angels understood, and they all turned to face the maelstrom. Paul was rooted to the spot.

"I will not ask Paul to face this alone," Lucifer said. He tried to shake off someone's hand, but it set itself firmly on his wrist. He looked round into Satan's wise eyes.

"Do not try and talk me out of this," he said, his jaw line setting resolutely. "I will do whatever I have to in order to save this realm."

Joseph smiled. "I know you will," he replied. "You are Satan's best friend, and Paul is mine. I value both of you, and would very much like both of you out of this alive, please."

"I will not promise you anything I cannot give," Lucifer said, more touched than his friend would ever know. "But I promise you that Paul and I value the safety of our worlds, and we won't let Alcyone destroy either of them."

He walked across the white expanse, trying to ignore the vibrations that were pushing through his body, emanating from the vortex. They were generating significant noise, which got louder the closer he moved towards it.

Paul was staring up at the huge, whirling maelstrom of energy that had once been Alcyone, but seemed unable – or unwilling – to move. Occasional winds buffeted Lucifer – and Paul – as he reached his former host's side.

"She reminds me of a nova," Paul said. The noise from Alycone was great, but the two beings – human and angel – were still attuned to each other, and could hear each other without needing to shout.

Lucifer nodded. "They were born from the heat of super-novae, so that is a good analogy."

"What happens now?"

The angel shrugged. "I do not know," he replied. "She is angry, that much is certain, and this pure form can destroy entire galaxies. Without a sacrifice, perhaps that's what she intends to do. She thinks it is the only way to cleanse our realms; by starting again."

Paul shook his head. "This is wrong," he said. "This is so incredibly wrong."

"Then let me die."

Paul turned his head to face the angel.

"No! You shouldn't die just because she's demanding it. Life is far more complicated than that, isn't it?"

Lucifer smiled. "Sometimes."

"You are my brother," Paul whispered. "All this time, you have lived inside my head, and never once have you demand-ed anything from me."

"You are my brother as well," Lucifer replied. "I never asked for anything, because you deserved to live."

Paul shook his head, sighing. He knew what he had to do, and he wasn't willing to ask anyone else to do it.

*Alcyone must be stopped.*

"You've given me that chance at life," he said, "and I've loved every minute of it. But now it's time for me to give you the same."

He looked over his shoulder at his human friends. "Tell Joseph and Lauren …" He swallowed. "Tell them the same. Tell them I love them."

Lucifer wasn't often confused, but he was in that moment. "You can tell them yourself, my friend," he said. "Alcyone's plan will take time. We have an opportunity to consider our response."

Paul didn't reply. He was looking hard at his friends for a moment, as if trying to memorise every last detail about them, and only then did he look back at Lucifer and look him in the eye.

"No…" Lucifer whispered. He suddenly realised what Paul was thinking. "No! I will not allow it!"

"Whether you allow it or not," Paul said, "this is what is going to happen. This is how I choose to end my life … and allow you the chance, finally, to live yours by breaking the link between us."

All of a sudden, he smiled – and it was a genuine, truthful smile. "Finally," he said, "I know what my purpose in life truly is. Remember me, won't you?"

Before anyone could react, Paul ran forward. Lucifer was dimly aware of shouts of alarm – some of them from his own throat – but it was too late. Paul jumped and disappeared into the heart of the supernova.

The angel's knees collapsed from under him; he couldn't tear his eyes away from the spot in the terrible, silent whirlpool of darkness where Paul had entered. Nothing else around him mattered except for that blackness, that terrible spot in the huge circle that just kept on swirling.

Nothing changed. The supernova continued growing vaster and vaster against the whiteness of the background. The sounds and vibrations continued to grow stronger, until he could barely hear himself think any more.

"Please," Lucifer whispered. "Don't let your sacrifice be in vain."

He had to blink a couple of times in case he had made a mistake.

In the black and red anger of the maelstrom, a different colour suddenly appeared. First green, then blue, then the other colours of the spectrum – followed finally by white. It was only a small speck at first, but then it started to grow … and grow.

His body started to shake, and he looked round to find the source. He realised that he was still on his knees, and that a pair of hands was shaking him. Lucifer looked up into Satan-Joseph's tear-stained face.

"What did he say?" the hybrid demanded. "Lucifer, what did he say?"

Lucifer struggled to find the words for a moment, then shook his head clear and said, "He's saved us all," he replied. "He's done this to save us."

If his friend understood, then he didn't show it. Perhaps it was impossible to understand.

"We've got to get out of here!" Joseph exclaimed. "We've got to go now! Everyone else has gone, Lucifer, we're the only two left! We've got to go, or we'll be killed!"

Lucifer wanted to protest. He wanted to stay and be with the human who he had learnt to love like a brother. But then he remembered Paul's last expression.

It broke his heart to think it, but he knew it was time to leave.

"Let's go," he said.

# Heaven ... and the Astral Plane

"It's beautiful."

Kirby was entranced with the view out of the Celestial Observatory. Paul had described it to him, of course, but how could he fully explain the wonders of this place to anyone?

*I'm dreaming,* he thought for the hundredth time. *I've got to be dreaming.*

"Can he hear me?"

Rachael Kirby laughed. "Not when he's so focused on something. There's only one way to get his attention."

Rachael stepped up behind him and cuffed her brother round the back of the head.

"Ow!" Kirby exclaimed. "Who the f –"

He cut his sentence short as he turned and saw who stood in front of him: his sister and Lucifer were there, amusement creased on their faces.

"That stung," he ended lamely.

Rachael shrugged. "Like I'm bothered. I'm a spirit," she said. "Human problems don't worry me anymore."

Kirby smiled and relaxed. Despite the fact he had been looking out over the wonders of the cosmos, it was even better to see his sister.

A thought suddenly caught him and he chuckled.

"What is funny?" Lucifer asked him. "Have you seen something out there that amuses you?"

"No, not at all," Kirby replied, "although I'm flattered that you'd think I could notice anything from this view. There's a lot of cosmos."

He laughed even more at that, but the laughter died off as neither Rachael nor Lucifer seemed to get it. He cleared his throat.

"No," he went on quickly, "it's just … a spirit, a human and an angel, stood together in Heaven." He shook his head. "There's nothing in that sentence that even begins to make sense to me."

This time, Rachael did laugh, and even Lucifer couldn't help but smile.

"It was time for things to change," the angel replied. "This is a good change."

Kirby shook his head and looked out over the screen. In the distance, the huge supernova was still there, hanging in space like a beautiful and dangerous star. Now, however, it looked muted, and was gradually sinking back into itself; Michael and Lucifer were convinced that, in time, it would fade into the darkness of the cosmos.

"What will happen to her?" he asked over his shoulder.

"Alcyone?" Lucifer said. "In truth, I do not know. A human has … merged with one of the Seven Sisters. That has never happened before. This is a new beginning for *them* as well."

Rachael folded her arms around herself as she looked out at the nova along with as her brother. "But what happened to Paul? Did he…"

"As I have said," Lucifer interrupted, "it has never happened before. All the inhabitants of Earth will know is that a new supernova has appeared in the sky. If I am truthful, that is all I understand. Anything else would be wild speculation."

The three of them fell silent and drew comfort from the companionship. Rachael took her brother's hand and they exchanged a contented glance. They each knew that this wouldn't last. Kirby would soon return to Earth to find out if any of the recent chaos had spilled over to his world; but, right here and now, they had each other.

Lucifer was lost in his own thoughts. He kept thinking of Paul, the man who had kept the angel safe inside his head, and then sacrificed his life so that countless others – *including me* – would live. He was distracted by a hand slipping into his – he looked round and saw Rachael smiling at him.

"I think there are a lot of positives to spirits and angels living together," she said.

Lucifer inclined his head. "We will see," he said, and smiled back.

—◆●◄—

"So, let me get this straight. Lucifer's now back in Heaven and Micah all but forced him to be the new president of the republic, the war's over, Michael's a peacenik, and heaven and the astral plane are now united. Have I missed anything?"

Joseph thought about it for a moment, then shook his head.

"Nope, you're pretty much spot on," he said. "Except for the bit about Michael. He's still leader of the armies, but he's certainly seen the error of his ways."

Lauren frowned. "I thought that Michael had some sort of revelation on the battlefield when he confronted Evan Somerville?"

"No, it's much more…" Joseph hesitated. "You know what? It might not be that complicated. I just don't understand it."

*There's a lot I don't understand right now*, he thought.

What he *was* certain about, however, was that Michael had appeared at just the right time. As they had all watched Paul run into the dark supernova that was Alcyone in all her fury, and it began its transformation into something life-threatening, Michael had taken charge and helped them all escape.

It was only then, when Michael had rescued them all, did he realise that Lauren, Rachael and Christina were in Heaven alongside the angels. Michael spoke to each of them in turn, quietly and thoughtfully, and the next thing any of them knew was that he had spoken to Micah and as a result, the war was over.

Joseph and Lauren were sat together on the steps in the Ruling Chamber, facing away from the empty throne.

Lauren sighed contentedly, and rested her head on her brother's shoulder. "Christina got back to Earth safely?"

Joseph nodded. "Yeah. Lucifer argued that she was caught in the crossfire. She wanted to lead what was left of the Seekers of Truth, and I think that's swayed it in the end. Lucifer wants to see if there's a way of working with them in the future."

Lauren sat up. "I could argue that I was caught in the crossfire, two years ago."

"You want to go back to Earth, do you?"

"No, I just…" She shrugged. "I was just saying."

"Good." Joseph's wings seemed to shrug by themselves as the feathers ruffled on his back. "I'd hate to lose you so soon after I've got you back … and so soon after –"

He choked up all of a sudden. His head dropped and tears began to fall. Lauren understood, and her own eyes welled up at the thought of Paul. Silence filled the hall until Joseph rubbed a hand across his face and cleared his throat.

"What do you think happened to him?" Lauren asked.

"I think…" Joseph chuckled. "I'd like to think he's kicking arse, wherever he is."

Lauren laughed. "Me too." She sighed. "I've still got so many questions."

"So have I," Joseph replied. "Let's deal with them some other time."

"Sounds like a plan."

Joseph looked out over the Ruling Chamber. His grief for Paul was still there, just beneath the surface, but so was another emotion – one that he hadn't expected.

Hope.

Lauren looked sideways at him, seeing a slight smile form on his face. "What do we do now?"

Joseph's mind was suddenly alive with possibilities. "We start planning for tomorrow."

www.ingramcontent.com/pod-product-compliance
Lightning Source LLC
Chambersburg PA
CBHW061618210726
48287CB00001B/182